LONE WOLVES

short fiction

by

George C. Chesbro

Published by
Apache Beach Publications
New Baltimore, New York 12124
June 2003

ISBN: 1-930253-15-X

by George C. Chesbro

The Mongo novels

Shadow of a Broken Man
City of Whispering Stone
An Affair of Sorcerers
The Beasts of Valhalla
Two Songs This Archangel Sings
The Cold Smell of Sacred Stone
Second Horseman Out of Eden
The Language of Cannibals
In the House of Secret Enemies (novellas)
The Fear in Yesterday's Rings
Dark Chant in a Crimson Key
An Incident at Bloodtide
Bleeding In The Eye of a Brainstorm
Dream of a Falling Eagle

Other novels

The Keeper
Veil
Jungle of Steel and Stone
Chant
Chant: Silent Killer
Chant: Code of Blood
Bone
Turn Loose the Dragons
King's Gambit
The Golden Child
Crying Freeman
Prism

These stories originally appeared in the following publications:

"First Strike"
            Ellery Queen Mystery Magazine, Dec. 1991
"The White Bear"
            Ellery Queen Mystery Magazine, May 1992
"Lone Wolf"
            Ellery Queen Mystery Magazine, July 1993
"Haunts"
            Ellery Queen Mystery Magazine, Oct. 1993
"The Problem With The Pigs"
            Ellery Queen Mystery Magazine, June 1997
"The Lazarus Gate"
            Ellery Queen Mystery Magazine, Oct. 1996
"Unmarked Graves"
            Ellery Queen Mystery Magazine, Sept. 1997
"Priests"
            Alfred Hitchcock's Mystery Magazine, Sept. 1991
"Tomb"
            Alfred Hitchcock's Mystery Magazine, Oct. 1993
"Model Town"
            Unholy Orders, Nov. 2000

GARTH

FIRST STRIKE

The substance that had once crippled his mind and body had been gone from his system for years, but Garth Frederickson had been permanently changed. Some layer of emotional insulation had been stripped from him, leaving him rawly sensitive to emotional and spiritual signals sent by others. He experienced others' anguish and need as physical discomfort, a shortness of breath, and in the presence of people who would do harm he experienced a taste in his mouth not dissimilar to bitter chocolate. The poison's strange legacy was a sometimes cruel gift that he didn't question and couldn't explain—not to Mary Tree, his wife, and not even to his brother, who tended to make jokes about his "nose for evil."

The Broadway actor in centerfield caught the fly ball hit by the ballet dancer and threw home, but he was too late to prevent one of the three local politicians on hand for the celebrity softball game to benefit the sloop Clearwater and its efforts to clean up the Hudson River from tagging up at third base and coming home. With two outs for Mary's team, one of the five film actors who lived in Cairn stepped up to the plate, while one of the two film directors who were his neighbors prepared to pitch to him. The rock star coaching at third base, virtually unrecognizable without his elaborate hairpiece, shouted encouragement.

From his seat at the top of a bleacher section on the west side of the high-school athletic field, Garth watched as a short, husky man, incongruously dressed in an ill-fitting tan suit and wearing a black leather beret, emerged from the bleacher section on the north side and made his way around the cinder track toward Mary, who had come off the field after her turn at bat and was standing on the apron of the field autographing copies of her latest album that people had brought with them.

Garth, tasting bitter chocolate, was out of his seat and heading down toward the field as the stocky man in the baggy suit and black beret roughly shouldered his way through the knot of autograph seekers. He said something to Mary, and then thrust the bulky manila envelope he had been carrying into the hands of the startled singer, who shied and backed away a step. As the man reached out for Mary's wrist, Garth grabbed his shoulder, pulled him back, and spun him around. He found himself staring into pale-green eyes that first registered shock, then rage. A dark flush spread from his thick neck to his fleshy face, highlighting the alcohol-ruptured veins in his broad nose. He cursed in German.

"Security," Garth said evenly, using his free hand to display the card that identified him as a member of Cairn's auxiliary police force. "Wait your turn and keep your hands to yourself."

"Mind your business!" the man shouted in English laced with a heavy German accent. "Get your hand off me!"

"If you have something for my wife to sign, line up and wait with the others. If not, get the hell back to your seat. She's here to play softball. If you want to meet her, buy a ticket to the reception after the game."

The man reached into the sagging left-hand pocket of his suit jacket, withdrew a black snub-nosed revolver with an elongated skeleton grip, and pressed the bore against Garth's sternum.

Garth slowly released his grip on the man's shoulder and dropped his hand to his side as he calmly stared at his death in the pale-green eyes. He had always had an aversion to dying by accident—a bullet meant for someone else smashing into his brain, or being run over by a drunk driver—or by degrees, his body and mind being slowly crushed by disease. Being shot by a psychopath at a fund-raising softball game was surely also an absurd way to die, but his instincts about the man had been correct. Now the man's instability and his potential for harm had been unmasked.

With two Cairn policemen now flanking him, guns drawn and aimed at his head, Garth didn't think it likely that the man in the black beret would again be in a position to threaten Mary for a very long time, if ever.

Then the killing time passed, the murderous rage in the green eyes vanishing as suddenly as it had appeared, to be replaced by what might have been bemusement, and something else Garth couldn't identify. The man handed his gun by the barrel to Jake Goldberg, the Cairn policeman standing to his left. Instantly, Goldberg and Fred Searles, the second policeman, wrestled his hands behind his back, handcuffed him, and started to lead him away. Just before they disappeared around the end of a bleacher section, the man twisted his head around and smiled at Mary. "Please read what I gave you!" he called over his shoulder. "It will explain everything!"

It had happened so quickly that only the knot of autograph seekers had actually seen the confrontation, but these people were now talking excitedly to one another, and as word of the incident spread more and more heads began to turn in their direction. The action on the field had stopped and a few of the players were heading toward them.

Garth leaned close to Mary, who was white-faced with shock and breathing hoarsely. "You have to pull yourself together and get your team back on the field, love," he said in a gentle tone as he took the manila envelope from her trembling hands. "You don't want that guy interfering with what you all came here to do, and publicity about what happened will only encourage others like him. It's over. Go on now."

The tall, lithe woman with the long whitish-blonde hair and piercingly blue eyes swallowed hard and nodded. She took a deep breath, then turned and, shouting and waving her arms, led her teammates out onto the playing field.

Garth headed back up to his seat in the bleachers, thinking that if living was a dangerous business that nobody survived anyway, it was even more dangerous for celebrities, where in any of the crowds constantly surrounding them might be the one person

9

who would murder for no other reason than that his victim was famous and he was not—as if the act of killing was some kind of mystical rite that would somehow magically confer the fame and power of the slain upon the slayer. A quick inspection of the contents of the manila envelope served to confirm Garth's suspicion that the man who had been taken away in handcuffs posed a very real threat to his wife.

During the reception that followed the game, Garth stayed back in the dim light of an alcove near the auxiliary bar of the Hudson Shore restaurant, closely watching the many well - wishers who had paid for the privilege of being there as they flocked around Mary's table to speak to her or ask for her autograph. In a way, Garth thought with a grim smile, he could almost sympathize with the man in the black beret, for he, too, had been obsessed with the transcendent beauty and sensuality of Mary Tree for more than twenty years before they had actually met and fallen in love.

When the others were finally gone, he went over to the table, sat down next to his wife, and brushed his lips against her cheek. "You all done good, babe," he said. "Counting the proceeds from the reception, you and your friends netted more than three thousand for the Clearwater." He paused and stroked her long hair with the back of his hand. "What did he say to you, Mary?"

Mary put her arms around her husband's waist, rested her head on one of his broad shoulders, and shuddered slightly. "I know things like that happen to other people, but I never thought it would happen to me. God, Garth, when he pulled that gun and pointed it at you, I— If he'd killed you, it would have been because of me!"

"That's nonsense. What exactly did he say?"

She straightened up, shrugged. "He told me he'd been a fan of mine for a long time and he had some things to give to me that would prove it. He was starting to make a few obscene suggestions when you came along." She took Garth's hand and looked into his eyes. "His threatening you with that gun should mean that he'll be locked away for a time, right?"

"I hope so," Garth said, but in fact he was experiencing a distinct sense of foreboding.

Mary pointed at the manila envelope her husband had placed on the table. "I don't want to read any of that."

"It's filled with love letters, lousy poetry, and even some song lyrics—most of it very sexual, and all of it meant for you, sweetheart. This man's had you on his mind for a long time."

Mary shook her head and brushed a strand of hair away from her eyes with a hand that had again begun to tremble. "You know I get stuff like this in the mail all the time. If he was going to go to the trouble to write to me, why hang onto it for years?"

"Maybe because he was in a place where it wasn't safe to send fan letters to a pacifist folk singer. As soon as I get you home, I'm going over to the station to talk to Jake and Fred about our friend in the beret."

Michael Gannett, the soft-spoken owner of the Hudson Shore, suddenly appeared at his side. "There's a phone call for you, Garth."

"Who?"

"He wouldn't identify himself. He says it's about what happened earlier, and that it's important."

Garth hurried back to the alcove between the dining room and the auxiliary bar where there were pay telephones. One of the receivers was off the hook. He picked it up. "Frederickson."

"Kill him before he kills you." The voice was flat and oddly muffled, as if the man was making an effort to disguise it. "He will leave you no choice. Don't let happen to you what happened to the man in Orlando. Strike first."

"Who are you?" Garth asked, but there was a click and the line went dead. He hung up the phone and, determined to mask his sudden sense of urgency from Mary, walked back to the table and calmly asked her to wait for him in the restaurant until he returned.

He stepped out into the evening and then ran the two and a half blocks to the Cairn police station, where he found Jake Goldberg standing beside the doorway leading into a back room where there were two holding cells.

11

The policeman's face was flushed with anger, and he seemed startled to see Garth. "You must be able to read minds," he said as Garth approached him. "I was just getting ready to call you. Your guy got sprung."

Garth glanced at his watch. "How could he have made bail so soon? No lawyer—"

"It wasn't a lawyer who got him out. The Feds took him."

"When?"

"About thirty seconds ago. They walked out the back just as you were coming in the front."

Garth wheeled and ran out of the office. He went out the door of the station house, vaulted over the iron railing to his left, and landed in the center of the narrow asphalt driveway directly in the path of the car coming out of the parking lot in the rear.

The car's brakes screamed in protest as the driver slammed his foot on the brake pedal and the car came to a halt with the front bumper less than four inches from Garth's knees. Garth took a step backward, shielded his eyes from the glare of the headlights, and noted the car's license-plate number. Then he stepped forward again, leaned on the hood, and peered through the windshield at the three startled occupants of the car. Two men in suits and ties sat in the front. The driver was a young, solidly built man with blond hair closely cropped in a crew cut. The other man, heavyset and with a swarthy complexion, looked to be about fifty. The man with the black beret sat in the rear seat, unattended and without handcuffs.

The heavyset man jumped out of the car. "What the hell's the matter with you! You want to get killed?"

"My name's Frederickson," Garth said. "What I want is to know who you are, the identity of the man in your back seat, and where you're taking him."

The big man reached into the inside pocket of his suit jacket and withdrew a thin leather wallet which he flipped open to reveal a photo I.D. card and metal shield. "I'm Special Agent Baker, F.B.I. This is Special Agent Walker with me. You're interfering with Federal officers in the performance of their duty

12

and risking arrest and prosecution. Now do yourself a favor and get out of the way!"

Garth heard footsteps behind him. He turned his head as Jake Goldberg came up on his left, and then casually leaned against the brick wall of the precinct station and crossed his arms over his chest. The policeman's dark eyes were impassive, but there was the slightest hint of amusement on his face—he looked like a man who had stopped by to see a show. "As a police officer and your friend, Garth," he said, "I have to advise you that you should do what the man says. They're the real McCoy—I checked them out with the New York bureau before I released that joker into their custody. I had no choice, and you don't, either. I have everybody's names on the receipt I made them sign."

Garth shook his head. "Not good enough. Their passenger's name could be a phony, and I'll bet anything it is."

"Get out of the way!" Baker shouted, his face flushed and his eyes flashing. "This is your last warning!"

"That man harassed my wife and threatened me with a gun," Garth said, addressing himself now to the agent identified as Walker, who had also stepped out of the car. The man in the black beret was following the conversation intently, his head halfway out of the open back window. "He's broken the law as well as shown himself to be a threat to my wife and me—and you're chauffeuring him around like he's your honored guest. I intend to press charges against this man, and as a citizen I have a right to know exactly who he is and where you plan to take him."

"He's in Federal custody," Baker said. "And you're overreaching. Get out of the way."

Garth decided to fire the only real weapon he had in his arsenal, even if it turned out to carry only a blank. He might never have another chance to confront any of these men and he was determined not to let the man in the black beret vanish. "Maybe if his victim in Orlando had overreached, he'd still be alive."

Baker exchanged a startled glance with his younger partner.

13

"Make him go away!" the man in the black beret shouted out the car window. "What's the matter with you people! Just make him go away!"

"Are you going to make me just go away?" Garth asked. "The gun that man pulled on me was a weapon of choice for many members of the officer corps of what used to be the East German Staatsicherheit. I have no idea what he's doing in this country or why you think he deserves such royal treatment, but I guarantee that I'm going to try to find out if you spirit him away from here. The chances are he's a killer, just like the other Stasi who have disappeared from Germany, along with their leader. He's dangerous and I don't want him coming at my back on some dark night."

Walker shook his head and spoke to his partner. "Well, we're sure as hell going to have to take him in now."

Baker nodded curtly, then strode around the open car door, pulled his gun, and pointed it at Garth's head. "You're under arrest. Turn around, lean against the wall, and spread your legs."

Garth did as he was told. Baker patted him down and, removing the wallet from Garth's rear pocket, he handed it to Walker. "Check him out," he said. When Walker returned to the car and picked up the radio, Baker handcuffed Garth, turned him around, and then leaned close to his face. "Where the hell do you get your information, mister?"

"The newspapers," Garth replied evenly.

"That's not good enough. How do you know what weapons were issued to the Stasi?"

Garth glanced at Jake Goldberg, who smiled thinly.

"Hey, Avery," Walker called from the car, an odd note to his voice, "you'd better get over here. The Chief wants to talk to you right now, and he wants you to take the cuffs off Frederickson."

Garth turned around and saw Avery Baker look at his partner as if the man, or their superior, had committed some unspeakable gaffe. The Special Agent strode back to the open car window on his side, reached inside and took the radio handset from

14

his partner. He spoke into it, listened for a few moments, and then quickly got into the car, shut the door, and closed the window. The younger agent was staring at Garth through the windshield, his eyes betraying both hostility and strong interest.

Goldberg moved closer to Garth. "My money says those FBI boys are being told in no uncertain terms not to hassle Garth Frederickson. I'm glad you got here when you did. Pulling this guy out of our jail may be legal, but it's outrageous."

"It wasn't you who called me, Jake?"

"Somebody called you?"

Garth didn't reply. He watched Baker replace the radio handset in its cradle, then re-emerge from the car. The agent's swarthy face was impassive as he freed Garth's wrists and dropped the steel handcuffs into the pocket of his overcoat. "You and your brother carry a heavy reputation, Frederickson," he said tersely. "I didn't realize you were that Frederickson, and I'm sorry we had to meet under these circumstances. In any case, my superior says I should let you go, and I think it's because a lot of important people don't want to get either of the Fredericksons riled. You must know where a lot of skeletons are buried."

Garth smiled thinly, without humor. "Actually, it's my brother they're afraid of."

"Yeah, well, whatever the reason, I'm also to give you assurances that somebody from the New York field office will be around within twenty-four hours to speak to you and your wife about this matter in detail. In the meantime, it would be appreciated if you wouldn't discuss this matter with anyone. The Chief says you know him and that his word means something. You can call him on the car radio if you want."

Garth searched Baker's face. "I don't need to take anyone's word but yours," he said and stepped aside.

He watched as the car pulled out of the driveway and saw the German's face staring at him through the rear window. The pale-green eyes gleamed with hatred as his mouth moved, carefully articulating the words, *I will kill you.*

"I'd like to speak with you and your wife together," Avery Baker said in an almost apologetic tone when he appeared at Garth's and Mary's riverside home the next morning. The man seemed somehow different, less anxious to appear tough, and Garth suspected this was because he didn't have his young partner with him.

"Mary's in the other room," Garth said. "Come in.

Garth led the agent into the music room. Its walls of glass looked out over the Hudson; in the distance, sail and power boats glided over the rippled surface of the river. Baker nodded to Mary, who was sitting with one bare foot under her in a canvas director's chair, and said, "The man's real name is Gunther Francke." He looked back and forth between Garth and Mary. "As you guessed, Frederickson, he's a former member of East Germany's Staatsicherheit. And, as you noted, these people are not exactly beloved by their fellow citizens in that unhappy land. Thousands of them went into hiding after the collapse of the Communist regime there and many are now being actively recruited by various Intelligence agencies around the world." He paused and smiled ruefully. "I'm told we are most fortunate to have acquired the services of Herr Francke."

Garth said, "It sounds like the province of the C.I.A."

"It most definitely is." The evenness of Baker's tone was belied by the expression of distaste on his face.

"Then what are you doing with him?"

"The C.I.A. doesn't have a good track record in dealing with would-be defectors—and that's how Francke is classified, even though his country no longer officially exists. We're acting at the specific bequest of the State Department. One of the demands Francke made when he approached the embassy official that re-cruited him was that he would not have to undergo C.I.A. interrogation. The State Department asked us to put him in our Witness Protection Program while he is gradually debriefed and the information evaluated. That's proving to be a lengthy process. The CIA's laughing at us. They think we're fools, and they've washed their hands of him. In effect, we're acting as well paid babysitters. He's not a prisoner and we're under orders to protect him. Unfortunately, we haven't figured out a way to protect others from him."

"You mean to tell me," Garth asked incredulously, "that he killed somebody in Orlando and you simply moved him?"

"I'm not at liberty to discuss Mr. Francke's movements. I don't know where you got that information."

"Why is this one man considered so important?"

East Germany was a notorious haven and financial backer for any number of individual terrorists and their parent groups. As a result, the Stasi possessed an enormous amount of information about these people and the groups' infrastructures, including the names of dummy companies in this country specifically set up to aid terrorist movements in the United States. East Germany may no longer exist, but the terrorists and their infrastructures certainly do."

Garth shook his head impatiently. "Am I about to hear the same rationale that was used for bringing ex-Nazis, including known war criminals, into this country after the Second World War?"

"The analogy wouldn't be inaccurate," Baker said in a flat tone.

"Again, what's so special about Francke? The man is obviously unstable and proven dangerous. Throw him back and get yourself another fish. Like you said, there are thousands of them out there."

"Apparently not like this one. In the last days before the Communist regime crumbled, the Stasi destroyed or hid most of their files. The information we need now exists only in the heads of some of these men."

Garth grunted. "What evidence do you have that this guy knows anything?"

"The State Department says he was one of Markus Wolf's top aides. He had access to all the records, and they think there's a good chance he's telling the truth when he claims to have

17

memorized information about terrorist networks and front groups in this country."

"Claims? I take it he's not being exactly forthcoming with all this valuable information he supposedly committed to memory."

Baker shrugged. "We've been ordered to adopt a strictly custodial posture. The State Department says he's just trying to negotiate the best terms for staying in this country, and we're supposed to show him how good things could be if he fully cooperates. Do you see the dilemma?"

Mary, who had been listening to the conversation with growing incredulity, said, "Move him to another part of the country, far away from us! Garth says you've moved him once already!"

Baker slowly shook his head. "I haven't confirmed that information. Even if it were true, it would be irrelevant. Francke's decided he likes it here. The way he sees it, Mr. Frederickson, it was you who accosted him, and he was only preparing to defend himself. He is, of course, quite right when he points out that there are many people who would love to get their hands on him, or see him dead."

"He has a sexual fixation on my wife."

"Your wife is a beautiful, world-famous artist, sir. Writing letters—even obscene letters—is something I'm sure a good number of other people have done. Apparently Francke became a fan while listening to bootleg albums and tapes he'd confiscated from East German youths, and at border crossings. He began writing letters to her, but hung onto them for the obvious reason that it wouldn't have boded well for him to be caught writing fan letters to an artist of Ms. Tree's political leanings. In any case, he has made it clear that if we were to try to force him to move from here, the State Department will lose his trust and good will."

The F.B.I. agent glanced back and forth at Mary and Garth. He seemed slightly embarrassed. Finally he continued, "The State Department and the Bureau think you should move, or at least go away for a time, if his presence in the community bothers you.

Without admitting in any way that this man might pose a threat to the two of you, or anybody else, we're prepared to pay all reasonable expenses for up to a period of one year if Ms. Tree will stop giving concerts and the two of you go to another section of the country for an extended vacation, under the auspices of the Witness Protection Program."

"I think not, Mr. Baker," Mary said dryly.

They talked late into the night, discussing the intolerable impact it would have on their lives to wait indefinitely, anxiously wondering if and when the German would strike, descending on one or both of them without warning, at a time and place of his choosing. Not willing to accept that situation, they agreed that their best option was to test the man's intentions and freedom of movement. They had to lure him to them at a time and place of their choosing.

It was Mary who came up with a plan. Although Garth was initially opposed to it, the logic of her proposal was unassailable and she finally won him over by pointing out that any risk couldn't be greater than the one that already existed, for Gunther Francke certainly knew where to find them already.

On the afternoon of the day when the first posters announcing Mary's benefit concert for the Clearwater appeared in the riverfront communities, Garth received a second warning from the anonymous caller with the flat, muffled voice.

"The concert is a mistake that could prove fatal. Make sure you see him before he sees you."

On the night of the open-air concert, Garth waited forty-five minutes in the shadows of a copse of trees on a hill in Cairn's riverside park, scanning the faces in the crowd that had gathered. When he had satisfied himself that Francke was not on the field in front of the stage where Mary was performing, he went searching in the darkness of the park's perimeter. There he found Francke, sitting atop a large outcropping of rock where he had a clear view of the brightly lighted concert stage a hundred and fifty yards below. Beside him, barely visible in the shadows cast by the moon through the trees, were binoculars and a high-powered rifle with a telescopic sight and homemade silencer. Garth put a hand on his shoulder, and when Francke started to turn he hit him hard on the point of the jaw. He lifted the unconscious man, flung him across his shoulder, and carried him down toward the river.

Gunther Francke heard the water close by when, half an hour later, he awoke to find himself in a chair across from his enemy. Their left wrists were strapped together with duct tape.

"Are you crazy?!" he screamed. "What are you doing?!"

"Getting to know you."

Francke looked around at the walls of weathered wood, the windows looking out over the river. His gaze came to rest on a shelf built into the north wall where a Colt revolver rested between a tape recorder and a telephone. "Where are we?" he asked in a hoarse voice.

"A boathouse on my property," Garth replied. "You can try shouting if you'd like, but I doubt anyone's going to hear you. You know, half the Nazis the C.I.A. and State Department slipped into this country in nineteen forty-five weren't even college graduates, much less the rocket scientists they claimed to be. I'm just wondering if you're really all your hosts believe you to be. I think it's time someone pressed you a bit to establish your bona fides."

"You're crazy!"

"Exactly. I'm probably even crazier than you are, or than you think I am. You may want to bear that in mind as the days pass. I'm certainly crazy enough to kill you out of hand and dump you in the river before I let you harm my wife.

"Now that we've established that, we can get on with our other business. You've harassed my wife and threatened to kill me. I sensed you were a killer before you ever opened your mouth. The only reason I haven't put you out of everybody's misery already is because I have a nagging suspicion that's exactly what certain people would like me to do, and I don't care to do somebody else's dirty business—or to give up my life and freedom if I don't have to. Consequently, before we leave here, we're going to reach an

20

accommodation. You're going to tell me everything you supposedly know that your keepers are so anxious to hear. I don't have much of a taste for torture or I'd just beat it out of you. So I'm going to share your misery—no food, water, or sleep for either of us until you give me what I want. Then we're going to call your keepers, you're going to gladly accept new placement as far away from Cairn as they can take you, and neither my wife nor I are ever going to see or hear from you again. That's the deal."

Garth paused and motioned toward the revolver on the shelf. "If that all seems too complicated for you, you always have the option of going for the gun. But in that case—"

The man loosed a string of curses in German and jumped out of his chair. He lurched to the side, trying to drag Garth after him as he stretched out his right hand for the gun. Garth braced himself, and then swung his left arm in a counter-clockwise motion. The German screamed as his left arm broke at the wrist and just above the elbow. With pain swimming in his pale-green eyes, he sank to his knees, and then slumped on the floor as Garth used a pocketknife to cut the tape joining their wrists.

"You should have let me finish," Garth said evenly. "I told you I was willing to suffer with you for as long as it took, but I was about to warn you that all bets were off if you went for the gun."

Francke rolled back and forth on the splintered wood floor, cradling his shattered arm. "I need a doctor!"

"You were ready to kill me, and maybe my wife, too. I'll get you a doctor when you tell me what I want to know. Don't bother lying. You'll find out that my craziness includes a pretty good sense of when people are lying. Tell me the truth, and I'll know it."

"I don't know anything!" the German screamed in agony. "I'm not Gunther Francke! The papers are forged! Call a doctor! I can't stand the pain!"

Garth stood over the man for a few moments, studying him carefully. Finally he nodded. "I believe you," he said as he walked over to the shelf and turned on the tape recorder. "Now all you have to do is provide enough detail about who you really are and how you managed to assume another identity."

When the man had finished supplying information to his satisfaction, Garth braced his broken arm with a crude splint, and then called the house. Mary answered in the middle of the first ring.

"The man's ex-Stasi, all right," Garth told her, "but he was just a minor functionary, a prison guard in charge of interrogation who beat up enough political prisoners to know he was going to be in big trouble in the post-Honneker regime. He killed the man whose papers he's holding, went to our embassy in West Germany, and offered his services. Once he got over here, he got carried away and made the mistake of overplaying his hand. Then he couldn't stop. Now maybe they'll send him back to Germany and get him out of our hair. I've got it all on tape. Call an ambulance, and then the FBI office in—"

"Baker and Walker are here, Garth."

He found he wasn't surprised.

"They didn't know where you were, and I didn't tell them, but they're certain you have the German. Where do you want to meet them?"

"Tell them to come down here."

"There's another man with them, Garth."

"Who?"

"He didn't introduce himself. He's waiting outside the house."

"He'll be coming down whether we want him to or not," Garth said.

He headed up the path leading to the house as the three men approached. The unidentified man was tall and lean, with cold black eyes and gray stubble on his cheeks. He was wearing khaki chinos, sneakers, and a bulky green windbreaker with a Chicago Bears logo. As they met halfway, the man in the windbreaker brushed past Garth without looking at him or saying a word.

"Here's the tape." Garth said as he handed the cassette to Avery Baker. "His real name is Wolfgang Ingwers, and you already know more about terrorist networks than he does."

"Your wife told us," Baker said, meeting Garth's gaze as he accepted the cassette and dropped it in his pocket. "We'll check it out. If what you say is true, he's out of here."

There was a soft, almost imperceptible chugging sound from the direction of the boathouse. Baker and Walker exchanged startled glances, and Garth realized that it hadn't occurred to the two FBI agents that the unshaven man who had been sent to them was a CIA assassin. Garth had known as soon as he'd seen the man that the German was indeed about to be out of there.

The younger agent started toward the boathouse. Baker started after him, but Garth grabbed his arm. "You tell the Company man down there to clean up his goddamn mess," he said in a low voice. "I mean that literally. I don't want any sign of the body—not a drop of blood on the floor. You understand?"

"I'll make sure he gets the message. My guess is that a disposal service is waiting nearby. Take your wife out for a drink, Frederickson. When you get back, your lives will be the same as they were before."

"No, they won't," Garth replied tersely. He glanced toward the boathouse to make sure there was no one within earshot. "Thanks for the calls, Baker."

The agent responded with a curt smile and Garth continued on up the path toward Mary.

THE WHITE BEAR

Grizzlies and brown bears were really the same creature, Mary Tree learned from the man who had appeared unannounced at their front door, and both smelled like the rotting meat that was their preferred diet.

Half of Jacob Andover's face was a wasteland of scar tissue, and his surviving eye seemed too bright, as if there were fever smoldering in him. He appeared emaciated, but somehow still projected an aura of strength; he was a feral creature of gristle and bone, with permanently tanned skin and a Seattle Seahawks cap pulled tightly onto his head. Although she had met him for the first time less than an hour before, Mary already considered him perhaps the second most remarkable man she had ever known, the first being Garth Frederickson, her husband, who sat next to her on the beige couch in the music room of their home overlooking the Hudson River, listening as Jacob Andover talked, telling tales of ice and cold and bears, moose, caribou, wolves and wolverines, of pink living rivers of salmon, and the beluga and killer whales that came to feed on them.

So much of her husband remained hidden from her, Mary thought; there were secrets in his past shared, if at all, only with his brother, and so she was impressed but hardly surprised to find that, before their marriage, Garth had frequently spent summers in the Alaskan bush prospecting for gold in a particularly dangerous area known as the "forty-acre tract," near a town named Chicken. Nor was she surprised to learn from Andover that one summer Garth had camped on a sandbar which he shared with a grizzly sow and her two cubs; her husband certainly had a most unusual effect on people, including strange men like Jacob Andover, and so it seemed only natural to her that the grizzly sow wouldn't have been bothered by his presence. Finally, she wasn't surprised that Andover, when he knew he was dying, had traveled six thousand miles to seek out Garth.

"It's just the damndest thing," the scar-faced man with the bright green eye said with an air of almost childlike wonder in the face of something so awesome he was still unable to fully comprehend it. He grinned, revealing a set of even, white teeth that were apparently his own and which seemed at odds with the rest of his appearance. "I hadn't seen no color for months. I was running low on funds and getting real tired of the bush, and I figured I needed a change of scenery. I used a contact I got and went up on the North Slope to work the pipeline and make me some money. Big mistake. Garth, you know how I feel about keeping a clean camp, because if you leave stuff lying around, sooner or later some bear's gonna' pay you a visit when you ain't expectin' it. You get in the habit of tidying up. I was at the airport in Anchorage waiting to catch one of the commuter flights to the Slope. I go into the men's room to take care of my business, and I notice one of the trashcans is full to overflowing with paper towels. I go to push it down and stick myself in the hand with this hypodermic needle somebody tossed in there. Didn't think nothing of it at the time. If I'd known then that that little needle prick was going to be the end of old Jacob, I guess I wouldn't have been in such a hurry to catch my plane. Hell, I probably wouldn't have believed it would kill me anyway. It took this last bout with that funny kind of pneumonia and a collapsed lung to convince me I'd better start taking care of my last bits of business."

Garth remained very still, watching the other man, but Mary sat bolt upright on the sofa.

"Oh, God, Jacob," Mary said, shaking her head. "I'm so sorry."

"It's all right, ma'am," Andover replied. His lips again drew back from his teeth, this time forming more a grimace than a grin. "To tell you the truth," he continued more softly, "I don't much like people feeling sorry for me. It makes me real uncomfortable, so I'd appreciate it if you wouldn't do any crying on my behalf."

"Jacob, Garth and I do volunteer work for a self-help group of people with exactly the same kind of illness. Why don't you consider coming . . .?" She allowed her voice to trail off when Jacob Andover raised his hand and slowly but firmly shook his head.

"Thank you, Mary, but Garth will tell you that I was never much for joining groups. Your husband's about the only man I've met in twenty years I could stand to be with more than an hour when I wasn't drunk."

"He's come to terms with it, Mary," Garth said in a low voice, without taking his eyes off the other man's face. "Jacob's come to say goodbye."

Jacob Andover stared back at Garth for a few moments, and then said, "Yeah, that too."

"What else, Jacob?"

The gaunt prospector, trapper, and hunter reached down to the stained, torn, canvas duffel bag on the floor between his feet and opened it. He took out three bulging drawstring pouches made from moose hide and a magnificent knife of blue-gray steel with a handle carved from walrus tusk. He set the items aside on the floor, zipped up the bag, and chuckled. This triggered a coughing attack. He quickly took a handkerchief out of his pocket, covering his mouth as he looked away in embarrassment. Finally the spasm passed. He wiped his mouth, looked back at Garth, and smiled wryly.

"Since you are the only person I was able to spend more than an hour with when I wasn't drunk, and since you're the only human in twenty years who made me feel good to be human, I figured that makes you my sole heir. For me, the biggest kick in prospecting was always in finding the color, and I never did get around to spending much of it, what with living in the bush and all that. Even when I did need money, I preferred to keep the dust and nuggets around to remind me of why the hell I was working so hard. This is part of my last will and testament. I want you to have the gold and the knife, which I always knew you had a keen eye for. I'd have brought you my rifle, Magnum, and shotgun, but I figured they wouldn't let me carry them on the plane, so I gave them to the bartender and two of the waitresses at the saloon in Chicken."

"Thank you, Jacob," Garth said quietly. "I appreciate that. I'll take the knife, which I have always had a keen eye for, but you'll need the gold for medical expenses. You know you're going to die soon, and you've accepted that, but there's no reason for you not to make the most of the days, weeks, or months you have left. There are drugs and other treatments that can help you."

"And you're welcome to stay with us, Jacob," Mary said, moving closer to Garth and taking his hand. "You have a refuge in which to die with dignity, if you care to accept it."

Jacob Andover was silent for some time, glancing back and forth between the man with whom he had spent so little time but to whom he felt so close, and the beautiful folk singer with waist-length, whitish blond hair and blue eyes who was the man's wife. Finally his eye misted, a single tear formed and rolled down his sunken cheek. "I thank you for making me that offer, Mary," he said in a low voice, "but I won't be needing to take you up on it. Now that I've decided what my last will and testament is going to be, I'm anxious to get on with the rest of my business before I check out. Garth, the gold stays here, but I have to ask you to wait a few days for the knife. I'll make sure it gets to you."

Garth took his hand from Mary's, and then leaned forward on the sofa, resting his elbows on his knees and staring hard at the man sitting in the wicker chair across the room. "What is it, Jacob?" he asked. "Why else are you here?"

The other man was again silent for a time, as if considering the question. Then he said, "You remember, Garth, how you and I used to talk about the differences between living in Alaska and back East here?"

Garth brushed his hand back through his thinning, shoulder-length, wheat-colored hair, and fixed the other man with his brown eyes. "I seem to recall we mostly talked about the different sources of danger, the things that can get a person killed."

"That's right. In Alaska, it's the environment that's most likely to kill you if you're not careful. In winter, when it's forty below, you can run your car off the road or wander off a trail and freeze to death in no time at all. In the East, you couldn't really get lost if you were trying to; there's almost always a house, more likely a whole neighborhood, or a road with traffic, just over the next hill. In Alaska you can get your head torn off by a bear a mile or so into the bush, or get stomped to death by a moose in your driveway. The danger there comes mostly from the environment, but you can take steps to protect yourself—carry a survival pack in your car, make a lot of noise when you hike in the bush, and look out the window to see what may be standing on your front lawn before you go outside. Here, it's the damn people crowding all around you who are dangerous, and you never know when somebody's sneaking up behind you to mug, rape, maim, or kill. To me, this is a far more dangerous place to live than the forty-acre tract."

"I couldn't agree more," Mary said evenly, glancing at Garth.

"Well, I've certainly killed more than my share of animals, but I always did it in self-defense, or for food or hides, or something else I needed. I could never see no sense in gunning down some moose or bison, because they're so stone dumb they'll just stand there and look at you while you do it. I was never much interested in killing for the sake of killing, if you know what I mean."

29

"The people who do that sort of thing call themselves sportsmen," Mary said dryly.

"I did me enough hunting in the war to last me a lifetime, and I never did know if the men I killed there deserved to die. But it occurred to me while I was over there that if I ever did really want to hunt something—say, for sport, or any other reason—it would be a man, and it wouldn't bother my conscience none because the man I hunted would be some son-of-a-bitch who deserved to die."

"Jacob," Garth said quietly, "do you really think I'd want that knife after you've used it to kill a man?"

"Well, I guess I'd say that depends on who it was I killed."

"No. You'd be wrong."

Jacob Andover's eye narrowed. "The way I hear it, you and that real smart little brother of yours have killed a whole lot of men."

"Men who were trying to kill us, Jacob. Like the bears you've shot. Who do you want to kill?"

"T. L. Michael Mason," the other man replied evenly, and smiled thinly. "He enough of a son-of-a-bitch for you?"

Garth exchanged glances with Mary, then leaned back on the sofa and crossed his arms over his chest. "You know."

"Yeah, I know. You're after the thieving, murdering bastard yourself. Janie Aglook told me how you and your brother are working for one of the tribal corporations, trying to prove not only that it was him and his men who sacked that village, but that he's been pulling stunts like that for a long time. I'll bet half of that collection of artifacts he's got were stolen, but you won't get many Inuits, Indians, or Aleuts coming to New York City to complain about him."

"How do you know Dr. Aglook?"

"I never told you that story?"

Garth shook his head. "You were never much of a talker, Jacob. You seemed pleased to seek out my company and just sit for a time, or listen to me talk, so that's how it went."

30

"You got that right," Andover said with a curt nod. " 'Nam messed up my mind pretty good. After I left there, I couldn't stand to be around people. A lot of us were like that, and a lot of us went looking for wild places where we could be by ourselves and just sort of do what we pleased so we wouldn't hurt so damn much. I headed for Alaska."

"So did a lot of other Vietnam vets," Garth said quietly.

"Yeah, but I went a lot *farther* into Alaska than the others. I wasn't content to just camp out in the bush. I had nightmares bad, and keeping on the move helped some. I just kept heading north. Who knows? Maybe I was looking to get killed, and I almost did. After three or four years of wandering, living off the land, I made it all the way up to the Circle. A polar bear caught me out on the ice, scalped me like they do, bit through my rib cage, and damn near tore off my left arm. He must have figured I was dead, 'cause he dragged me off to an ice cave and left me to ripen up for a few days. I was found by some Inuit—Janie's people. They put me on a sled, took me back to their village, and healed me up. I'm probably the only white man you'll ever meet who actually likes Inuit ice cream. Anyway, you can imagine my surprise when I wake up one morning, half out of my mind with fever, to find this pretty young Eskimo woman sitting beside my bed, holding my hand, and talking to me in perfect English. With a Boston accent, no less. Sounded like a Kennedy.

"Later, I found out that she'd been adopted by some hotshot Eskimos on the tribal corporation board, and they'd made sure she got some top schooling. When I met her, she'd just gotten her Ph.D. in cultural anthropology. She'd spent years studying Inuit in general, and this particular group of Inuit. She wrote papers about them. Finest woman I've ever met. If it hadn't been for her visits two or three times a year, I'd probably have forgotten my English."

Mary asked, "You came back by yourself when you were better?"

"Heck yes, ma'am. I didn't need Janie to show me how to get back. And I didn't mind living with the Inuit; I liked their lifestyle. Life up on the Circle was real simple. I'd go off hunting by myself a lot, but I always brought back meat and hides to share with the tribe, so they accepted me. They even gave me an Inuit name, called me the White Bear.

"After a few years up there on the Circle, I started feeling a little better, so I headed back south. Worked on the Slope for a while, and then I went into the bush to prospect for gold. While I was living with the Inuit I learned to do a little scrimshaw, carved ivory and bone—not too good, mind you, but I enjoyed doing it. I carved a polar bear once, gave it to the couple who'd cared for me when I was mangled up. It was such a bad carving that most of those Inuit would have laughed if they weren't so polite, but the couple appreciated my effort, and said they'd keep it always as a treasured gift. Inuit don't lie about things like that. Now, your T. L. Michael Mason claims he got all his Inuit artifacts and carvings through legitimate trading outlets. He also claims he and his hunting buddies were never in that village that was sacked. He's a damn liar on both counts, because that bear I carved is right now sitting in one of the glass display cases in the lobby of that big building he owns on Fifth Avenue."

Garth uncrossed his arms and sat bolt upright on the sofa. "Can you prove that, Jacob?"

Andover shrugged. "Well, anybody who knows about such things would know that bear wasn't carved by any Inuit artist— Mason ain't the expert he claims to be. It also happens to have my initials carved into the bottom. You tell me if that proves he and his men sacked the village, raped a couple of women, stole their carvings and raw ivory, and killed a man."

"It would certainly help bolster the prosecution's case. Look, if you'll give me a deposition—"

"I already started all that deposition stuff with some lawyers in New York Janie sent me to. I'm supposed to talk to them again next week. It was Janie who contacted me and brought me here, and it was Janie who told me where to find you here in Cairn. Nice town. That's some river out there."

32

"If you're working with lawyers for the tribal corporation, Jacob, then you're doing all you can. I'm investigating other leads concerning stolen artifacts that, together with your bear, could at least prove that Mason is a thief and a liar. Let it go."

"I gave them the deposition, and they say they want to talk to me a few more times after they talk to other people. They want me to testify at his trial, if there is one, but there ain't much chance I'll live that long. Each morning now when I wake up it's a surprise to me. Most days it's a big disappointment. You want to know what's going to happen to Mason? Nothing. That's what. I ain't been out of touch for so long as to forget how lawyers do their business, and Mason's got plenty of those. They'll say there's no way to prove the couple I gave the bear to didn't give it away to some other Inuit who sold it."

"Dr. Aglook has Inuit who'll testify that the two planes that landed near their village bore the logo of Mason's corporation, and they'll identify him as one of the raiders."

Andover made a dismissive gesture with his trembling right hand. "Ten minutes after a lawyer gets one of those witnesses on the stand, he won't know the difference between a logo and a logjam. The lawyer will say all white men look the same to an Inuit. The Inuit will end up looking foolish. That's the way it's going to go. The way I figure it, part of my last will and testament is to give my death to serve some good purpose. I don't give a damn about all those bodyguards Mason has, because I don't mind getting killed. It's what I want. My life's been pretty worthless, when all's said and done, but I'd like my death to mean something. All I need to do is get close enough to Mason to cut his throat, and then justice will have been done."

"It's not going to work out, Jacob," Garth said softly.

The other man raised his head slightly and frowned. The too-bright light in his one eye seemed colder. "No? Why not?"

"Because I can't let you do it."

"And just how do you think you can stop me?"

33

"You have to understand that this isn't the bush," Garth replied in the same soft tone. "Here, neither of us can just go about taking care of our business any way we please."

"I can."

"No. I'm a private investigator licensed by the state of New York. I'm currently involved in a case that's before the courts, and that limits my actions in certain ways. Information you give me isn't privileged. I can't learn of a plan to murder the man I'm investigating, and not notify the authorities. I could be brought up on criminal charges myself. In short, Jacob, I'll stop you by calling in the cops."

The other man's half-face grew even paler. "You'd call the cops on me?"

"I've said it."

"You think I'm wrong, Frederickson?"

"It doesn't matter what I think, Jacob, only what I do. I don't care to discuss it any longer. I need to hear from you that you don't intend to pursue Mason outside of the legal process."

Jacob Andover abruptly rose to his feet and picked up his duffel bag, leaving the three pouches filled with gold dust on the floor. He walked stiffly to the door of the music room, hesitated, and then turned back. "I thought much better of you before I came here, Frederickson," he said in a rasping voice. "I won't be seeing or talking to you again." Then he walked quickly out of the room.

Mary, her face mirroring her distress, started to rise to go after him but stopped when she felt the pressure of her husband's hand on her thigh. She looked inquiringly at Garth, who raised his hand slightly to indicate she should wait. Although puzzled, Mary had learned from experience that Garth had certain very special sensibilities about certain things, and she nodded her assent.

A few seconds later they heard the screen door at the front of the house open and close, indicating that their visitor had left. Garth continued to wait almost two minutes before he finally rose and motioned for Mary to follow him. They walked through the house and out the front door. Mary glanced past Garth down the walk and saw the hunched shape of Jacob Andover sitting on the

34

steps leading down to the sidewalk and street. His frail shoulders were shaking as if he were crying. She turned toward Garth to ask how he had known the other man would not be going far, but her husband was already walking toward the slumped figure. He knelt down, put his powerful arms around the weeping man, holding the scarred head to his chest. Mary knelt down on the other side of Andover and gently stroked his back.

"I'm so ashamed," he sobbed into Garth's shoulder. "I'm so damn tired all the time. Sometimes it's all I can do to get out of bed. I was just hoping I'd have enough energy left to pay back Mason for what he did to the people who saved my life. God, Garth, I was even hoping you might help me. I don't think I can manage it by myself. Right now I don't have enough energy to get down to the street."

"You'll stay with us, Jacob," Garth said, lifting the frail man in his arms and starting back up the walk to the house. "We'll talk about what can be done about Mr. Mason."

They never did get around to talking about what could be done about T. L. Michael Mason. Garth and Mary cared for Jacob Andover, gave him a place to live, food, and comfort. On days when Jacob was feeling stronger, he would take the Red-and-Tan bus into New York City to confer with the tribal corporation lawyers, or take walks, or run errands. Two weeks after his arrival in Cairn, the newspapers carried reports of his death at the hands of a gang of teenagers who'd tried to rob him as he was walking in Central Park. Jacob had killed two of his attackers, and severed the spinal cord of a third.

Mary was troubled when she found her husband smiling as he read the accounts of the attack and deaths. "Garth," she said in a curt tone she had never before used with him, "do you think what happened to Jacob and those kids is *funny?*"

"No," Garth replied evenly. "It's not exactly what I would describe as funny, but it does make me feel good."

Mary shook her head. "Garth, I can't believe it's you saying that. I don't understand at all."

His smile vanished so suddenly that Mary, despite her knowledge that Garth was not angry, felt a slight chill. "Listen to me, Mary," Garth said in a quiet, even tone. "We share love, but we haven't really known each other for very long, so you're still getting to know me. For you to understand why I feel good about what's happened, you must first understand why I don't feel bad. Jacob Andover was a very strange and dangerous man, but he never hurt anyone who wasn't trying to hurt him. He had a strong, if primitive, sense of justice, and his presence in the world did not cause a blight. He was dying, slowly and painfully, in a way that was totally humiliating to him. He wanted to make his death count for something, and now it has. Those 'kids,' as you called them, have arrest records dating back years, juveniles charged as adults. They were rapists, robbers, and killers. They were on a rampage in the park that day, beating up and robbing, or sexually molesting, anyone who got in their way. From all the evidence cited in the news reports, the lives of the two youths Jacob killed in self defense, and the one he maimed, were irredeemable; they would have spent the rest of their lives hurting and killing people until they were put away in prison for good, or until somebody stopped them another way. Jacob stopped them. They went after Jacob because they thought he was helpless, not realizing he was a wounded bear every bit as dangerous as they were, or more so. They got what they deserved, and when Jacob died at their hands he took the evil and blight of their lives out of the world with him. It's what Jacob, who was a decent man, wanted. That's why I like the way things worked out. Now, if you feel sad or upset, and you appear to, I'd like you to explain that to me."

Mary stared at her husband for some time before turning and walking slowly out of the room. A half minute later she reappeared in the doorway.

"Garth?"

"Yes?"

"Do you still own the claim where you spent the summer with the grizzly sow and her cubs?"

"Yes. I never mentioned it because Alaska's a very long way away, the area around Chicken is rough. It's not the sort of thing I thought you'd have the slightest interest in."

"Would you take me there some time? Show me how to live in the bush and pan for gold? I'd like to learn."

Garth smiled warmly. "Sure," he said, and took his wife in his arms.

LONE WOLF

He hadn't thought they'd risk releasing the animals, for free of their brutal handler and running as a pack they would be unpredictable, seemingly posing as much danger to his hunters as to him; but when he saw the three dark shapes glide through a patch of moonlight next to the high-voltage fence separating him from the river on his right he knew he'd been wrong, had underestimated the hatred and desperation of the men who would kill him. He cut to his left, started to climb the steep embankment toward the rock face fifty yards above him, grimaced with pain when he felt his left ankle give and twist in the loamy soil. He went down on his right side, brought his left leg up, and tentatively touched the ankle. It did not seem broken, only sprained, but in his situation it made little difference, for immobilization here among the trees and thick brush surely meant death, if not in a blunt needle-spray of gunfire, then with his throat torn out by the fangs of the creatures who might or might not be stalking him in their mutilated silence. He willed himself to move, rolling over on his back and awkwardly crab-walking up the slope, dragging his left leg. He expected at any moment to hear a rustle in the brush that would presage his death, but there remained in the woods only the sound of his own heavy breathing as he struggled upward. Then he emerged from the tree line at the edge of the sloping field of broken rock at the base of the sheer wall of trap rock that was the eastern face of an abandoned quarry that formed the western boundary of Floyd Kunkel's inherited riverfront estate. He twisted around onto his stomach and snaked his way through the sharp riprap up to the base of the escarpment, where, exhausted, he sank down behind a large boulder and gasped for breath. He wiped his bleeding palms on his thighs, and then gently kneaded his sprained ankle as he looked around him. From here he could see above the trees to a shimmering, silver-coated section of the river near where Mary had been the first to sight the exhausted animal swimming in the middle of the deep channel, struggling against both tide and current, directly in the path of an oncoming tanker.

"Garth," Mary cried, pointing to the bobbing patch of dark fur off their starboard side, "there's a dog out there! We have to save it!"

Garth Frederickson glanced up at the steel shrouds on either side of the fourteen-foot catamaran where plastic telltales fluttered in a wind that remained between fifteen and eighteen knots, coming directly from the southwest. In order to avoid the tanker approaching from the north, he had just tacked out of the deep channel, sailing to the port side of a large, green buoy that marked the edge of the shipping lane in the vast, four-mile-wide section of the Hudson River between Piermont and Haverstraw, New York, that the first Dutch settlers had called the "Tappan Sea." They were on a run, with the wind at their backs. Their speed would increase considerably if he fell off to either port or starboard, left or right. On their port side, across the river, was Rockland County and their home in Cairn; to fall off to starboard was to invite an abrupt and brutal end to their lives.

"The tanker's too close, Mary. There isn't time."

"There *is* if you turn now! We'll be on a reach! We can make it! You can't just let it be run over!"

"I'm not about to risk my wife's life for a dog."

"They'll turn when they see our sail!"

"That's a seventy-five-ton tanker, Mary, not a sports car. In the position they're in now and at the speed they're traveling, they can't swerve to avoid the dog or us. The ship's too big. You know that."

"Garth, listen to me," Mary Tree said in a voice that had suddenly grown low and husky, quavering and desperate. "You know how crazy I get about animals. It's just very important to me for us to try to save that dog. *Please* just try."

Garth turned his head slightly in order to look at his wife, who was sitting next to him on the port side of the catamaran. Strands of her waist-length, silver-streaked blond hair had worked free of the cotton band that held it in a ponytail and were whipping across her face. Tears welled in her sea-blue eyes, rolled down her cheeks. She was rhythmically pounding her fists in helpless frustration against the front of her heavy life jacket. Garth knew what he had to do. His wife's exquisite madness was the sometimes-dark engine that powered her music, and her vehement passion for small as well as great things was one of the reasons he loved her so much. At this moment the most important thing in the world to her was not her life, or even his, but saving an animal that was on some inexplicable and hopeless mission, swimming, struggling against the tide, toward its certain death. He would feel bad if the dog were run over and ground up by the tanker's propeller blades, but it was Mary who would enter the soul and body of the dog in recurring nightmares, Mary who would suffer the bone-smashing collision with steel, feel the river filling her lungs, hear through the water the deadly song of whirring blades of steel.

"Swim to the buoy," he said as he swept her off the catamaran

40

with his left arm at the same time as he pulled on the tiller to turn the cat ninety degrees to starboard.

He ducked under the swinging boom, slid across the cat's canvas trampoline to the opposite side as the wind filled the sail and the starboard hull began to lift out of the water. He sheeted out the sail slightly, released the traveler to the three-quarter's mark, and then anchored his feet in the hiking straps and leaned far back in order to counterbalance the force of the wind that was sending the cat streaking like some misshapen white arrow directly into the path of the oncoming tanker. Mary shouted something at him, but her words were lost first in the hiss of the port hull slicing through the water, then drowned out completely by the ominous, deep-throated bray of the tanker's horn warning him away.

Despite the brisk breeze, the surface of the river was relatively smooth, allowing Garth to plane, flying the starboard hull on which he was sitting a foot or so above the water and increasing his speed. He glanced up once at the tanker, which had become a moving wall of steel filling the horizon, then looked away, focusing his vision and all his concentration on the furry, dark head bobbing just above the surface seventy-five yards away. He had dismissed from his mind fear of being crushed by the tanker the moment he had committed and veered sharply to starboard; he would simply either make it under the bow of the tanker or he wouldn't, and it wouldn't take many heartbeats for him to find out which was going to be the case. The task at hand required all his attention, for it was a complicated one; if he miscalculated, he could shoot right past the dog, which would make it all a wasted exercise; or the sudden addition of weight as he pulled the dog from the water could cause the cat to flip backward, and they would both die anyway.

The tanker was almost on him now, its great horn wailing its mournful dirge even as the ship's bow wave rolled under his port hull, lifting the cat slightly. Above him, at the edge of his peripheral vision, he glimpsed perhaps a half-dozen men standing at the railing, shouting and waving their arms, urging him on. The tip of the flying starboard hull passed just in front of the dog's head. He sheeted in the mainsail hard, causing the hull on which he was sitting to begin to rise even higher into the air. The small cat would have flipped over if at the same time he hadn't arched his back, reached down and grabbed a handful of fur and skin on the neck of the animal struggling in the water behind and below him. Pain shot up his arm and into his back as the sudden tug of the animal's weight combined with the speed of the catamaran insulted bone and muscle and threatened to pull his right shoulder from its socket. The raised hull of the cat abruptly slammed down into the

41

water Garth hauled the animal up out of the water and onto the center of the trampoline. He sheeted out instantly and shifted his weight to prevent the cat from flipping over backward, and then the surge of the ship's bow wave carried him away from the tanker, just inches from the painted steel wall that now rushed past him. When the wake had passed he came about and began the series of short tacks that would take him back to the green buoy where Mary was, and as he looked into the glazed, golden eyes of the exhausted animal beside him, noted the long, spindly legs and large feet, he realized that the animal he had rescued from the river was not a dog.

"It's a wolf," Garth said to his wife the next day when she came around the side of the house to the area where he had staked the animal next to the river on a heavy chain wound around a boulder erupting from their beach a few yards above the high-tide mark. He had been working the animal all morning, repeatedly wrestling it to the ground, cuffing it sharply on one side of the head and then the other when it tried to resist.

He waited for a response, but Mary Tree simply stood and stared at him, her limpid blue eyes moist, her face a kind of diary of unspoken thoughts. Garth straddled the wolf, squeezing its rib cage with his knees, and smiled at this woman whom he loved so much, the only person besides his brother who had ever made him feel complete. He had always found this professional folk singer terribly fragile, often conflicted and inarticulate without a guitar in her hands and with no music to accompany her words. She had spoken little since the day before when he had picked her up at the buoy, but she had expressed her feelings most adequately with her body, clinging to him throughout the rest of the day and into the night, repeatedly taking him into her until finally, exhausted, they had fallen asleep.

At last she said in a small voice, "A wolf?"

"Yep. Somebody's idea of a pet." He grabbed the thick leather collar he had put around the wolf's neck, brought the animal's head back, then used the fingers of his left hand to part the fur on its throat to reveal a circular scar the size of a quarter. "Its vocal cords have been cut. I guess his owner didn't want him bothering the neighbors."

Mary winced, put a hand to her cheek. "My God. How cruel." She came forward, knelt down on the sand beside Garth, a few inches from the large, dark gray head with its bright golden eyes. "It's beautiful."

The animal started to turn its head in Mary's direction. Garth pressed down on the back of its neck, and then cuffed it lightly on the side of the jaw. "Yes. It's most likely a hybrid, with a little dog

42

in it—but not much."

"Is that why you play so rough with it?"

"I'm not playing. Remember that this is a wolf, Mary, not a dog. They may look alike, but there the similarity ends. This fellow can snap your face off, and it will if you don't constantly pay attention to what's happening when you're around it. You can't domesticate a wolf. You can live with one, but you have to know the rules. The first rule is that you must physically dominate it, and you have to keep doing it, because a wolf will keep testing you. This morning's workout was intended to show him who's leader of the pack around here."

Mary reached out and stroked the animal's fur, then rested her head on her husband's shoulder. "Garth, I... I..."

"I know what you want to say, Mary. It isn't necessary."

"Yes it is. I have to get it out. I can't imagine what I was thinking about yesterday. I just kind of went out of my mind when I saw this guy out there in front of the ship. But that's no excuse for the way I behaved. I can't believe I made you . . . Garth, I almost killed you."

"Hell, you could have been killed too. You weren't exactly expecting me to dump you in the river. Besides, you didn't make me do anything. I wasn't very happy with the situation either. It was the right thing to do, and we did it."

"You did it. And I not only let you risk your life, I damn well insisted on it."

"Mary, I really do under—"

"Oh, Garth, I love you so much. Truly, I don't know what I'd do without you. In so many ways, I feel I owe you everything."

"Come on, sweetheart, you were famous long before my brother introduced us."

"When you met me I was a has-been, and hiding out here in Cairn. You gave me back my confidence."

Garth waved his hand in a dismissive gesture, kissed his wife the cheek, and then, still keeping a firm grip on the wolf's collar, stood up. "Move back a little. I want to take our friend here to the vet get his shots, in case he hasn't had any, and I have to go get the muzzle I bought him."

"I'm all right here. He seems friendly enough—which is a wonder considering the way you've been swatting him around. Let me stay here with him. He has to get used to me as well as you."

Garth thought about it, nodded. "Okay. Scratch him behind the ears; he likes that. But keep a firm grip on the chain, right behind his head, and don't put your face close to his."

When Mary gripped the chain as he had instructed her, Garth released his hold on the animal's collar, and then went back up the

43

beach and into the boathouse to get the muzzle and heavy leather leash he had purchased earlier in the morning. When he returned he found Mary staring down at a stain on her pants leg.

"Garth," she said with a nervous laugh, "he peed on my leg!"

Garth walked quickly to where Mary was standing, grabbed the wolf's collar, and forced it down onto the sand. He turned it over on its back, sat on its stomach, and then gripped its throat with both hands.

"Garth—?!"

"I know what I'm doing, Mary. I'm not punishing it—but you have to do exactly as I say. Bite him on the nose. Hard."

"What?! I can't do that."

"Well, you're going to have to if this animal is going to stay with us. When he pissed on your leg, he was challenging you. That was his way of seeing if he could push you around. Now you have to push back—only harder. If you don't, you'll constantly be in danger. I'll turn it over to the animal shelter rather than risk having it attack you, and they'll almost certainly end up having to put it down. This animal could be a big problem. If you want him to live, you have to show him you're the boss, if you want yesterday's rescue to mean anything, you'll do as I say."

Mary slowly knelt down, bent over toward the wolf's head, hesitated.

"Do it!" Garth said sharply. "It's for his own good! Bite him hard!" Mary closed her eyes, opened her mouth, closed her teeth gently on the moist, black leather nose, then snapped her head back in alarm when she heard an anguished, raspy whimper from somewhere deep within the animal's chest.

Garth released his grip on the wolf's throat, got up off its stomach. The animal turned over, but remained flat on the sand, its head down between its forelegs. Garth grunted with satisfaction, and then fitted the muzzle over the wolf's jaws and replaced the tether chain on the collar with the leather leash. "That wasn't very hard," he said, stroking his wife's cheek, "but I think it may have done the job."

"How do you know so much about wolves? Mining for gold in Alaska?"

"Partly. Actually, it was my brother who taught me that little trick."

"Your *brother?*"

"Uh-huh. You know the story about the lobox, but you've never seen it. One of these days we'll visit one of the closed, experimental breeding pens at the Bronx Zoo and I'll show you the fellow *he* took on. In the meantime, we've got to figure out what we're going to do with our own beastie here. Call *The Journal*

44

News, have them run an ad in the Classified ---.make it an eighth of a page, with a border around it. Have it read: 'Unusual Pet Rescued From River. For Information Call—' and give our number."

"You're going to give him back?"

"Hardly. You might also want to make a run to the butcher."

"Meat for the wolf?"

Garth laughed, and described a circle in the air with his finger to include the three of them. "Wolf has already had tonight's pork chops for his breakfast," he replied, and would later recall his words with a certain grim amusement when he was trapped with an entire pack of the creatures that could, sooner or later, be considering him as a candidate for a meal.

Throughout the night he had seen pairs of eyes glowing among the trees at the edge of the rock fall as members of the pack came and went, but none of the animals attempted to negotiate the treacherous slope of broken rock to get at him. He knew that in the wild wolves will go to extreme lengths to avoid contact with humans, so all things being equal, he should not be in great danger of imminent attack. But all things were not equal. These hybrid wolves were not in the wild; they were trapped, like him, in a giant enclosure where he was the only pork chop around, and he had no idea when they had last eaten. In addition, they had been brutalized, first as cubs by having their vocal cords cut out, and then, presumably, through the kind of training that had conditioned in them the savage reactions he had observed in the animal he had rescued from the river. In short, the behavior of these animals, as individuals and as a pack, would be unpredictable. And he had only the rocks he held in each hand to defend himself against the pack's fangs and the guns of the men who would come during the day.

As dawn broke he found one animal, a male who was either very hungry or intent on establishing territory, standing at the edge of the rock fall and looking up at him. Almost five minutes passed, and then the wolf bared his fangs and started up toward him, picking its way carefully through the sharp riprap. Garth casually tossed the rocks he was holding in the wolf's direction, and then picked up two more. He was not so much concerned with holding off the wolf, which could not maneuver well in the broken rock, as he was with the stalking animal giving away his position to Kunkel's young, would-be storm troopers, perhaps led by Franz Heitman, who had certainly begun fanning out through the enclosure at first light. The worry became academic when a burst of fire from an automatic weapon caused the animal to spin around and bound back into the trees.

Garth recognized the young man who emerged from the tree line

45

twenty-five yards away, to his right, as one of the two companions of the acne-scarred man whose jaw he had broken at Hook Mountain in Nyack. Then he had worn black leather, but now he was dressed in an ill-fitting khaki uniform with the group's lightning-bolt-and-cross patch on the left sleeve. Although the morning was cool, with a steady breeze from the river, the young man's shaved head glistened with sweat, and his hand trembled slightly as he raised his Ingram MAC 10 machine pistol and aimed it at the spot where Garth sat behind the boulder.

"That's a lot of firepower you're carrying there, kiddo," Garth said easily, "but the problem with it is that it sprays bullets all over the damn place. Be careful you don't shoot your dick off."

"You're not such a big shot now, are you, Frederickson?" the man said in a tight voice that cracked. "Get down here!"

Garth wriggled his damaged left ankle in his boot. It was still decidedly sore, but there was no longer the stabbing pain that had disabled him before. It would hold his weight. "I can't. I twisted my ankle."

"Get up or I'll kill you!" the man shouted, his eyes glinting with both hatred and fear as he started to advance up the slope toward Garth.

"So kill me. What do you have to lose, except twenty to twenty-five years tacked onto the prison sentence you're already likely to get? You'll certainly make Kunkel and the man you call Otto, not to mention your birdbrain buddies, happy, at least in the short term, because right now they're probably trying to figure out what to do with me if *they* find me. Like you said, I'm a big shot."

The man advanced another ten yards, and Garth threw a rock with a hard sidearm motion, aiming at the man's head. He missed, but the sharp stone sailing past his left ear made the man flinch, and then stumble on the rocks at his feet. By the time he recovered, Garth was on him, punching him in the throat, then on the side of the head. The man fell, hitting his head against a boulder, and did not move. Garth did not check to see if he was dead or alive, for he didn't care. He picked up the machine pistol, checked to make certain that the specially treated cloth he carried in his jacket pocket was hidden yet secure, and then, limping only slightly, headed down into the trees. Now that he had a weapon, he was no longer interested in running or hiding, or trying to find a way to escape from the enclosure. He would see how these young men and their masters, who dreamed of the deaths of so many, liked it when they faced their own deaths at the hands of a man who loathed them as much as they loathed their intended victims. And he knew there was an outraged veterinarian who would very much approve of his present course of action.

46

"You know," Sarah Bleekman had said, eyeing Garth suspiciously as she removed the needle from the flank of the muzzled animal that lay on the examining table under the tall man's firm grip, "what you've got here is mostly wolf."

"I do know, Doctor," Garth replied evenly, stroking the animal's quivering hide as the veterinarian prepared a second hypodermic. "It's a hybrid. It's got some dog in it, but not much—maybe five percent or less, just enough for some breeder to leave a paper trail that would make it legal to own in some states."

"Not in this state," the round-faced woman with short, dark hair replied in a clipped tone that displayed her severe disapproval. "It doesn't belong here. This is a very dangerous animal. You need a special license to keep one, and then you have to show a special reason. Wanting to own an unusual pet to impress the neighbors isn't good enough."

"I appreciate the information."

Sarah Bleekman studied the famous man with the shoulder-length, wheat-colored hair and dark brown eyes who stood across from her on the opposite side of the examining table. He had, she thought, a mysterious, perhaps mystical, aura of gentleness combined with an implacable toughness, was probably not afraid of anything, and would be very dangerous to the wrong kinds of people. This was the first time she had ever spoken to Garth Frederickson, but like virtually everyone else in Cairn, she knew who he was; he was a celebrity, like his folk singer wife, whose career had blossomed the sixties, been eclipsed, and was now once more in ascendance. She had read the newspaper stories and heard the wild rumors about this man who, teamed with his even more famous brother, ran what was probably the world's best-known private investigation agency, an enterprise that seemed to virtually specialize in bizarre cases that made headlines. But she often saw Garth Frederickson and Mary Tree in town and they never acted like the celebrities they were, never put on airs. She certainly did not believe all the stories she'd heard about the fantastic exploits of the Frederickson brothers, but if even half of them were true, Garth Frederickson was a brave man indeed. He did not seem like the type of man who would need to keep a dangerous pet to bolster his ego. "Did you have his vocal cords cut out?"

"No. As a matter of fact, I was going to ask you if you knew any other veterinarian in the area who might have been persuaded to perform such a procedure."

She shook her head, and then tears misted her eyes. "Then it doesn't belong to you?"

"I fished it out of the river yesterday. It was going someplace, or was after something, that was very important to it; he'd been swimming against the tide and current to the point where he was exhausted. Even if he hadn't been about to be run over by a tanker, I believe he would have kept swimming until he drowned, or his heart burst."

"Do you know where he was going, or what he was after?"

"No."

She finished, patted the animal's flank and stroked its fur. "Except for the fact that it's been mutilated and can't communicate vocally with its own kind, it's healthy. And now he's had his shots against rabies and distemper. But you do agree that it isn't a suitable pet?"

"I thought I'd said so," Garth replied quietly, holding the wolf's leash tightly as the animal bounded off the table and looked up at Garth with its golden eyes. "How much do I owe you, Doctor?"

"You saved his life, and I gave him his shots. We'll call it even. May I ask what you plan to do with him?"

"Try to find a suitable home."

"That won't be easy, Mr. Frederickson. The only suitable home for this animal is in the wild, and he can't go back there."

I don t think he's ever been in the wild; my guess is that he was bred. Are you recommending that I have him put down?"

Sarah Bleekman quickly shook her head. "I'm not recommending that at all."

"Then I'll just have to do the best I can, won't I?"

"Let me know if I can help you. Seeing what's been done to this animal makes me very angry."

"You can let me know if anybody else with a wolf comes to see you, or if you can think of a skilled amateur who might have cut this animal."

"I will. You might want to touch base with the police or Animal Control about having this animal."

"Oh, I certainly plan to."

Jeffrey Bond, the Cairn chief of police, was in his office, a grim expression on his face as he sorted through a small pile of crudely printed posters and pamphlets. The thickset man with the crooked nose looked up as Garth knocked and entered, and then smiled thinly and motioned Garth to a chair.

"Got a couple of minutes, Chief?"

"For you, my friend, I've always got a couple of minutes." He paused, pushed the pamphlets and posters aside with a gesture of distaste. "Besides, I'm tired of looking at this garbage."

"What kind of garbage?"

"We've got ourselves a neo-Nazi outfit in town. They call them-selves Angry Cross. They opened up a storefront down at the end of Main Street, staffed by a bunch of skinheads. They're trying to turn Cairn into Creep City. They seem to be having an influence on some of the more dysfunctional members of our little community, and we're getting a rash of synagogue and Jewish cemetery desecrations. I can't stand it."

"Bust them."

"Can't. Protected speech."

"Defacing synagogues and desecrating cemeteries isn't protected speech."

"No, but we have to catch somebody actually doing that, and then tie them to Angry Cross. We haven't been able to do that so far—but we will." Bond cursed softly under his breath as he swept the papers onto the floor, then sighed as he turned back to Garth. "How's your smart little brother? Usually he's up here every weekend during the summer, but I haven't seen him around lately."

"My smart little brother is over in Europe taking care of business with some corporate clients while I hold down the fort here."

"What can I do for you, Garth?"

"A couple of things. First, I want to report what I think could be a crime in progress.

"And what crime do you think could be progressing?"

"I've got a hybrid wolf out in my van. I fished it out of the river yesterday."

"What the hell is a hybrid wolf?"

"A big, bad wolf with a little dog bred into it. They breed them legally in Alaska, where they're a hot item as pets. I've got a small mining claim in Alaska, and I used to spend some time there before I got married, so I've seen a lot of hybrid wolves. They're dangerous."

"How dangerous?"

"Keeping one as a household pet would be about the equivalent of bringing a leopard, or a bear, into your home; you could do it, but you'd best not be prone to carelessness."

"So it's very dangerous," Bond said with a curt nod. "And that makes it illegal in New York State. Any tags on it?"

"No. And there's more to it. This animal had its vocal cords cut, and it's an old scar. That indicates to me that the owner, or breeder, planned from the time it was a pup on bringing it into a heavily populated area. When you hear a wolf howl, you know it's no dog—and wolves howl a lot. It would be bound to attract attention. Cut their vocal cords, and they don't howl. Maybe only this animal was cut, and then delivered on special order. But maybe not."

"You're suggesting that a breeder may be attempting some market expansion?"

"I think it's possible that mutilated wolf cubs are being shipped

49

down here from Alaska to people willing to pay a premium for them, or even that they're being bred around here. Now, some people might ask, who the hell would want to keep a wolf in the city, or in a town like Cairn? Well, you and I know there are lots of folks who think they might want a wolf—but especially people who are into intimidation, personally or professionally."

Bond slowly nodded. "Like drug dealers thinking to make a switch from pit bulls as the attack dog of choice to wolves."

"The thought occurred to me, and I wanted to share it with you."

"What are you going to do with it, Garth?"

"If I turn it over to the shelter or the state police, my guess is that they'll eventually feel they have no choice but to destroy it. Mary would certainly not be pleased, and I'd hate to think I saved it from drowning only to have it killed. It's not the animal's fault that it was brought here, or that its vocal cords were cut and it can't be put out into the wild. I'd like to try to find a home for it, maybe with one of my friends in Alaska, or in one of the western states where they're legal. But I need some time. I have no right to keep a dangerous animal in Cairn for any length of time, and I don't want to. I was hoping you could give me some kind of short-term special license."

"How much time do you need?"

"Hard to say, Chief."

"How about a month?"

"That should be more than enough."

"You've got it. I can't do anything in Cairn that would supercede the laws of New York State, but I'm going to have to get some very specific information on laws regarding a hybrid wolf, and that could take me just about a month. In the meantime, I'll give you a letter specifying the conditions under which you found the animal, the fact that you immediately brought it to my attention, and so on. You may consider yourself the holder of a temporary permit to keep it—at least until I officially tell you otherwise."

Garth left his friend feeling satisfied with the situation, and he felt even better later in the day when Mary spent the afternoon with the animal, feeding it, walking it around the house, frequently wrestling it to the ground as he had taught her, and even occasionally gently nipping it on the ear to drive home the point, or illusion, of her dominance. Garth judged that the wolf now respected Mary, accepted her as master, and even liked her. He could also plainly see that Mary was quickly growing very attached to the wolf, not as a symbol of an endangered species about which she cared passionately, but as an individual. That worried him, but he would attend to the problem of their inevitable separation when he had to. In the meantime, he was satisfied that Mary would be safe with the wolf when he was not around. His usual good judgment in such matters made the wolf's reaction the next morning when Mary came down to the beach where he was working it even more startling.

"Garth, there's somebody on the phone calling about the ad. He says—" The wolf s reaction was so quick and unexpected that Garth was caught totally by surprise. The animal had been lying on its side, tongue lolling out as Garth brushed his coat, but when Mary appeared he suddenly sprang to his feet, bared his fangs in a savage, silent snarl, and leaped forward. It was brought up short when it reached the end of its chain and fell down, but it immediately got up again and lunged at her. But then Garth was on its back, pressing it to the ground, gripping it by the throat.

"Get back around the house!" he shouted at Mary.

Trembling, eyes wide with shock, Mary slowly backed away until she was around the side of the house, out of sight. Gradually the wolf stopped its struggles and grew very still, its body limp. It closed its eyes, made breathy mewling sounds in its throat. Garth released his grip on the animal's throat, but kept his hands in front of him as he slowly got up. The wolf remained on its side, limp, softly mewling—almost, Garth thought, as if it were ashamed. He retrieved the muzzle from the boathouse, put it on the unresisting wolf, and then went to his wife.

Mary was wearing a jacket against the mild morning chill, but she had her arms wrapped around herself, as if she were cold. She was still trembling and ashen, her blue eyes flooded with tears.

Garth stepped forward, held her tightly.

"Garth, what did I *do*?!"

"Nothing," Garth replied, then stepped back and thoughtfully studied his wife standing in front of him in her black leather jacket with its white leather piping and long fringes on the sleeves and bottom. "Take your jacket off."

"What?"

"Take off your jacket. Put it on the ground."

"Garth, there's a man on the phone."

"He'll wait, or he'll call back. Just do as I say, please. I want to see something."

Mary was thoroughly puzzled, but she did as her husband asked, removing her black and white leather jacket and tossing it behind her on the lawn.

Garth nodded, continued, "Now pull yourself together. Wait about a minute, and then go back around to where the wolf can see you. It's important that you don't show fear; act as if nothing had happened."

"All right."

Garth walked back down to the beach where the wolf was still lying on its side, head resting on the sand, staring almost wistfully out at the river. Garth knelt down beside it, scratched it behind the ears. A few moments later Mary, a determined smile on her face, strode purposefully around the side of the house. The wolf saw her at once, but its reaction this time was totally different from what it had been less than five minutes before. It rolled over on its stomach, and slowly got to its feet and shuddered. With head down and tail drooping, it slouched toward her, and when it reached the end of its chain it dropped to its belly, once again resting its head on the sand.

Garth was too far away to stop Mary as she abruptly walked to the wolf and dropped to her knees beside its head. "You have been a very bad boy," she said sternly, wagging a finger in its face and cuffing it lightly on the jaw. Then she lay down on top of the animal and draped her arms lovingly around its neck.

Garth stood close by, watching the wolf's reactions carefully, and he didn't object when Mary removed the animal's muzzle. On his way back to the house he picked up the jacket off the lawn, then put it at the back of the top shelf of a closet before going to the phone.

"Yeah."

"You took your goddamn sweet time, pal."

"You want to tell me what's on your mind, or do you want me to hang up?"

"I'm calling about the ad in the paper. You've got something that belongs to me."

"What?"

"A wolf."

"Right."

"I want it back. I'll give you a couple of bucks for your trouble."

"Where are you?"

"Blauvelt."

"I'll meet you at Hook Mountain in Nyack, in the parking lot down by the beach, in half an hour," Garth said, and then hung up without waiting for a reply.

He checked on Mary, who was playing with, "working," the wolf, then went to his car and drove south to the state park in Upper Nyack, where he was waiting, sitting on a picnic table, when the wolf's owner arrived in a battered, rusting Jeep with two bumper stickers proclaiming White Power and a large window decal depicting a white bolt of lightning flashing across a red cross on a yellow background. The three young men in the car looked like identical triplets with their shaved heads; they were dressed

52

alike in studded black leather jackets, pants, and boots, and even wore the same contemptuous sneers.

The man driving the Jeep got out, looked around, settled on Garth, and swaggered over to him. Garth put his age at twenty-three or four. His face was a map work of purplish acne scars that almost matched his maroon eyes. He stopped in front of Garth, put his hands on his hips.

"You the guy I talked to on the phone about the wolf?"

"Yep."

"Where is it?"

"Home."

"What the hell-?!"

"The ad said to call for information, which is what I'm looking for. I'm not here to give the wolf back. I want to know how you got it."

"It's none of your damn business," the man replied in a tone that was marked as much by surprise as anger. Then he signaled to his two companions. "You must be out of your mind, pal."

The other two identically dressed young men sauntered across the parking lot, stopped on either side of the scar-faced man to form a wall of flesh and studded black leather.

The wolf's owner leaned very close to Garth. "Now, what were you saying about not giving me back my wolf?"

"It's my wife's fault that I can't give him back to you," Garth replied easily. "She's an animal lover, and she doesn't like the way you've been treating him. She wondered how he happened to end up in the river."

"He ended up in the river because I kicked his ass off my friend's boat," the scar-faced man said with a humorless laugh that was filled with malice. "I've got two of 'em, and they were acting up and pissing all over the place. Now I can't do anything with the other one, and I'm thinking of blowing the bitch's brains out. I may shoot this one too if it doesn't come around, but that'll be my choice. Now why don't you come along with us? We'll go to your house to pick up my wolf, and then we'll bring you back to your car."

It explained what the wolf was doing in the river, Garth thought, as well as its desperate struggle against tide and current; it was swimming in the direction where its mate had gone. "I don't think there's room in your Jeep for all of us," Garth said, and when he saw the owner's two companions reach into their pockets, he slammed his foot into the groin of the man on his right, then abruptly shoved off the table as he brought the heel of his right

53

hand up under the scar-faced man's jaw, breaking it. The wolf's owner slumped unconscious to the ground next to his writhing companion. Garth stepped over the body, then turned to face the third man, who was standing as if frozen to the spot, his mouth open. Finally he brought his hand, which held a knife, all the way out of his pocket. He flicked his wrist, and a six-inch blade snapped out of the handle.

"That's a mistake," Garth said to the young man who would later come upon him on Floyd Kunkel's estate after pointing him to it. He stooped down over the scar-faced man at his feet and unbuckled the thick leather belt the man wore, snapping it from around his waist. Then, lazily swinging the buckle end of the belt over his head, he slowly advanced on the young man holding the knife. "I doubt very much that you've ever killed anyone, my young friend. You like to try to scare people to death. I'm just the opposite; I don't care if you're scared, but I will kill you if you don't drop that knife. Look around, and you'll see lots of people staring at us. They'll testify that I was attacked by three skinhead thugs. No problem."

When the man suddenly threw the knife to the ground, turned and started to run for the car, Garth snapped, "Hold it!" The man stopped, slowly turned back. Garth pointed to the two men on the ground. "There's no littering here. Take your garbage with you."

Still lazily swinging the belt, Garth sat back down on the bench and watched as the man with the large, muddy brown eyes helped the man Garth had kicked in the groin to his feet. Together, they carried the scar-faced man back to the Jeep, threw him in the back, and quickly drove away. Garth noted the plate number, intending to pass it on to Jeffrey Bond, whom he found waiting for him when he returned home. The Cairn chief of police was sitting in the music room with Mary, who looked pale and upset.

"We've got a problem with your wolf, Garth," the policeman said, rising to his feet as Garth entered the room. "A report just came in of an incident up in Ulster County. Yesterday an animal described as a wolf was let loose in a synagogue. There was a group of men, a minyan, praying in there. The wolf attacked. It killed one man, managed to get at his throat, and chewed up three others pretty good before somebody managed to get to a phone and call the police. They came and shot it."

Garth looked away as he felt sorrow well in him at the thought of the shock and horror the men must have felt as a gray juggernaut of death suddenly exploded into their midst. He would never understand the thinking of those responsible for the releasing of the wolf, but he did understand hatred. He hated. He despised

54

these purveyors of hatred and death to the core of his being, and their very existence offended him. They were the human pustules on the face of life his mother had spoken of so often to his brother and him when they were children, the holes in the world through which good escaped and evil entered. He looked back at Jeffrey Bond, said, "The attack took place yesterday. It wasn't our wolf."

Bond stared at Garth for a few moments, slowly blinked. "That's an odd reaction."

"What's an odd reaction?"

"You don't seem surprised."

"I'm not surprised." Garth reached into his pocket, took out the slip of paper on which he had written the plate number of the Jeep, handed it to the policeman. "That's the license-plate number of a Jeep that I think belongs to the wolf's owner. He may live in Blauvelt, but if he doesn't, it should be easy enough to find out where he does live. I just met him and two of his buddies. They're skinheads, neo-Nazis probably allied with the Angry Cross people who run your friendly little bookshop here in town. You should have the Orangetown Police check this guy out, because he says he has another wolf—a female."

Bond studied his friend's face, nodded. "I'll certainly do that. How did you come to meet these skinheads?"

"I put an ad in the paper about the wolf. One of them answered it."

"You were thinking of giving the wolf back?"

"I was thinking of trying to find out who's breeding those animals here, or carting them down from Alaska."

"I appreciate your bringing this matter to my attention," Bond said carefully, narrowing his eyes slightly. "Everybody knows that you and your brother are the best private investigators in the business, but this has become a personal thing with you. Now, why don't you call your friends in Alaska like you said you would, and let me do my job?"

"I'm not interfering with the police, Jeff. And I am looking into this on behalf of a client."

"You didn't tell me that. May I ask who it is?"

"Mary, give me a dollar."

Mary looked at her husband in surprise. "What? My purse is in the bedroom."

"Jeff, lend Mary a dollar, would you?"

The police chief sighed and rolled his eyes, then took out his wallet and handed Mary a dollar bill, which Garth immediately took from her. "I'd hate to have you think I was acting like an amateur, Chief," Garth said with a slight smile. "Now Mary's officially my client. She's a very serious animal rights person, and this business of wolf captivity and mutilation offends her."

"That's right," Mary said, stepping close to her husband and kissing him loudly on the cheek.

The police chief grunted, shook his head. "Why don't you two righteous animal lovers take me to see this hairy friend of yours?"

Garth and Mary led the police chief out of and around the house to where the wolf was staked. The animal looked up, immediately leaped to its feet, bared its fangs, and charged to the end of its chain, where it was yanked back. It charged again, ears back flat against its head as it struggled to get at the man standing between Garth and Mary.

Jeffrey Bond paled, took a step backward, and reached for his gun.

"Jeff, no!" Mary cried, clutching the policeman's arm. "Don't shoot him!"

"To call that animal dangerous is a serious understatement, Mary," Bond said in a low, tense voice. "It would be irresponsible for you to give it to anyone, in Alaska or anywhere else. There's no place for it. It's going to end up being killed anyway, so you may as well let me do the job for you right now and get it over with before it kills somebody. There are people who walk along this beach."

"It reacted to me the same way once, Jeff! There's something wrong with him! Somebody's done something to him to make him react that way!"

Bond kept his hand on his gun as he stared at the animal that was still straining at its chain, clawing at the sand under its feet, trying to get at him. "What are you talking about?"

"I don't *know* why he came at you like that, Jeff! But-"

"I think I do," Garth said as he took his friend's arm and gently but firmly led him back around the house. "Give me your jacket and hat, Jeff."

"What the hell are *you* talking about?"

"Just give them to me. Please."

Bond hesitated, but finally removed the articles of clothing and gave them to Garth, who put them on and walked back down toward the beach. There was no reaction from the wolf, which was what Garth had expected. He returned to the side of the house, gave the blue jacket and hat back to the police chief. "It's not the uniform," Garth said. "My guess is that he came at you because you're black. He's been conditioned to attack blacks - - and Jews, when he thinks he sees one.

"What?"

"You said the wolf up in Ulster County attacked a group of men inside a synagogue. A wolf won't normally attack people. Unless it was cornered, which I seriously doubt, it would have slunk all over that synagogue, hidden under pews, whatever. That wolf had been conditioned to attack those men, probably because of what they were wearing, the same as this wolf was conditioned to attack you because of the color of your skin. If I'm right, we're talking about more than the illegal importation and the keeping of dangerous animals in the state. Now we're looking at murder, and conspiracy to commit murder. Somebody's using trained animals as murder weapons."

"How do you know all this?"

"I know something about wolves, and the rest is an educated guess based on my observations of this wolf's behavior. Give me time and I'll prove it. The way the wolf reacted to you isn't the wolf's fault, any more than having its vocal cords cut was its fault. If it was conditioned, it can be unconditioned. If you want to see that I'm right, have Orangetown pick up that creep in Blauvelt and sweat him. And you can pick up whoever it is that's running that hate factory in town. I think it's Angry Cross people who are responsible for these wolves. If the police don't act quickly, I predict there are going to be more wolf attacks, and more deaths."

Bond thought about it, gave a curt nod. "God knows you and your brother have some kind of track record at nosing out things like this. I'll look into it. I'll also check with the local cops upstate and see if I can't get the state police interested. In the meantime, you've got a week to get rid of that animal."

"The wolf may be material evidence."

"Then the state police can take it, along with the responsibility."

"You said I had a month," Garth said to the policeman's back as the other man headed up toward the driveway.

Jeffrey Bond stopped, turned back. "Garth, you said the animal was dangerous, and you were right. I'm sorry, but right now I'll be responsible if some kid in this town gets eaten. If that wolf gets loose, or, God forbid, some kid walking the beach comes too close to it and gets hurt, it's my ass—because I know you're keeping it here. One week. Start making your calls to your friends.

He called a friend and neighbor, an Orthodox Jew who lived in the next block. When he had the item he had asked to borrow, he went to his computer, punched in the code for DMV listings, and in a few minutes had the name and address of Conrad Regent, the Jeep's owner, who was just coming out of his mother's house where he lived when Garth pulled up in front. It was not the acne-scarred man, but the skinhead with the mud-colored eyes, and when he saw Garth he bolted for the Jeep parked in the driveway. But Garth was on him before he could get in, knocking him across the hood of the Jeep, wrapping the black and white fringed *tallis* around his neck, dragging him across the lawn to the curb where his van, with the wolf inside, was parked.

"I brought your friend's pet back," Garth said quietly. "I've had a change of heart, and thought it was time you were all reunited."

"It'll kill me if you put me in there!" the young man said in a strangled whisper as he clawed at the prayer shawl wrapped around his throat and gazed in wide-eyed horror as the wolf snapped and clawed at the window separating them. "It'll be murder!"

Garth pressed the man's face up against the saliva-streaked glass, rested his hand on the door handle. "Murder?" he said easily. "This is your friend's wolf. He wants it back, doesn't he? In fact, you came to help him pick it up, and you didn't seem all that nervous then. Is there something wrong?"

"You... know! It's the shawl! The wolf's trained to go after anyone wearing one!"

"And people with dark skin?"

The young man with the shaved head nodded.

"Who trains them?"

"I don't know!"

Garth banged the man's head against the window, and the wolf redoubled its efforts to get at him, fangs striking against the glass.

58

"Otto!" the man shrieked.

"Otto who?"

"Just Otto! That's what everybody calls him! He raises and trains them, cuts their vocal cords when they're cubs! He works for Mr. Kunkel!"

"Who's this Mr. Kunkel?"

"Floyd Kunkel! He's the one who gives away the wolves! He's the head of Angry Cross!"

Garth yanked on the prayer shawl, throwing the man to the pavement. "Where do I find Floyd Kunkel?"

The skinhead averted his eyes, swallowed hard. When he spoke, his voice quavered slightly, as if he were about to cry. "He lives in Cairn. He's got a big mansion down by the river, next to the quarry."

"Why does Kunkel give away the wolves? What are you supposed to do with them?"

The man had told him, and the rage that had surged through Garth then returned now, blotting out the pain in his ankle as he marched purposefully through the wooded grounds of Floyd Kunkel's estate, heading back to the mansion that afforded the only exit from the enclosure. He came across three of Kunkel's uniformed Angry Cross skinheads standing in an open, grassy area separating a firing range and an obstacle course. Garth made no effort to avoid the men as he stepped from the trees and walked at a fast pace directly toward them. The men saw him, started. The man on the left raised his weapon, and Garth shot him in the head. The other two men threw down their machine pistols, turned and ran. Garth tossed the MAC 10s into a clump of brush and continued on in the direction of the mansion, toward the little man with the ill-fitting toupee and the most dangerous storm trooper of them all, the real one, the professional soldier who was behind everything, the savage mercenary who would kill not only him, but also his brother, and even his wife, who had gently stroked his back as he'd checked his camera with its zoom lens and the miniature tape recorder strapped to his waist.

"I think what's been done to those animals upsets you even more than it does me."

"It certainly does upset me," Garth replied evenly as, satisfied that his equipment was in order, he replaced the camera and zoom lens in their case.

Mary wrapped her arms around her husband's waist, rested her head between his shoulder blades, and hugged him. "I love you so very much, you very strange man.

Garth laughed, reached back, and patted his wife's bottom. "Now there's a wonderful compliment."

59

"There are so many things, so much feeling deep inside you that you never show to other people."

"Well, whatever it is you think you see, I'm glad you approve."

"If you know who's breeding the wolves and giving them away, why don't you just go to Jeff and tell him?"

"That's exactly what I intend to do before the end of the day. But what you have to remember is that Jeff, as good a cop as he is, is only the head of a town police force. He'll need all the help he can get to shut these people down, and it has to be done quickly, before anybody else gets mauled or killed. There's only so much Jeff can do on his own, and there are strict legal procedures he has to follow. Judging from the place he owns, Kunkel has a lot of money, and the first thing he's going to do when the police start showing interest in him is to hire a squad of sharp lawyers. Then the state police will come and impound our wolf, which will probably eventually be destroyed. The only killing that we know of that's connected with the wolves and Angry Cross took place near Kingston, which is a hundred miles outside Jeff's jurisdiction. We don't know how many more wolves there are out there, where they are, or the mental state of the crackpots who have them. Kunkel isn't going to give out those names to the police until he's under a lot of pressure, after a long time. Meanwhile, I don't want to wake up one morning and read in the paper about another wolf in a synagogue, or let loose on a playground filled with black children."

"You think you can make him give you the names of the people he's given wolves to?"

"I'm going to try."

"But how?"

"Sweet reason," Garth said with a smile as he gently pulled away from his wife's grasp, turned and kissed her before heading for the door.

"Garth, *you're* the lone wolf around here!" she called after him. "You and your brother are just the same. And when the two of you work together, what you have is a two-headed lone wolf."

"He'll love that description."

"You're not going to take a gun?"

Garth paused in the doorway, turned back. "I'm not planning on killing anyone—and if I was, I wouldn't be doing it in our home town. My guess is that the publicity wouldn't do anything for our privacy, and I don't think it's the kind of publicity your record company or music publisher would much appreciate."

"Garth—?!"

"I'll be home before dinner."

"Where does this Floyd Kunkel live?"

60

"Way too close," Garth had replied, and in less than ten minutes was pulling onto the rutted dirt access road threading along the side of the abandoned trap rock quarry at the edge of Cairn. He drove as far as he could go on the weed-choked road, then got out and with the camera case slung over his shoulder, clambered up the rock fall at the base of the escarpment where great mechanical behemoths had once sheared huge slices of stone that would eventually be crushed and used for the building of roads in New York City. He managed to climb a few yards up the wall itself to a ledge, where he sat, legs dangling over the edge, and looked down onto Floyd Kunkel's property. Through the zoom lens he could see that the spacious grounds included a shooting range, as well as a military-style obstacle course where perhaps a half-dozen men in tan uniforms were working out. At the southern end of the property was what appeared to be a kennel, with more than a dozen wooden shelters. Staked outside each shelter was a dark gray animal. Surrounding the entire complex were double chain-link fences, and the inside fence appeared to be electrified.

Garth shot two rolls of film, concentrating on the animal pens, and then climbed down. He put the camera and rolls of film in the trunk of his car, and then drove around to the front of Floyd Kunkel's mansion, parked at the top of the circular driveway. There were a number of cars in a parking area off to the side, and one enclosed van with Alaska license plates. He activated the tape recorder strapped to his waist, then went up to the front door of the Victorian mansion and knocked.

The man who came to the door was no more than five foot three or four. He had a wispy brown moustache that only served to highlight his sallow complexion, and he wore a bushy, absurd-looking toupee that came halfway down over his forehead. His dark eyes were like the button eyes of a doll, without light, the eyes of a man in whom things had died, dreams and ambitions and a sense of self-worth, and then, like a crippled phoenix, had been resurrected as murderous hatred.

"Floyd Kunkel?"

"Maybe," the man replied nervously. "What do you want?"

"My name's Garth Frederickson. I'm a neighbor, and I'm here to try to do you a favor."

"Go away," Kunkel said, starting to close the door. "Whatever it is you're selling, I don't want any."

"It's about those hybrid wolves you've got in your backyard," Garth said, planting a large, strong hand on the door and pushing it back open. "The favor I'm doing is inviting you to come down to the police station to give up the names of the people you've given those hybrid wolves to. That won't stop the lawsuits that are going to cost you this house and everything else you own, but that kind of cooperation just might keep you out of prison."

Floyd Kunkel's pinched mouth opened and closed, and his button eyes opened wide. "Wh—? I don't know what you're talking about!"

"Yes, you do. You've been training those animals to attack blacks and Jews, and then giving them away to your punk skinheads like membership cards, or merit badges. One of your boys decided to test his out to see if it would really do what you said it would. It did. It makes you a kind of accessory to murder. In the interest of saving time, why don't you just give me the names? How many wolves have you given away?"

The door abruptly swung all the way open, and Garth found himself looking at his own death. He had come to this place filled with contempt for spiritually crippled men he considered weaklings and cowards, but Franz Heitman was neither weak nor a coward. And the ex-Stasi agent had every reason in the world to want to kill him.

"'Otto,' I presume?"

The man with the very pale blue eyes and close-cropped blond hair stepped back, but kept the gun in his hand pointed directly at Garth's forehead. "Do come in, Frederickson."

"Fancy meeting you here, Franz. Interpol's looking very hard for you, you know, just like the citizens of your former country. There are a lot of people who'd dearly love to get their hands on you."

"You don't say? I guess I'd better stay in the United States for a while longer.

Kunkel, a bewildered expression on his face, looked at the German. "Otto? Why does this man call you Franz? How does he know you?"

"Leave us!" Franz Heitman snapped.

Garth turned to the slight man with the bushy toupee. "You know who you have working for you—or think you have working

62

for you?" he asked just before the white-eyed man brought the barrel of the gun up against the side of his head.

When he regained consciousness he found himself tied to a straight-backed chair in what appeared to be a small den or office. He was very much surprised to find he was still alive.

"So what's up, Frederickson?"

"You tell me, Franz. What's a professional murderer and torturer like you doing hanging around with a bunch of wimpy, wannabe Nazis? They're all amateurs; you're the real McCoy. What the hell are you up to?"

The white-eyed man sitting across from him behind a desk leaned back in his swivel chair, pushed aside the tape recorder he had removed from Garth's waist, and then folded his hands behind his neck. "I owe you and your smartass little brother, Frederickson. The two of you put five bullets in me."

"Yeah, Franz, but you know how hard it is to kill a snake. You're actually looking quite fit, I'm sorry to say."

"Speaking of your smartass little brother, where is he? It's funny, isn't it, how I have trouble picturing one of you without the other? Wherever there's one Frederickson, the other usually can't be far behind."

The reason he was still alive, Garth thought. The German wanted to know who might be covering him, and who else might know about the wolves. He knew that Franz Heitman was unlikely to believe anything he said, so he decided he might as well tell the truth. "He's in Europe."

"You don't say. Who are you working for? Who hired you to look into this wolf business?"

"Nobody."

"Nobody? Then why are you here?"

"I found one of the animals you carved up drowning in the river. What had been done to it pissed me off, so I decided to try to find out who was behind it. One thing led to another."

The German grunted. "You know, I think you may just be telling the truth. You told that fool Kunkel you were a neighbor. You live here in Cairn?"

Garth felt his heart begin to beat faster, and he struggled to keep his face impassive. "No. Whom are you really working for?"

The other man laughed. "The usual suspects, of course."

"Abu Nidal's people? Saddam? Castro?"

Heitman smiled thinly. "Why go to the trouble of trying to smuggle bands of foreign-speaking terrorists into the United States when you have whole groups of American terrorists here all ready and willing, with just the slightest nudge in the right direction, to do all your work for you? It's true that your Klansmen and Nazis

63

aren't too bright, but I've found that to work to my various employers' distinct advantage."

"We don't have the Europeans' centuries of practice at hating and murdering our own people. You let the wolf loose in that synagogue, didn't you?"

"A test of my training methods, with a most satisfactory result. Now it's time for a Day of the Wolf. The people who have the wolves are simply waiting eagerly for me to give the word. Of course, I must pick a suitable occasion—perhaps Rosh Hashana, or Yom Kippur, when there are lots of Jews wearing prayer shawls on the streets. At the same time, a number of the wolves will be let loose in black neighborhoods. I believe it will make quite a splash, in a manner of speaking."

"For what reason, Heitman?"

"You think Kunkel and his skinheads need a reason? They just want to kill blacks and Jews, and they think that using the wolves is a way for them to get away with it."

"You sold them the idea, of course."

"Of course."

"What's *your* reason? What's the point? You're a professional killer, not a goofy ideologue.

The other man shrugged. "Striking terror into the hearts of your enemies is always its own reason. You know the theory. That's my job. My employers consider the United States their enemy; terrorism is not only their weapon of choice, but also their only weapon. There will be other operations like the Day of the Wolf. As you know, I'm rather clever at manipulating fools like Kunkel and his skinheads, and putting things like this together. The United States is a very big country, and I plan to keep busy here for some time."

"How many wolves are out there, Franz?"

"Enough," Heitman said, glancing at his watch and rising. "I'll leave you to your own devices for now, while we wait to see who may show up looking for you. I really do hope it will be your smartass little brother."

Left to his own devices, Garth practiced one other thing his brother had taught him, *muzukashi jotai kara deru,* which could be roughly translated as "extricating oneself from knotty situations," and which was a Japanese technique of muscle tensing and relaxation. What Garth had dismissed as a joke, or at most a parlor trick, his brother had used to save their lives inside a Swiss castle, and only then had Garth insisted that his brother teach him. What would have taken his brother ten minutes took him an hour, but at last he was free.

What he wanted was a telephone, but if there had been one

64

in the office it had been removed. However, rifling through the desk drawers, he found a spiral notebook. Inside the notebook was written the name and address of a hybrid wolf farm in Alaska. There was also a list of men's names, addresses, and telephone numbers. The addresses were scattered all over the southern half of New York State, with close to a third in New York City. Twenty-five names, including that of a man in Kingston, had dark checks beside them. He ripped the pages with the names out of the notebook, folded them and put them in his wallet, then headed for the door, which opened out into a much larger study at what appeared to be the rear of the mansion.

He was halfway across the room when Franz Heitman entered. The German cursed and clawed for the gun in his shoulder holster, but by then Garth was running the rest of the way across the room, diving for a window. He put his forearms across his face and dived headfirst through the glass as a gun exploded behind him. He hit the ground on his left shoulder, rolled, and was up and sprinting across the well-manicured lawn toward a wooded area running along the base of the abandoned quarry. As he ran he thought of Mary, wondered what she was thinking and doing. He had said he would be home before dinner, and so by now she would be worried, perhaps already have called the police. He had told her where he was going, but that did not mean the police, without a proper search warrant, would be able to find him. Heitman would certainly have moved his car out of sight, and Kunkel would simply deny he had ever been there. There would be nothing Jeff could do.

His greatest fear, the anxiety that had gnawed at his heart throughout the long night, was now realized as he approached the house and saw Mary's station wagon parked at the back of the mansion, where it had been placed in plain view to tell him that Franz Heitman had his wife. He threw his gun off to one side and entered the house through the back door into the kitchen, where he found Floyd Kunkel's corpse on the floor, a single bullet hole in his forehead.

"I'm here, Heitman."

"Right this way, Frederickson," Heitman's voice called. "Straight ahead."

Garth walked down a corridor with walls decorated with garish Nazi posters, into the spacious living room of the mansion. Mary was sitting very straight in a chair that had been placed in the middle of the room a few feet away from where the German sat on a couch, legs crossed, an automatic pistol resting in his lap. The wolf, lying on its stomach at Mary's feet, raised its head and began to wag its tail as Garth walked in.

65

"I knew those idiots wouldn't get you, Frederickson," the German continued, glancing at his watch. "In fact, you're here just about the time I thought you would be."

Garth looked at his wife. "Are you all right?"

Mary nodded. "You?"

"Yes."

"By the way," Heitman said with a thin smile, "the police did come around looking for you. Kunkel told them he didn't know what they were talking about. What were they to do? When your smartass little brother didn't show up like I expected him to, I decided that you must have been telling the truth when you said he was in Europe. I remembered you also telling Kunkel that you were a neighbor, so I went into town and made some inquiries-told people I was a long-lost friend of yours who'd misplaced your address and phone number. Everybody knows you; people were very helpful in giving me directions to your home. Incidentally, you and your lovely wife have done some nice work with that wolf. It's downright docile. I think I'm going to keep it for myself."

"He came to the house," Mary said in a small voice. "He said you needed my help right away, and that I should follow him and bring the wolf. I didn't know what else to do but what he asked."

Garth nodded, looked back into the cold, blue-white eyes of the ex-Stasi agent. "I saw the mess you left out in the kitchen. You must be getting ready to move on."

"Indeed. You've managed to make things uncomfortable for me here. But first I want to make some phone calls, and you have the numbers of the people I want to call. I'm thinking that today would make as good a Day of the Wolf as any. You have the list of names and phone numbers?"

"If you were certain I had the list with me, I wouldn't be alive right now.

"The thought did cross my mind that you might stash the list away someplace after you saw your wife's car, just to annoy me. Did you? You won't annoy me for long. I'd hate to put a bullet in your wife's kneecap to prompt an honest answer, so why don't you just tell me where to find the list?"

"If I do, will you let Mary go?"

"Give me a break, Frederickson. You want me to insult you by lying to you? Interpol and various other police forces I can handle, but I don't need your smartass little brother dedicating the rest of his life to hunting me down. I can't leave any witnesses. I will promise that neither of you will suffer."

"Under the circumstances, that seems fair enough," Garth

66

said. He removed his wallet from his pocket, took out the folded pages, flipped them in the direction of the German. As the man reached out to catch them, Garth took the prayer shawl out of his jacket pocket and tossed it at the man's head. "You might as well take this, too."

In the instant before the billowing prayer shawl settled down over his head, the German's pale eyes went wide with shock and horror. He grabbed for the gun in his lap with one hand, while with the other he frantically clawed at the fringed black and white cloth, but by then the wolf, which had sprung to its feet at first sight of the *tallis,* was at him. Heitman screamed as he and the wolf toppled over backwards. Garth quickly walked around the overturned sofa, gripped the wolf's collar, and pulled him away from the German's head. The man had managed to protect his throat and was still alive, but his face was gone. Franz Heitman writhed on the floor, screaming, legs thrashing, his hands spasmodically reaching for, but never quite touching, his shredded flesh. Garth pulled the animal back around the sofa, brought it over to Mary, who gripped its collar while wrapping her free arm around its neck.

"Our wolf is going to need a lot of love and counter-training if he's going to unlearn the nasty habits he's been taught, which is essential if he's going to be allowed to live," Garth said to Mary as he walked across the room and picked up a phone to call the police and an ambulance. "Considering the fact that he's played a large part in saving a lot of people's lives, including our own, maybe we should keep him. I could look into getting a special permit, and we could build an appropriate enclosure. Would you like that?"

Mary, her eyes brimming with tears, simply nodded.

HAUNTS

"They're here!" Madame Bellarossa shrieked as the flames of the seven candles on the table guttered, and then Mary screamed, her voice joining the other woman's in a duet of horror, her features twisted with the same terror Garth had seen on Elsie Manning's face when he had found her huddled on the ground at his back door at three o'clock in the morning one week before, too weak to pound any more, scratching at the screen like a stricken cat.

"They want me to die, Garth!" the eighty-year-old woman had said in a strangled whisper as she clutched at the hem of Garth's robe.

Garth Frederickson looked around, saw nothing in the warm September night beyond the glow cast by his porch light, heard nothing but the sibilant whisper of waves washing up on the beach fifty yards away. He bent down, placed his hands under the woman's frail arms, gently lifted her to her feet, and held her as she trembled violently and grabbed the lapels of his pajama top. Despite the fact that he knew the answer, he asked, "Who wants you to die?"

"My ghosts."

"They can't hurt you here, Elsie," Garth said in a soothing tone, leading her into the house, where he eased her down into a chair at the rectangular butcher-block table in the kitchen. He took off his woolen robe and wrapped it around her, then went to the range to heat water for tea. He looked up when his wife appeared in the doorway. Her brilliant blue eyes still blurred by sleep, white-streaked, waist-length blond hair disheveled. Mary Tree was still

69

the most beautiful woman he had ever known, and the love he felt surging in him like a tide at the sight of her came as a welcome relief from the pall cast by the trembling old woman Garth considered to be ill with a kind of spiritual leprosy she had consciously nurtured, indeed reveled in and boasted about, for so many years, and which had now resulted not only in what Garth believed to be the most bizarre and perverse legal decision in the history of the country, but had also cost her the sale of her home and the money he knew she desperately needed, and might also be killing her. "Elsie's had a fright, Mary. She needs some time to rest."

The folk singer sighed sympathetically, then quickly walked into the kitchen and sat down next to the other woman, resting her large hands with their long fingers on Elsie Manning's still-quaking shoulders. "Oh, Elsie, Elsie, it's all right now. Everything's all right. Your ghosts?"

Elsie Manning seemed unable to speak. Her pale, watery green eyes were still wide with shock and horror as she stared somewhere over Mary's head, transfixed by her own private haunt that only she could see. Without her dentures in place her cheeks were sunken, and her mouth formed an 0 as she slowly nodded her head.

The kettle began to whistle. Garth prepared three cups of tea, brought them to the table, placed one in front of Elsie. "Sip some of that, Elsie," he said, smiling reassuringly. "It will make you feel better. Just be careful; it's hot."

Mary placed her hands around the old woman's, helping to steady them as Elsie lifted the cup to her mouth and sipped some of the steaming brew. When she set the cup back down, her hands and body did not seem to be trembling as much, and her pale green eyes had come back into focus. "I just don't understand it," she said weakly. "I've lived in that house all my life, and the ghosts were always so friendly. They were young lovers who committed suicide in an upstairs room rather than let their parents force them apart. They loved my parents, and they loved me. Sometimes, when I was a child, I'd see them sitting at the foot of my bed, all

70

aglow, smiling at me. Sometimes they'd sing lullabies to put me to sleep. I always felt so comfortable with them. They kept me company. Now... they hate me because I want to sell the house and leave them. I feel their hatred, know that they want me to die. They send cockroaches."

"You called the exterminator about the cockroaches," Garth said. "Didn't he take care of them?"

Elsie nodded tentatively. "Yes. But they came back. I was too ashamed to tell you. The exterminator came again, but the cockroaches were back a week later. Now they're all over the house. And rats, and terrible smells. Garth, you and Mary have been in my home; you know I keep a clean house. And then the phone will start ringing at all sorts of odd hours. I'll answer, but there'll be nobody there. I hang up, and the phone starts ringing again. Sometimes that will go on for hours, all night. I just can't fathom how spirits who had been so loving could have turned so spiteful."

Garth and Mary exchanged glances, and Garth reached across the table to touch the old woman's liver-spotted hand. "Elsie, you've been under tremendous stress since what happened with the buyer you had. I don't think you've ever really understood that most people aren't as comfortable with ghosts—friendly or otherwise—as you are. Humans are a very superstitious breed, and Americans are just as superstitious as the rest of the world. For years, you've been enjoying your haunted house, talking about it to anybody who would listen. You loved the attention when the local paper would run a story on your haunted house every year. But now you want to move into a retirement community where all your needs will be taken care of—staff to prepare your meals and clean your apartment, and doctors to look after you—and you need a lot of money to get into the place where you want to go. You've already lost one buyer who offered a fair price and gave you a sizable binder because a week before the closing he got wind of the fact that the house was supposedly haunted. We may agree with your attorney that the binder should have been yours because he reneged, but incredibly, the judge ruled that you should have told him the house was haunted. In effect, the state of New York has offered a legal opinion that yes, there really are such things as haunted houses, and one of them happens to be in Cairn. And now you have a worse problem because the wire services have picked up on it, and it's become a national news story. You'll probably continue to be deluged with phony seers, sages, astrologers, psychics, and professional magicians who've discovered they can pick up a lot of free publicity simply by issuing a press release saying they're thinking of buying your haunted house. But they don't want your house, and most couldn't begin to afford the three quarters of a million it's worth. They just want the attention. And nobody else wants your house, at least not at the moment. What you have to do, Elsie, is give the story time to die down. Eventually you'll find another buyer, because it's a fine old house sitting right on the Hudson River, and there aren't too many of those. But—above all else - - you have to stop advertising the fact that you think it's haunted."

"I don't think I have much time," the woman said in a hollow voice. Her eyes had once again gone out of focus, and she put a shaking hand to her throat. "Tonight one of them touched me- -here. It woke me up. They were both there, in hooded robes, standing next to my bed in the moonlight. I could see them just as clearly as I see the two of you right now. But this was different from the other times when they've come to me. They've never worn hooded robes before, never hidden their faces. And they've never touched me before. The hand on my throat was so *cold,* like it had been in ice water. I didn't think he was going to let me up, but he did, and that's when I ran over here. I—" She abruptly stopped speaking, looked hard at Mary, then at Garth. "I know you don't believe me. You think it's all my imagination. You've always been too polite to say so, but I know you think I'm just a batty old woman."

"Elsie," Garth replied in an even tone, "I don't find what you believe any more improbable than the things believed in by ninety-nine percent of the population of Cairn, or the country, and I don't consider most of my other friends and neighbors batty."

"But you don't believe there are ghosts in my house, do you?"

"That shouldn't surprise you."

"But one *touched* me tonight, Garth!"

Garth sighed. "Elsie, Mary, my brother, and I have faithfully attended every one of your Halloween séances ever since Mary and I settled in Cairn—in fact, we've felt honored to be invited. We find them great fun. My brother would be the first to tell you that he'd love nothing better than to meet a ghost, sit down with it, and have a nice long chat about whatever."

"But your little brother doesn't believe in ghosts."

"No, he doesn't believe in ghosts either. But he's open to the possibility of anything because he believes in mystery, and he'd be highly amused to find out that he's wrong, and that there really are such things as ghosts. But the fact of the matter is that there have never been any visitations at the six séances we've been to, not a peep from anyone or anything that wasn't present and accounted for."

"It's because you and Mary and your little brother don't believe in them. They won't appear if you don't believe in them."

Garth caressed his wife's cheek with the back of his hand, and then rose from the table. "Elsie, I'm going to get dressed and go check on your house to make sure there's nobody there."

The old woman stiffened in her chair, clutched at Mary's arm. "No, Garth, don't go! There's no use! You won't find anything. They won't appear to you. It's me they're after."

Suddenly Elsie Manning began to cry—not in racking sobs, but softly, more now in hopeless despair than the terror she had displayed earlier. She closed her eyes, threw her head back, and opened her shrunken 0 of a mouth in a silent howl of torment as a steady stream of tears welled from between her eyelids and coursed down her cheeks. Garth had gone around the table, wrapped his powerful arms around the woman, and held her as close as, a week later, he now held Mary, who had collapsed from her chair to the floor. Mary's limbs twitched spasmodically, and her eyes railed in her head. Garth kissed her cheeks, gently rocking

73

his wife back and forth in silence that was broken only by Madame Bellarossa's heavy breathing and Elsie's quavering voice offering a prayer. Finally Mary grew still, opened her eyes. "They're here, Garth. My God, they really are here in this room with us."

"Are you all right?"

"I'm so cold ..."

"Don't try to talk. Just rest here. I'll get you a blanket."

"No, Garth. There's no time. They won't wait."

"Let her speak," Madame Bellarossa said in a low voice that had grown slightly hoarse. "It's important. Mary's been chosen as the messenger."

Garth nodded to the portly black woman with the crimson lipstick and huge hoop earrings who was leading the séance, then looked back at his wife. "What happened?"

"They . . . came to me, Garth. I felt them."

"Felt them how?"

Mary swallowed hard, licked her lips. "At first there was just this terrible cold. I'm all right now, but for just a moment there I felt colder than I ever have in my life. And then they came into my thoughts, started to tell me why they're so angry. It has something to do with selfishness, and terrible greed."

"They think Elsie's being greedy just because she wants to sell her home? All she was asking for was what had been appraised as its fair market value."

Mary shook her head. "It's not that."

"Then what greed, Mary? Whose greed?"

"I. . . . don't know. I think they were about to tell me all of it, but then I passed out."

"They're still here in the room," Madame Bellarossa said in a distant monotone, slurring her words slightly. "They want us to know, but the circle has to be restored."

Garth looked up at the black woman; her eyes were half closed and her arms stretched out over the table as if she were in a trance. The black man standing stiffly beside her, Jeffrey Bond, was staring at Mary, his mouth half open and his eyes filled with amazement. Both John and Linda Luft, the young, blond, dark -

74

eyed married couple who looked so much alike they might have been brother and sister, had stepped back from the table and were standing at the very edge of the flickering pool of candlelight. Linda Luft's eyes were glazed with shock, and she was very pale. Her husband, too, looked pale in the dim light, but the lines of his mouth were drawn down in a frown of skepticism. Elsie was standing at the opposite end of the table from Madame Bellarossa; the old woman's eyes were closed, and her thin lips continued to move in silent prayer. The only person at the table who had remained seated was Harry Parker, Garth's friend, a professional magician and world-renowned debunker of psychic charlatans and supernatural occurrences. Parker seemed perfectly calm. He was leaning back in his chair, thick arms folded across his barrel chest. His face was impassive as he stared back at Garth, who asked, "Anybody else see, feel, or hear anything?"

Jeffrey Bond coughed, cleared his throat. "I felt the cold," he said, looking around somewhat sheepishly at the others. "I got a blast of it right on the back of my neck. It was just like Mary said; for just a moment, it was the coldest I've ever been in my life. And we all saw what happened to the candles." He paused and again looked around the table at the others. "Didn't we?"

"You're the expert, Harry," Garth said to his friend. "What happened to Mary and Jeff? What's going on here? Mass hysteria?"

The big man with the blue eyes and close-cropped black hair slowly blinked and seemed about to reply when he suddenly started. "I'll be damned," he said in a quiet but thoroughly astonished tone as he slowly unfolded his arms and looked down at his chest where blood was slowly seeping across the front of his white shirt, staining the cotton fabric as red as the dawn that had announced its presence and begun to push away the night the previous week when Garth, Mary, and Elsie Manning had sat around the butcher-block table in Garth's home.

"I guess I should go home now," Elsie had said in a small voice. She was still very pale, but she had stopped trembling. Mary had brushed the woman's hair, and this had seemed to calm her.

75

"I've bothered you people long enough, woke you up and kept you up all night."

"Elsie," Mary said, gently squeezing the other woman's hand, "you're a dear friend, not a bother. And you're welcome to stay here as long as you want."

Elsie slowly shook her head. "It's still my home, at least until I'm able to sell it. I belong there. They don't come during the day anymore, not since they turned mean."

"I'll walk you home," Garth said, rising from his chair.

Garth took a flashlight, but it wasn't needed. As they walked along the beach, the shortest and easiest route to Elsie's home an eighth of a mile away, the sun appeared in the east over the Westchester hills across the river, causing the waters of the Hudson to glow first reddish orange, then golden. By the time they reached the three-story Victorian mansion that was Elsie's home, it was day. Garth opened the door, walked with Elsie through the large, lushly carpeted living room decorated with antique tapestries into the dining room, which was dominated by a heavy oak table in the center.

"Thank you, Garth," Elsie said with a sigh, easing herself down into a chair. She removed his robe from around her shoulders, handed it back to him. "Thank you for everything."

"Are you going to be all right?"

"Garth, I don't know what to do."

"You know I'm not the one who can help you with your ghost problem, Elsie."

"I don't know who else to turn to."

"Maybe a priest or minister."

"They don't believe me either," she replied, bitterness creeping into her voice. 'They only believe in their own ghosts." She paused, shook her head, and once again tears misted her pale eyes. "Even though I know you don't believe there are ghosts here, you're the only person I can feel comfortable with anymore talking about it. I'm so afraid, Garth. What should I do?"

Garth pulled another chair out from the table, sat down, and leaned close to the old woman, looking intently into her eyes. "Stop believing.

"…What?"

"The ghosts in this house live off you, because of you. Stop feeding them with your belief and they'll go away."

"But Garth, one *did* touch me! He put his hand around my *throat!*"

"He touched you because you believe he touched you, because you believe there are ghosts and that they *can* touch you." Garth suppressed a sigh, brought his chair even closer, and took both the woman's hands in his. "Elsie, we all have our haunts. Haunts are just bad memories. It's when we don't recognize them for what they are that we start to give them the power to hurt us in the present."

Shadows moved in the woman's pale eyes as she stared back at Garth. Finally she asked, "You have haunts too?"

"Of course. But I don't ask them for stock tips, I don't let them sit on my bed, and I don't let them wrap their fingers around my throat."

"Would you tell me one of your haunts?"

"I grew up on a farm in Nebraska. I was maybe nine or ten when one day my favorite uncle, Uncle Bill, for no reason that anybody could fathom, up and left our Methodist church and joined a fundamentalist sect that was into handling rattlesnakes as a way of demonstrating their faith. About two weeks after he joined, Uncle Bill was bit in the throat by a rattler, and he died. The people in the sect he'd joined said he'd died because he lacked sufficient faith."

"Do you believe he died because he lacked sufficient faith?"

"Of course not. He died because he lacked sufficient brains. You have to be very careful what you believe, Elsie, because you become what you believe. Think of it as a question of mental hygiene. My Uncle Bill became a victim of his own belief system, exactly the same as you've become a victim of yours. Belief in

77

gods or ghosts is like a brain fever; some have it, some don't, and some only pretend to have it because it seems to them that everyone else around them has it, and they don't want to be different. Just as with what happened to you, the fever is passed from generation to generation, and so all over the world we have tens of millions of people believing in ghosts they call God, Satan, Mohammed, Buddha, Jesus, devils, or angels. But some infections are more virulent and dangerous than others, and they'll bite you just as surely as that rattlesnake bit my uncle. For whatever reason, your belief system has turned on you. So stop believing before it does you more harm. Or change it. If you insist on believing in the supernatural, why don't you try something a little less toxic, like Unitarianism, or Reform Judaism, or maybe Zen Buddhism?"

Garth waited for some response from the woman, but there was none. Elsie's mouth opened and closed repeatedly, as if she wanted to say something but could not find the words. It did not surprise Garth, who gave the woman's hands a gentle squeeze, then leaned back in his chair and sighed. He knew from the confusion swimming in the woman's eyes that she had no real comprehension of what he was talking about, and the stunned expression on her face was not unlike that on Harry Parker's as he sat at this same table a week later during the interrupted séance and stared down at the bloodstain spreading across the front of his shirt. There were shocked gasps from the others around the table, and Linda Luft screamed. Garth eased Mary down on the carpet, then rose to his feet and strode quickly around the table toward his friend. He stopped when Harry Parker held up his hand. "It's all right, Garth," the burly man said in a tone that was at once distant and disbelieving, yet firm. "I'm okay."

"For Christ's sake, Harry, you're bleeding."

"Not anymore," the magician and investigator of the paranormal replied in the same distant voice. He unbuttoned his shirt to show his bare chest. The thick, wiry hair there was matted with blood, but there was no longer any seepage. "I'm not even cut. The blood must have come right through my pores. Wow."

78

"It's a sign," Madame Bellarossa intoned. Her head was tilted back now, her arms still extended out over the table. "They want to be taken seriously."

John Luft cleared his throat loudly. When the others turned to the young man with the blond hair, dark eyes, and thin face, he took his arm from around his ashen-faced, trembling wife and tapped his watch. "Uh, I really think Linda and I should be toddling off. It's getting pretty late."

Suddenly Madame Bellarossa's head came forward and her eyes opened wide. "That could be dangerous!" she snapped. "They haven't finished telling us what they want us to know!"

For the first time since the séance had begun, Elsie spoke in words not offered as a prayer. She seemed composed now, determined. She looked directly at John and Linda Luft and spoke in a soft but firm tone. "I understand now that this thing will have to be done if there's ever to be peace in this house. They've spoken to Mary this time, not to me, but I sense that they won't harm us- - as long as they can finish their story. But they want the two of you here. If we listen to all of it, I think they'll go away at last. God knows I need to sell this house, but in good conscience I can't allow anyone else to move in here until this is resolved. Especially not a nice young couple like you. I certainly understand your fear—but if you don't stay and continue, then I can't let you have the house."

"That's just fine with me," the young woman said in a quavering voice as she turned toward the living room. "I'm out of here."

John Luft grabbed his wife's arm, pulled her back beside him. His bright eyes reflected the flickering candles as he looked around at the others, and then finally settled his gaze on Elsie. "You're saying that this could be like a kind of exorcism? If the ghosts tell Mary what's on their minds, and Mary tells us, then they'll leave the house when you leave?"

It was Madame Bellarossa who answered. "That is correct."

"Then let's do it," Luft said, virtually pushing his wife back down into the chair she had jumped out of when Mary had collapsed.

"Hoo, boy," Harry Parker said, flapping the ends of his shirt in an effort to speed the drying of the blood that had soaked it, "I've been exposing phony-baloney occult scams for most of my life, but I've never seen anything like this. I don't mind telling you I'd really like to see how it all comes out."

"No," Garth said as he walked back to where Mary was still sitting on the floor, looking dazed. He put a hand under her arm, helped her to her feet. "Let's not do it."

The others stared at him in stunned silence, which Mary finally broke. "Garth? What's wrong?"

"I'm sorry, Elsie," Garth said to the old woman. "It's your house, and your ghosts, but it's my wife they're using as a mouthpiece - - and they knocked her to the floor to get her attention. That's a bit rough, and it's not at all my idea of how to start a pleasant conversation. Neither is making Harry bleed. If they want to talk to me, that's fine, but I'm not letting Mary sit back down at that table. The only hand she's going to hold for the rest of the evening is mine."

"Garth," Mary said, a quiet urgency in her voice, "it's all right. I want to do it - - for Elsie, and for John and Linda. I want to help end all this. They don't mean to hurt me; they don't want to hurt anybody. They're just very *angry*. They want to be heard."

"That is correct," Madame Bellarossa whispered.

Garth shook his head. "If they need a lawyer, then let them talk through me."

Mary said, "They won't. They'll only talk through me."

"Why?"

"I don't know," Mary replied, and then put her arms around her husband and gently kissed him on the cheek the way she had when she'd drifted up from sleep and found him awake the night after he had discovered Elsie cowering outside their back door. "Whom are you calling?" she had asked dreamily.

"Elsie."

80

"Garth, it's past midnight."

"That's why I'm calling. I've been trying to reach her for the last fifteen minutes. There's no answer."

"Remember she said she heard the phone ringing all the time. Now she's probably not answering the phone, even when it really is ringing. With Elsie, I'd say that's a healthy sign."

Garth hung up, waited ten seconds, and then dialed again. "I'm worried about her. I want to talk to her, make sure she's all right."

"Garth, let the poor woman *sleep*. If her ghosts were hassling her, she'd be over here just like she was last night. You're starting to act like you believe in them."

"I believe in terror, Mary," Garth said evenly, hanging up the phone and rising. "That's what I saw in Elsie. I had an uncle who died from what he believed, and I don't want the same thing to happen to Elsie. I'll be back in a little while."

He quickly dressed in jeans, a sweatshirt, and sneakers, took the flashlight from a shelf in the kitchen, and then went out into the night, down to the beach. A full moon painted the river silver and silhouetted the Victorian mansion that loomed up out of the darkness into a sky of midnight blue as he approached it. He knocked on the door, waited, and then knocked again, louder. When there was no answer, he retrieved the spare key he knew Elsie kept behind a potted plant on the porch, opened the door, and let himself in. He started as he swept the beam of his flashlight across the hardwood floor of the foyer and a moving, shiny carpet of cockroaches skittered away in all directions. There was a strong smell of rotting garbage.

"Elsie?!" he called. "Don't be afraid! It's Garth! I've come to make sure you're all right!"

There was no answer. He reached to his left and flipped a light switch, but the house remained shrouded in darkness. From somewhere upstairs, barely perceptible, came flopping and scratching sounds, as if someone or something with long nails was hopping around and slapping bare hands or feet against the floor.

81

He went to the foot of the stairs and the flopping and scratching sounds grew more pronounced.

"Elsie?!"

There was another flop, the crash of a lamp or dish hitting the floor, and then he heard a soft moan. He immediately bounded up the stairs, heading for the old woman's bedroom on the second floor. The door was closed. He yanked it open, stepped into the room.

Garth Frederickson was a man who had faced death a hundred times, and he no longer feared anything, but he was thoroughly startled when something slimy, soft, and heavy smacked into the side of his head and claws raked his cheek. He stumbled and went down to one knee as the thing fell off him and leaped away into the darkness, landing fifteen feet away with a sharp slapping sound. But the shock passed as he realized almost immediately what the thing was, and even as his heartbeat rapidly began to return to normal, anger, swift-running and hot, rose in him.

He got back to his feet and swept the light around the room until the bright beam found Elsie huddled on the floor beside her bed, her arms wrapped around her. Her face was purple, and she was rapidly opening and closing her mouth in a desperate struggle to breathe.

"It's Garth, Elsie," he said, flashing the light on his face as he quickly went to her. He set the flashlight on a dresser, where it illuminated half the room, and then lifted Elsie up and sat her on the edge of the bed. He braced one hand against her back, then gently pressed on her chest, released the pressure, pressed again. "Breathe, Elsie. Come on, now; breathe. I'm here now. Nobody's going to hurt you."

"The ghosts . . . "

"I'm pretty sure your ghosts have finished their work for the night and gone home. If they are still in the house, I guarantee I'll break their necks and make real ghosts out of them."

82

There was a scratching sound in the half of the room still in darkness, and then a heavy slap. The woman's eyes went wide, and she again began to hyperventilate.

"I'm going to take care of that in a minute," Garth said easily, "just as soon as I get you breathing normally. It won't do for you to have a heart attack. I'm here, and I'm not going to let anyone hurt you. I'm going to see what I can do about taking care of your ghost problem. Now take a deep breath and tell me you're not afraid any longer."

Gradually, the woman's color and breathing became more regular. She took a deep, shuddering breath and slowly let it out. "I'm not afraid."

"Tell me again."

"You're here, Garth. I'm not afraid."

"Good," Garth said as he rose from the bed and picked up the flashlight. "Now just sit there; be calm, and keep breathing normally."

He stepped to the foot of the bed, swept the light around the floor, finally spotted the thing in a corner. In three quick strides he was across the room. He bent down as the creature was about to leap away, gripped it firmly around the haunches, picked it up. Thick, powerful legs with webbed feet clawed at the air as the animal writhed in Garth's hand.

"Oh, my God," Elsie said, putting her hands to her mouth. "What is it?!"

"Just what it looks like, and it certainly didn't come out of the Hudson. Do you need to use the bathroom right away?"

"I. . . don't think so."

"Good," Garth said evenly as he casually tossed the creature into the bathroom adjoining the bedroom, then closed the door. "I'll take care of it later."

"Do you believe me now about the ghosts, Garth?"

"I most certainly do, my dear, and I plan to do a little exorcising. Listen to me: I'm going downstairs to get the lights back on; it'll take me about five minutes. I want you to just sit where you are, keep taking deep breaths, and think happy thoughts. I'll be right back. Things are going to be all right now. Okay?"

"O. . . Okay."

The living carpet of cockroaches scattered from the beam of light as Garth descended from the second floor and crossed the living room, flipping light switches as he went. The smell of rotting garbage grew more pungent as he went down into the basement. He opened the circuit-breaker box, flipped all the switches that had been turned off, and the lights in the house came back on. Next he moved around the cavernous, dust-filled basement, brushing aside thick, intricate tapestries of cobwebs as he went. The wine cellar that hadn't been used in decades was empty, save for a mound of broken black plastic bags that was piled to waist height, spewing garbage. River rats as big as woodchucks scurried away as Garth swept the beam of his flashlight over the expanse of rotting food. He found a second cache of garbage in a tool room, and in another five minutes found an unlocked basement window. He locked the window, and then went back up to the second floor, where he found Mary, dressed in jeans, sandals, and a baggy sweater, sitting on the bed next to Elsie.

"We owe our friend and neighbor an apology, Mary. She really has been haunted, and somebody did, in fact, touch her neck—probably after soaking his hand in ice water. Now I plan to do a little haunting of my own."

"What the hell is that?!" Mary said, jumping off the bed as the creature in the bathroom smacked against the door.

Garth opened the door, went into the bathroom, and once again grabbed the animal, which had landed in the bathtub. He brought it into the bedroom, held it up. "It's just a big frog."

Mary's eyes went wide as she stared at the creature, and she laughed nervously. "A *very* big frog!"

"It is that. I'd estimate this guy weighs upwards of fifteen pounds, and, unless it was stolen, it set Elsie's ghosts back about a thousand dollars. These big guys come from South America. You may remember a few years back when some guy imported one and tried to enter it in that famous frog-jumping contest. It was finally disqualified after a lawsuit, but not before it had eaten half the competition."

Mary shook her head. "Garth? I saw all the cockroaches downstairs, and the whole place reeks of garbage. You and I *do* know that Elsie keeps a clean house. What's going on here?"

"Elsie's going to tell us," Garth replied, tossing the giant frog back into the bathroom and once again closing the door. He went to the bed, put his hand on the old woman's shoulder. "Elsie, you said once before that you couldn't afford to, as you put it, sell the house for a song. But somebody has been trying to buy it for a song, haven't they?"

"Well, I don't ..."

"Did somebody come to you and make an offer after the stories about this house appeared in the papers and you couldn't get any more buyers?"

Elsie brushed a wisp of white hair away from her eyes and looked up at Garth. "Yes - - a really nice young couple. They came to see the house two or three times, looked all around from the attic to the basement. They made me an offer, but it was way too low. How did you know?"

"Being in this house must enhance my psychic powers. Elsie, I want you to tell me all you know about this nice young couple."

She did, and in a few days Garth had compiled sufficient information from computerized bank files, motor-vehicle records, credit bureaus, former employers, real-estate agents, the former owner of the house in an expensive section of Westchester where John and Linda Luft now lived, and their current neighbors, to visit the Luft home, where there was a large For Sale sign stuck in the front lawn.

"John Luft?"

The young man who had answered the door stared at Garth, making no effort to hide the suspicion in his dark eyes. He had the look of a man who was suspicious of a lot of people, and with good reason.

85

"Yeah. Who are you?"

"My name's Garth Frederickson. I'm a friend of Elsie Manning. She asked me to come around and speak to you."

At the mention of Elsie's name, the suspicion left John Luft's eyes, instantly replaced by an expression of innocence and charm. "Elsie Manning. What a lovely old lady. How is she?"

"Actually, she's not doing too well—that house is really too much for her. She's very anxious to sell it, and you and your wife were the last people to express an interest. That's why I'm here."

Now other things moved in Luft's eyes, greed and triumph. He started to laugh nervously, cut himself off, licked his thin lips. "Uh, sure. Come on in."

Garth entered the house and followed John Luft, who was walking jauntily and snapping his fingers, into a living room decorated with huge, garish, abstract paintings that Garth judged were expensive, but of dubious artistic merit.

"You want a drink or something?" Luft continued, motioning for Garth to sit down in an overstuffed chair.

"No, thanks," Garth replied, easing himself down into the chair and casually crossing his legs.

"Garth Frederickson," Luft said as he sat down on a sofa and studied the rangy, powerfully built man with shoulder-length, thinning, wheat-colored hair and soulful brown eyes who was also studying him. "You're pretty well known, right?"

"Am I? I don't have the slightest idea."

"Yeah. I've seen your picture in the papers. You're a private investigator. You're married to Mary Tree - - my wife and I love her music, buy all her records - - and you've got a weird little brother who's even more famous than you are."

Garth smiled thinly. "It sounds like you've got me pegged."

"Uh, how come Elsie sent a private detective to talk to me?"

"She didn't send a private detective; I'm here as her friend and neighbor. She asked me to speak with you on her behalf."

"She's . . . ready to sell the house?"

"Yes. Are you and your wife still interested in buying it?"

Luft again licked his lips, swallowed, and cleared his throat. "Is she willing to accept the last offer we made her?"

"Two hundred thousand dollars, yes."

The other man leaned back on the sofa, grinned. "How about that?"

"You've got yourself quite a bargain, Mr. Luft; two hundred thousand dollars for a house worth three quarters of a million. Considering the neighborhood you're in, you'll probably get more than enough from the sale of this house to buy the one in Cairn outright."

"Yeah, well, Linda and I have been pretty lucky with our real-estate investments. We got this house at a good price, but for a very good reason. We were ready to go into hock up to our eyebrows to buy it, and then our building inspector discovered not only that the well on the property is polluted with toxic waste, but also that there was a big termite infestation—lots of structural damage. There were other major problems as well. The owner was so disgusted that he just wanted out. He accepted our second offer. We've put a lot of money into fixing up this house."

"I'll bet you have."

"Had to take out a huge home-equity loan to pay for the repairs. That's why we couldn't afford to offer Elsie any more than we did. But then, I figure we're doing her a favor. What with what happened with the court case and all, she's really in a jam. Nobody else wants to buy it, and she needs to go to a nursing home."

"Aren't you a little nervous about moving into a haunted house?"

Luft laughed—a kind of high-pitched giggle. "Are you putting me on? Don't tell me *you* believe in ghosts."

"Elsie's willing to sell you the house, for the price you offered—but there's one condition. If it's not met, there's no sale."

Luft's eyes narrowed. "What condition?"

"You and I may not believe in ghosts, but Elsie does. And she feels responsible for the ghosts in that house. You might say she wants to clean up her home before she sells it to anybody—

87

especially a nice young couple like you and your wife. You and I know it's crazy, but she insists on it. She wants to exorcise the ghosts, and she intends to do it with a séance. You and your wife must agree to be a part of it, since you're the ones who'll be moving into the house."

Luft's dark eyes shone with amusement. "She wants us to meet her *ghosts?!"*

"She insists on it. The séance will be tomorrow night, eleven o'clock. I hope you and your wife can be there."

"Can we *be* there?!" Luft threw back his head and laughed, held his stomach. "God, we wouldn't miss it for the *world!* Wait until I tell Linda we're going to a séance tomorrow night in order to clean the ghosts out of our new home. She'll *love* it!"

"I hope so," Garth replied evenly, and wondered now, as he held the woman's hand in the restored circle at the candlelit table, if Linda Luft and her husband were enjoying the experience as much as the man had believed they would. The woman's hand was clammy and trembling, slick with sweat.

"I feel them coming closer, Mary," Madame Bellarossa whispered. "Yes," Mary said in a soft, dreamy voice. "I feel them too. . . very close. They're so angry—but not with Elsie. And they're not the ones who've been doing the terrible things to her. There are others . . . undead. Not dead. Greed; it's all about greed, incredible selfishness, a young couple who think they're entitled to anything they want just because they want it, no matter who's hurt. I see money, pieces of paper... stocks! Yes! The man used to be a stockbroker, but he was fired for churning accounts, and suspicion of embezzlement. He stole. . . Wait! I see something..."

Garth looked up as a light began to glow in the darkness near the ceiling. The light resolved into a rectangle, and then became two figures in hooded robes, bathed in moonlight, approaching the house from the beach, opening a basement window. Linda Lull snatched her sweat-soaked hand from Garth's grip.

"That's enough!" John Luft shouted at almost the exact moment when the giant frog sailed out of the darkness and landed in the center of the table, knocking over half the candles, then hopped away toward the living room.

Garth rose from his chair, reached for the light switch on the wall behind him. The lights in the dining room came on. John and Linda Luft, their faces the color of old parchment, were standing back a pace from their overturned chairs, almost directly beneath the suspended screen with its mounted, remote-controlled rear projector, gaping at the people around the table who stared back at them now with undisguised hostility and contempt.

"I guess this is the part where we find out if the butler did it," Mary said in a low, steely voice.

"I don't have a butler," Elsie said, her voice quavering with rage as she glared at the couple across the table from her.

"That wasn't us!" John Luft shouted, pointing a trembling finger at the screen above his head. "We didn't put the robes on un—!"

"Shut up!" Linda Luft screamed at her husband, punching him in the chest with her fist. "You *idiot!*"

John Luft grew even paler, took another step backward, then looked over at Harry Parker, who seemed to have lost interest in the proceedings now that the illusion he had helped create had been played out. He had taken off his shirt and was removing an apparatus of tubes and blood-filled capsules from around his lower waist. "Actually, I kind of like this house," the big man mumbled to no one in particular. "It has atmosphere. If the frog's part of the deal, I may buy it myself."

Elsie slowly rose from her chair, pointed a finger at the Lufts. Her entire body was trembling with rage. "How *could* you?!" she said. "How could you be so mean?"

Now it was Linda Luft's turn to lose control. Her face turned crimson as she stepped toward Elsie and screamed, "You shut up too, you old bitch! What do you want with the house or the money? You're going to die soon, you hag! Why can't you let somebody else enjoy it?"

John Luft gripped his wife's shoulders, pulled her back from the table as he glared at Garth. "You set us up,

Frederickson!" he said, his voice shimmering with both anger and fear.

"Set you up?" Garth replied mildly. "You're damned lucky Elsie didn't have a heart attack; you'd be facing manslaughter charges." He paused, nodded toward Jeffrey Bond, who had a deep frown on his face as he stared at the young couple. "I introduced you to Jeff, but I don't think I mentioned that he's the Cairn Chief of Police. Madame Bellarossa is his wife, and her real name is Carol. She's quite a well-known actress. Without her wig and makeup, I'm sure you'd recognize her."

"You can't prove a thing!" the man shouted at Jeffrey Bond.

"That remains to be seen," the police chief replied evenly. "We have a videotape of these proceedings, for what that's worth. Also, my friend Garth found the fellow you paid to mess up that guy's house that you're living in now, and then pose as a building inspector to give him the bad news. It seems he kept the sales slips for the acid you had him buy and inject into the wood joints to make it look like the owner had termite damage. The police across the river have a warrant out for your arrest. In addition to that, there'll be a process server around to see you in the morning. You're looking at a whopping lawsuit, in addition to any criminal penalties. I think I'll let Westchester have you for now, and that will give me time to ponder all the charges I'm going to hit you with when they're done."

The lights in the living room came on. John and Linda Luft started, then wheeled around to see two uniformed policemen and the two young stagehands, friends of Carol Bond, who had handled the special effects for the evening's performance standing in the archway between the two rooms. The giant frog was over in a corner contentedly munching on what appeared to be a mouthful of cockroaches, survivors from the exterminator's visit earlier in the day.

"The charges won't stick!" John Luft screamed at Garth as he and his wife were handcuffed. "They can't prove anything! You're going to be sorry! I swear I'll get you!"

90

"Boo," Garth said.

THE PROBLEM WITH THE PIGS

The first of the three shots fired in rapid succession grazed Charlotte's neck, the second ricocheted off the pavement, and the third hit Garth in the left thigh, just above the knee. As Charlotte squealed in surprise, pain, and anger, Garth clutched his wounded leg, staggered a few steps, and then went down to his knees in the otherwise deserted parking lot at Nyack Beach State Park. He glanced up, squinting in the bright light of the early spring morning, and saw a tall, gaunt man in a ski mask and carrying a rifle leaning on the stone wall beside the narrow road leading down to the beach from Nyack's Broadway. As Garth watched, the masked gunman straightened up and walked unhurriedly down the road, obviously intending to finish him off at point-blank range. The man was a lousy shot, Garth thought with a grim smile, and this seemed an odd and unprofessional way to carry out an assassination. Not that it made any difference; one assassin's bullet would do the job just as well as another. He certainly had plenty of enemies who wished him dead, but there weren't many amateurs in the lot, and he wondered which of these had finally tracked him to Cairn, taken note of his daily six-mile run to the beach and back, and selected this time and place to kill him.

There had been a time when he had never gone on the street unless he was armed, but those days were past, and now he rarely carried a gun, except on those rare occasions when he was working a particularly dangerous case. He was helpless now, crippled, and a stationary target in the middle of an empty parking lot. To his left was the Hudson River, its shoreline still clotted with ice. The trees on the side of Hook Mountain, which stretched toward the azure sky on his right, were barren of leaves and would provide no cover even if he could reach them. To his immediate right, perhaps fifty feet away, was the entrance to a two-story building that had once housed a factory for a company that had blasted trap rock from the sides of the mountain, crushed it in the facility, then shipped the scrapple by barge down the river to the stone-hungry boroughs of New York City. The building would surely provide sanctuary, but the wide, swinging doors at its entrance looked to be securely padlocked.

Garth thought it highly unlikely that the gunman was interested in Charlotte and Precious, but, fearing that the man might kill them anyway, out of spite, he removed the loops of their leashes from his right wrist, then slapped them on their haunches, trying to drive them toward the trail behind him that snaked along the shoreline. They refused to go. Squealing raucously, both pigs nudged at his arms and shoulders, as if to prod him to his feet. Bracing himself on Charlotte's back and grimacing against the pain that shot through his leg, Garth struggled to his feet, and then lurched toward the entrance to the building. The gunman, who had just entered the parking lot from the road and was perhaps fifty yards away, raised his rifle and fired, but the slug bit into a stone corner of the building, which momentarily shielded Garth from the line of fire. He could hear the man's running footsteps on the pavement as he lunged at the guardians to the darkness inside where he would be safe. The swinging doors, which had no brace besides the heavy padlock, creaked and gave a bit, but with his wounded leg Garth could not generate sufficient speed and leverage to smash them open. In a few seconds the gunman would round the corner of the building and kill him.

Garth was preparing to lunge once again when suddenly there was a loud thump below him and the doors shook. He looked down and was astounded to see Charlotte, knocked back on her haunches and the top of her head bleeding from the force of the blow she had delivered, get to her feet. She wobbled a bit, but she backed up, and then once again charged the door, this time with Precious running at her side. Garth timed his lunge with theirs, and the force of his own weight and three hundred pounds of pig did the trick. The old, dry wood around the padlock cracked and gave way, and Garth tumbled after the pigs into the darkness.

As Charlotte and Precious scampered away toward the opposite end of the building, Garth pulled himself back down a narrow space between two enormous pieces of rusting machinery that appeared to be portable conveyor belts. When he had been swallowed up by darkness, he leaned back against a steel tread, removed his belt, and cinched it around his leg to serve as a tourniquet. Through spaces in the undercarriage of the conveyor belt on his left he could see the bright rectangle of light that was the entrance. The gunman had not appeared in the doorway, and Garth did not expect him to; he would be a fool to stalk a man in darkness, or to hang around. The park was small, and there were houses less than a quarter of a mile away where the shots could have been heard. Hikers and motorists looking for a spectacular view and a break from their day used the park year-round, and both state police and Orangetown cops patrolled the area regularly, as had been the case two weeks earlier when Sam Beeman had eased his cruiser up beside Garth, rolled down the window on the passenger's side, and called, "How are the girls?"

"Just fine," Garth called back. "If you've got a minute, I'll show you their latest accomplishment."

"Sure," the baby-faced Orangetown policeman said, pulling his car over to the side of the road and getting out. "I want to talk to you anyway."

Garth pulled two ears of barbecued corn from a plastic bag he carried in his waistpack. Charlotte and Precious pricked their ears and grunted expectantly. "Sit," he said, and the pigs sat. "Roll over," he commanded, and, somewhat laboriously, they managed to roll themselves over. Garth fed them the corn, turned to the policeman, and continued, "Pretty impressive, huh?"

"Damn," the young policeman said, taking off his cap and running a hand back through his thinning brown hair. "I see they like their corn *and* the cob. I didn't know pigs did tricks."

"Pigs are smarter than your average dog—just not as eager to please. You need a lot of corn, and you have to get them when they're hungry—not really a problem, since they're hungry most of the time."

"I thought it was your smart little brother who was so good with animals."

"He does the big critters—lions, tigers, bears, and elephants. I do pigs."

"And a wolf."

"Wolves don't do tricks—but they're amused when *you* do."

"I also thought Vietnamese potbellied pigs were supposed to be cute little pink things; Charlotte and Precious are two cute big gray things. What do they go, a couple of hundred pounds each?"

"Bite your tongue, Sam. They do start off as cute little pink things when they're young, but, like all pigs and people, they get bigger if you feed them. They both weigh in at about a hundred and fifty now. Charlotte was about fifty pounds overweight when Marge bought her a couple of years ago to keep Precious company. That's when I volunteered to take her out for a fitness trot two or three times a week. Precious insisted on coming along, and it's become kind of a habit. I get a kick out of them, and I enjoy their company. What did you want to talk to me about, Sam?"

The policeman sighed, shook his head. "We've got a problem with the pigs."

"Who's got a problem?"

"A guy by the name of Peter Erckmann—just moved to Cairn, bought the old Hurley mansion. He filed a zoning complaint against Marge. Claims the pigs make too much noise and keep him awake at night."

"That's absurd. They don't make any noise, and they're probably asleep every night before he is. They don't bother anyone. Marge got Precious as a piglet for the kids in her day-care

96

center to raise as a pet. Charlotte came along later. The kids love the pigs, and the pigs love them. They're even housebroken. All they do is wander around in their pen all day, an4 then go to their place in the basement at night. The neighbors around here have never complained, and the Hurley mansion is a block and a half away."

Sam Beeman shrugged resignedly. "What can I tell you? Who knows what he's got against the girls? But there is a zoning ordinance in Cairn that prohibits the keeping of wild or farm animals, so he's on good legal ground."

"Mary and I keep a hybrid wolf that's a lot more dangerous than Charlotte and Precious. The village board gave us a variance. Why can't they do the same for Marge?"

"Maybe they will—but it's not certain. Your wolf was a special case. You didn't buy it to keep as a pet—you fished it out of the river. It had been mutilated, and you and that wolf were responsible for saving lives after those neo-Nazis set up shop in the county. People were grateful, and there was a lot of emotion. There was no place to send the wolf, so the board let you and Mary keep it. The variance you got may actually work against Marge; the board may not want to make another exception. Anyway, I just served Marge with notice of the complaint, so you're going to find she's upset when you get back with the girls. I figured you'd want to know."

Marge Proctor, the pigs' owner, was indeed upset, and when Garth arrived home he found that his wife, the folksinger Mary Tree, was too. Mary was in their soundproofed music room practicing a new ballad she had written with her band. Garth tapped on the glass and waved as he walked down the hallway outside, then stopped when Mary urgently signaled to him. She put down her guitar, said something to the three people in the room with her, and then hurried out into the hallway. Her long, gray-streaked yellow hair gleamed in the sunlight pouring in through the skylight above their heads, and her blue eyes flashed with anger.

"Have you heard what that man is trying to do to Charlotte and Precious?"

97

Garth nodded. "I just left Marge."

"How can he do that?" Mary snapped, clenching her fists. "Marge's house is their home. Marge will never find anybody. to take them both in, and no other place would be the same anyway. Those are friendly, intelligent, and loving animals, Garth, and they're so attached to each other! They have feelings, and they'll be so sad if they're separated and sent away!"

"I spend more time with Charlotte and Precious than you do, my love," Garth said quietly, gently caressing his wife's cheek. "You don't have to tell me that they have feelings."

"What are you going to do about it?"

Garth shrugged. "Marge and I were talking strategy, and we'll start with a little PR work. We'll organize a letter-writing campaign; it shouldn't be hard to get the parents of the children who have been in Marge's day-care center to speak up in support of Charlotte and Precious, and then the neighbors will testify that the pigs have never bothered anyone. We'll round up a lot of sup- porters to attend the next board meeting, and maybe we can per- suade the trustees to give Marge the variance she needs."

"That's all?"

"All? What do you want me to do, Mary?"

"Your brother would think of more to do."

"He might think of it, but he wouldn't do it. And he wouldn't want me to do it. In fact, his greatest concern would be that I might overreact. You expect me to go thump on the guy?"

"I think you and your brother have thumped people for less."

Garth frowned slightly as he studied his wife. "Not over pigs and charges of a zoning violation. That's an odd thing to say to me, Mary."

"I'm sorry," the woman said softly, averting her gaze as she rested her hand on her husband's chest.

"Cairn is our home, Mary, which means Erckmann is our neighbor. I don't want it to appear as if I'm throwing my weight around, literally or figuratively. I very much value our privacy, and I prefer my famous wife to get all the publicity and attention. The people who'd be interested in me and my whereabouts aren't exactly fans."

"I know," Mary said in the same small voice. "You're always concerned about my safety."

"I didn't tell Marge this, but I'll tell you. If all else fails, we'll bring on the lawyers. If the board won't give her a variance, Frederickson and Frederickson will take on her and her pigs as clients, and I guarantee the matter will be tied up in the courts right up until the day when both Charlotte and Precious have died of happy, comfortable old age. I just don't want to pull that kind of stunt except as a last resort. Okay?"

Now Mary looked up at him, and Garth could see shadows moving in her eyes. "Garth, there's more to it. This Peter Erckmann is an evil man."

"Why? Because he doesn't like Vietnamese potbellied pigs?"

"Because he exploits people's fears, and he harms them. It's not just Charlotte and Precious who need your help. He has to be stopped."

"What's he doing, and how do you happen to know so much about him?"

"Marge filled me in when she called. Erckmann's a psychologist who now runs a practice consisting exclusively of group therapy sessions for people who think they've been abducted by aliens. He wrote a bestseller, which explains how he could afford to buy the Hurley mansion. He's started up a group here in Cairn, and Burty Bennett's his star abductee. Burty's parents must be paying for it."

Garth shrugged. "So Erckmann's one more alien-abduction con man, but his victims know exactly what they're paying for when they go to see him. I don't blame Burty for wanting to believe he was abducted by aliens; he'd rather do that than face up to the fact that he fried his brains on angel dust when he was a teenager and has spent the rest of his life wandering around the streets of Cairn clawing at his skin to try to dig out the worms he feels crawling under there. A whole lot of people are very unhappy with their lives, Mary, and they want somebody besides themselves to blame for it. Alien kidnappers make dandy scapegoats. What Erckmann is doing isn't illegal. I can do my best to protect Charlotte and Precious from him, but it's impossible to protect people from themselves."

Mary shook her head stubbornly. "A year and a half ago Bill Stiller lost his management job with IBM. He couldn't find another job with a salary even close to what he'd been making, and he started going to hell with himself—having affairs, drinking heavily, putting on a lot of weight. He ended up in Erckmann's therapy group.

Garth's response was another shrug. "He sounds typical."

"What about Bill and Pat's daughter, Jenny? Would a seven-year-old fit the profile of a typical victim?"

Mary watched her husband's face darken, and she knew she had finally captured his attention and interest.

"Explain," Garth said softly.

"One day while Pat was working late, Bill took Jenny with him to one of his therapy sessions. Erckmann did a number on her, claimed that by talking to her he could tell that the whole family had been abducted and experimented on, and that Jenny and her mother were repressing the memories. Pat found out about it and went through the roof. She threw Bill out of the house and started writing letters to the editor and passing out fliers attacking Erckmann. But the damage to Jenny had already been done; she's been having nightmares about being abducted by aliens."

"And she's likely to have them for the rest of her life," Garth said in a voice just above a whisper. "The son of a bitch has implanted memories of events that never happened, and those phony memories could twist her life completely out of shape as she grows older. They could destroy her."

"Jenny used to be in Marge's day-care center, and Marge has been advising Pat. She's even written a few letters herself, and she has the academic credentials to back up what she says about Erckmann harming a child. Marge thinks that's the real reason Erckmann filed a complaint against the pigs—to punish her."

100

Garth abruptly turned and walked away, and Mary felt a twinge of fear. Garth would not use violence on behalf of the pigs, but he certainly would to protect a child. That was why she had told him the story, but now she was suddenly having serious reservations about what she had done. She felt manipulative and slightly guilty. She knew that her husband could be unpredictable and extremely dangerous in certain situations, when something or someone he cared deeply about was in jeopardy, and when he was in that frame of mind he took no prisoners. This was precisely such a situation. She knew from Garth's reaction that she had succeeded in arming him like a guided missile and pointing him at Peter Erckmann, but now she wondered what price might have to be paid. Her fear was not assuaged when she woke in the middle of the night to find Garth, in his robe, standing at the window and staring out at the moon-washed Hudson River. "I'm sorry, sweet-heart," she said, rising and going to him, resting her head between his shoulder blades as she wrapped her arms around his waist. "I was very upset this morning. I love you so much. Sometimes I think of you and your brother as the righters of all wrongs, and I know you can't be that. I shouldn't have laid all that business about Jenny on you. You can't undo what's already been done."

"Don't be sorry, Mary," Garth said in an even tone, taking his wife's hands in his and squeezing them. "I would have been angry with you if you hadn't told me and I'd found out about it later. The problem isn't one of putting Erckmann out of business, because there are dozens of people like him. A way has to be found to heal the girl."

"It's not helping anybody for you to be losing sleep over this, Garth."

"I'm not losing sleep; I'm thinking. You and Lothar have the same manager. His house has been dark all week, so he must be out on tour. Why don't you give your manager a, call in the morning and find out where he is? Lothar owes Frederickson and Frederickson a big favor; even if he didn't, I think he'd want to help me out on this."

Mary frowned, looked at the back of her husband's head silhouetted in the moonlight. "I know where he is," she said, thoroughly puzzled. "He's in Atlantic City. He's got a month-long gig at Trump Palace. I'm supposed to be watering his plants."

Garth nodded. "I'll give him a call in a few hours, find out when he has a day off."

Mary shook her head. "How on earth is a master magician and illusionist going to help you in this situation?"

"I need an introduction to some aliens," Garth replied, and two weeks later he reflected on the fact that the gunman, who had suddenly appeared at the entrance to the building where he lay in the darkness, was certainly no alien, at least not one from another planet, although he could very well be in the country illegally. On the other hand, he knew that if the man were ex-KGB or Stasi, or renegade CIA, he would have been killed with the first shot.

Garth loosened the tourniquet around his leg, but immediately tightened it again when he felt blood gush from the bullet wound; there was no sense in worrying about gangrene when there was a good chance he could bleed to death. The last time his past had caught up with him here had been when an old enemy who had been with the Stasi in East Germany had unexpectedly landed in Cairn, but that meeting had been accidental. Very few people who were not his friends knew that he lived in Cairn and was married to Mary Tree, and, their home number was unlisted. In Cairn, as in neighboring Nyack, local residents were fiercely protective of the host of celebrities in their midst. It was always possible that he had been tracked from the Frederickson and Frederickson offices in New York, but he did not think that was the case here. He was definitely dealing with an amateur, and even before the man, now half in shadow inside the building, took off his ski mask to reveal half a shaved skull painted with Mercurochrome Garth was beginning to strongly suspect that the source of this problem was much closer to home, possibly linked to the tall, stooped, and heavyset man with brooding, hawk-like features, musty smell, and big feet who'd held up Garth's business card as he'd walked into Garth's home office and announced, "I've

102

been doing a little checking on you, Frederickson. You and your smart little brother are pretty famous private detectives. You two have been involved with some pretty weird business."

And was about to be again, Garth thought, and said, "It's my smart little brother who's the famous one. Most of the time I just hold his coat. And you're involved in some pretty weird business yourself."

The hawk-faced man narrowed his eyes, which were the color of shale. "In the note you sent with your card you said you had something important to show me, and that I should come here at this time if I wanted to see it. But this is really about those pigs, isn't it? I was told you're friends with the woman who owns them, and I was warned to watch out for you. Well, you're wasting your time. I didn't spend almost three quarters of a million dollars for a house so that I could have pigs living in the next block."

"Why don't you sit down, Mr. Erckmann?" Garth said, motioning to the chair set up in front of his desk. "I really do have something to show you, and as a reputed expert on alien abduction I think you'll be very interested."

Erckmann hesitated, then pulled back the chair and sat on its edge, leaning forward as if ready to bolt at any moment. "What is it?"

"First, let's get things straight between us. You're a fraud. You take disturbed people looking to shift the blame for their problems, you hypnotize them to elicit these so-called repressed memories, and then you helpfully add on a few details so that it sounds like everyone is telling the same story."

"I didn't come here to be insulted, Frederickson!" Erckmann snapped, jumping to his feet.

"Sit down, Erckmann," Garth said easily. "If you walk out of here before you finish hearing what I have to say, there's a very good chance you'll disappear—permanently—from the face of the earth before dinnertime."

Erckmann scowled. "Are you threatening me?"

"You have nothing to fear from me, Mr. Erckmann. It's my clients you have to worry about."

103

Erckmann slowly eased his large frame back down onto the chair. "Your clients?"

"The reason I know you're a fraud is because I'm in touch with the only aliens within thirteen light-years of earth, and they've never abducted anyone, much less harmed them."

Erckmann threw back his head and laughed—a harsh, guttural sound. "You must take me for a complete idiot."

"You think I'd make a statement like that if I couldn't prove it?"

The other man stopped laughing, looked warily at Garth. "How can you prove it?"

"With a simple demonstration, which we'll get to momentarily. But first let me give you some background so you'll understand just what's involved and why I asked you to come here. A year and a half ago my brother and I were contacted by these aliens."

"Ridiculous! How did they contact you?"

"E-mail, at our New York office. They understand, read, and write English very well, but they can't speak it. They must have bladders for vocal cords, because when they speak it sounds like they're passing wind. They hired us to do a job for them."

Erckmann laughed again, but this time the sound seemed forced, and he looked uncertain. "Why should they hire you?"

Garth shrugged. "As you pointed out, my brother and I have been involved in some pretty strange cases, so I guess they didn't think we'd be fazed by having as clients a couple of barrel-sized things with fur and tentacles."

Erckmann licked his lips nervously, then swung sideways in his chair and crossed his arms over his chest, looking at Garth out of the corner of his eyes. "I want you to know I don't believe a word of this, but I'll humor you by listening to the rest of your story."

"Possibly the wisest decision you've made in your life."

"How do they pay you?"

"Gold, of course. They mint some very interesting coins."

"What did they hire you to do?"

104

"Find them suitable hosts, and then keep an eye on them, act as bodyguards, to make sure they weren't disturbed while they were carrying out their observations. You see, once they enter a host body, they can't leave it or communicate with us for a period of twenty-seven of our months. They can communicate telepathically with each other, but not with humans—it seems we're too limited intellectually. That means my brother and I have to use our best collective judgment to decide what may be a threat to them, and what's in their best interests. They understand what I'm doing now, and I'm sure they concur with my decision—we'll both find out shortly. They were particularly interested in studying human development in very young children. Now, this is where you come in, Erckmann. The problem with the pigs you want to evict and separate is that they're not just pigs. They're host bodies for our alien clients."

Erckmann snorted loudly and crossed his arms even tighter across his chest. "This is absolutely absurd, Frederickson. I knew this meeting was about those pigs. If you think I'm going to with-draw my complaint because of this wild cock-and-bull story, then you're a very stupid man."

"Actually, this is a pig tale, Erckmann, and I'm not surprised at your reaction. I'd feel the same way. That's why I've suggested to the ambassadors that they arrange for you a modest demonstration. Considering what's at stake, I assume they've taken my advice. We'll see."

Erckmann smiled and shook his head, but his smile quickly vanished as Garth rose, walked across the room, opened the door to the office, and ushered in Charlotte and Precious. Precious, always the more curious and friendlier of the two, immediately padded over to Erckmann and began sniffing his shoes. The color drained from Erckmann's face, and he hastily drew up his legs.

"Mr. Erckmann," Garth continued, "I'd like you to meet the ambassadors. I wish I could tell you their names, but, for the reason I explained, that's quite impossible. Don't worry about that one: She's always anxious to meet new humans, and she's

105

probably taking field notes. But I wouldn't touch her. The other one is quite protective, and she's liable to take a nip out of you.

"I don't want to touch her!" Erckmann said in a strangled voice, gazing down in horror as Precious, still sniffing away, proceeded to circle his chair. "I just want to get out of here!"

"Just another couple of minutes, Erckmann. We're almost finished." Garth went back to his desk, opened a drawer, and took two ears of barbecued corn out of a plastic bag inside. He threw one to Charlotte, who immediately began to gobble it down. Precious abandoned her investigation of Erckmann and scampered over to Garth for her corn, which he gave her. Then Garth glanced back at Erckmann, continued, "After all, the ambassadors are housed in pig bodies, so they have pig appetites. They do love their corn, and the cob."

"I'm leaving!" Erckmann yelped, leaping to his feet. He rushed to the door, opened it, and then took a step backward when he found Jenny Stiller standing in the doorway.

"Mr. Erckmann!" the seven-year-old with the brown hair, blue eyes, and freckles said. "What are you doing here?"

"Uh, hello, Jenny," Erckmann mumbled as, obviously disturbed, he glanced quickly at Garth.

"You might want to stay just a little bit longer, Mr. Erckmann," Garth said in the same mild tone he had been using all along. "It's time for the demonstration. Come on in, Jenny."

The child skipped around Erckmann and across the room to Charlotte and Precious, put her arms around them. "Hi, Garth! You said I could come over and play with the pigs!"

Garth nodded. "Precious, yes. Charlotte's been a bit cranky, so I think she should stay here. You can take Precious outside. I've put Loner's muzzle on, so he's ready to receive company. Take Precious into his pen, and she and Loner can push the soccer ball around."

"Oh yes!" the girl cried, and giggled with delight as Garth snapped a leash onto the collar around Precious' neck and handed it to her. With Precious scampering along beside her, Jenny Stiller went out the side door to the path leading down to the beach behind Garth's home.

"Come on over here and see what happens, Erckmann," Garth said, rising and going to the window. "The view may give you a new perspective on things."

For a moment Garth feared that Erckmann would simply keep walking out of the office. Erckmann hesitated, and then tentatively stepped over to the window. Garth waited until the girl and pig came into view and were about to enter the enclosure where Garth's hybrid wolf was kept, then turned to Charlotte. "All right, Ambassador. If you agree with my recommendation for a demonstration, you can signal your ship now."

To Garth's considerable surprise and delight, Charlotte, as if on cue, grunted loudly. A moment later there was a wave of shimmering light outside the window, and Jenny, Precious, and the hybrid wolf winked out of sight.

Erckmann jumped back from the window, caroming off Garth, who had been standing right behind him. "It's a trick!" he shouted in a hoarse voice, putting a trembling hand to his mouth.

"I'll say," Garth replied dryly. "I wish I knew how they did it. Jenny and the animals have been transported to the aliens' ship. Jenny's been there before, and she loves it. I think they've got some kind of huge playground up there; I don't know for sure, because I've never been invited aboard. You're more likely to see what the interior of the ship looks like than I am. I'm just a hired hand, but you're a threat to the ambassadors' mission.

"Only fools and nut cases believe in aliens!" Erckmann shouted, his eyes wide. Tiny droplets of sweat had appeared high on his forehead.

"That's an interesting comment coming from someone who makes a living treating people you've convinced have been abducted by aliens, and it's a real hoot that you've bought a home and set up shop in the one place on earth where they actually do exist. Ironic, don't you think? If I were you, I'd start thinking about what accommodation I was going to make to them."

Charlotte, who had been keeping a wary eye on things, grunted again.

"I don't believe it!"

"I wouldn't believe it either if I were you," Garth replied casually as he pretended to sort through some papers on his desk, "but that's irrelevant. I'm not the one who's threatening the well being of the pigs housing the aliens' minds. I've done what I was hired to do, and that's all I care about. I'm not really concerned now with what you believe or do, but—just in case what I've told you is true—you might want to start getting your affairs in order. My suspicion is that you'll be abducted within a matter of hours. They won't harm you, but you will be living aboard that ship for the rest of your life. I'm sure you'll eventually get used to the sight of them."

Garth, his heart hammering, watched as Peter Erckmann walked to the door. He put his hand on the knob, but then hesitated. Finally he turned back to Garth, opened and closed his mouth a few' times, then said in a tight voice, "I'll withdraw my complaint against the pigs."

"Mmm. Smart move, Erckmann."

"Understand," Erckmann said quickly, "it's not because I believe you're representing any aliens, but just because I don't want to be bothered dealing with somebody who'd go to all this trouble just to protect a couple of pigs."

"It's always better to err on the side of caution; in this case, you have everything to gain and nothing to lose. You've definitely done the right thing. Now, just to be on the safe side, I suggest that you apologize."

"What?!"

"My clients' species is very big on courtesy and ritual," Garth said, reaching into his desk drawer and taking out an ear of corn, which he placed at the edge of the desk. "Tell the ambassador you're sorry, and give her that ear of corn. It will be a nice gesture." When Erckmann hesitated, Garth continued, "Go ahead and do it, Erckmann. You've already said you'd withdraw your complaint, so you might as well go whole hog, as it were. It's just

108

to make absolutely certain that the ambassador understands you mean her and the other one no harm. It's for your own good, a kind of insurance policy. After all, you might not like alien food as much as the ambassadors like corn."

Red-faced, Erckmann crossed the room, took the ear of corn from the desk, and held it out to Charlotte, who snatched it from his fingers. "I'm sorry," he mumbled, jumping back.

Garth shook his head. "Don't mumble, Erckmann. Be clear. Say, 'I'm sorry, Ambassador.'"

Erckmann swallowed hard, said to Charlotte, "I'm sorry, Ambassador."

"Good," Garth said curtly. "One last thing. Lay off Jenny and her family—and that includes her father. Tell him he can't come to your group any longer. My clients have plans for the girl, and they don't need her father messing up her head with nonsense about other aliens that don't exist. Now you can go."

Erckmann virtually ran to the door and out of the office, slamming the door shut behind him. Garth reached under his desk and flipped the switch there, then slowly exhaled and shook his head in amazement not unlike that he would experience two weeks later when the gunman who was stalking him, half hidden in the shadows, said "Garth, I got to kill you for what you did to me. You know you deserve it. Now c'mon out and let's get this over with."

"Burty? What the hell do you think you're doing? Why did you shoot me?"

"You were there on the spaceship with the aliens that took me and put the worms under my skin, Garth. I remember now. You're working with them."

Garth tightened the belt around his leg, cutting off the flow of blood that was pouring from his wound and filling his shoe. He was beginning to feel faint, but he willed himself to focus. He groped around him in the darkness until his fingers touched what felt like a crowbar or tire iron. "Burty, you horse's ass, I don't know what you're talking about, but I do know that I'm going to beat your brains out if you don't put that gun down. We have to talk."

The man with the permanent brain damage came further into the building, angling across the pool of sunlight and toward the sound of Garth's voice. "You were with the aliens when they experimented on me. Mr. Erckmann helped me remember. If I kill you, the worms will go away and I'll feel better."

Fighting the terrible weariness that was sapping his strength and making him want to do nothing more than lay his head down on the concrete and go to sleep, Garth, clutching the steel bar, inched forward in the darkness, toward the light. Waiting for Burty Bennett to tire of the hunt and go away was not an option; he would have to make a move soon, or he would die. "Burty, Erckmann's pulling your pud. He wants you to kill me because he thinks that will save him. I've got him on videotape saying that anyone who believes in aliens is a fool or a nut case, and then apologizing to a pig he thinks is an alien ambassador. That's not going to help him sell many more books. Your classmate Bill Stiller has seen the tape, and he's dropped out of the program. He's suing Erckmann, and he's subpoenaed me to appear in court with the tape. He thinks having you kill me is going to solve his problems."

For a moment it appeared that Bennett was coming to him, but the man stopped when he was a few feet away, looked to either side of him, then started toward the rear of the building, where the pigs could be heard rooting around in the darkness. Garth sighed, leaned back against the conveyor belt and smiled thinly as he recalled the look of wonder on Jenny Stiller's face when she had seen herself, a pig, and a wolf vanish in a wink of light, remembered the excitement in her voice as she had leaped off the sofa in Garth and Mary's living room, clapped her hands, and said, "Mr. Lothar made us all disappear! It's a trick!"

Garth let the tape run through the section with Erckmann offering his sincere apologies to Charlotte, then turned off the VCR and looked around at the others. Mary, sitting at the back of the room, smiled broadly, winked, and blew him a kiss. Bill and Pat Stiller sat side by side with their daughter on the sofa that faced the television set. The man was leaning forward and holding his

110

head in his hands while his wife, her face registering both anger and relief, gently stroked the back of his neck.

Jenny skipped over to Garth and put her hand in his. "That was so funny, Garth! Mr. Erckmann was talking to Charlotte just like she was a person, telling her he was sorry he tried to make her and Precious move away. Now everything's going to be all right!"

Garth nodded. "Yes. Now I think everything is going to be all right."

"What a wonderful trick!"

"Why don't you tell your mom and dad what happened?"

"I took Precious outside, just like Garth told me to," the child said, turning to her parents. "Mr. Lothar was waiting for me just outside the door. He took Precious and me around to the side of the house where there were other men, a truck, and a lot of lights and mirrors. He played with Precious and me like he always does, and he showed me some more magic tricks. We had a lot of fun. I didn't know he made it look like we disappeared. That was really neat!"

"Mr. Erckmann was playing tricks too, Jenny," Garth said quietly, stroking the girl's hair. "He just forgot to tell you that he was playing tricks. His trick was to make you think that maybe you and your mom and dad had been taken away by people from another planet, and then he tried to make you remember it, even though it never happened. He tried to fool you, like Mr. Lothar does. But he's not as nice as Mr. Lothar. You and your parents weren't taken away by people from another planet, Jenny. Even if people from another planet do visit us one day, I think they'll be too smart to want to hurt a little girl. You don't have to be afraid of something that never happened, Jenny, and you can stop having nightmares. Your mom and dad would never let anyone harm you."

"I know that, Garth. I'm not afraid anymore."

Bill Stiller, still holding his head in his hands, choked back a sob, and then said in a quavering voice, "I want a copy of that tape, Garth."

Garth put his hand on the girl's back, gently pushed her toward the door. "Loner's got his muzzle on, and I'll bet he'd love a good belly rub."

"Okay!" the girl said, and ran for the door.

Garth waited until Jenny was out of the house, then turned to the girl's father and said simply, "No."

Stiller sobbed again. "The man made a fool out of me, and he almost destroyed my family!"

"If that's how you see it, then you haven't learned a damn thing from this little episode. Erckmann didn't do anything to you or Jenny, Stiller. First you made a jackass out of yourself because you were filled with self-pity and looking for someone or something else to blame for your problems. Then you gave Erckmann a shot at your daughter. I didn't do what I did for the pigs, and I didn't do it so that you could see what an idiot you'd been; I did it so that Jenny could get her head straight. We all got very lucky. It was an incredibly long shot. The only reason Erckmann bit is because sometimes people like Erckmann who peddle nonsense get spooked when the same nonsense is peddled back to them. You're a big boy, Stiller, and I'm not about to help you try to destroy Erckmann. If you've got a beef with Erckmann for making a fool out of you, frightening Jenny, and almost costing you your marriage, you handle it yourself. I won't do anything to help you— not willingly. Do you understand what I'm saying?"

"I understand," Pat Stiller said, looking up at him. "Garth, I can't tell you how grateful I am for what you've done."

Garth nodded to the woman and walked from the living room, and days later, as he lay on the cusp between darkness and sunlight listening to the footsteps of the man who was stalking him, he reflected on the fact that it was Erckmann who was getting payback, and that payback could be Garth's life. He knew he had to make a move now, for to wait much longer meant that he would bleed to death. Even if he could walk properly, it would be useless to stalk the other man in the darkness, for that would use up all the energy he had left. His only chance was to make it out of the building, closing the doors behind him, and then attack Burty Bennett with the steel bar if he followed.

Garth cinched up the belt around his leg, struggled to his feet, then hobbled as fast as he could toward the entrance.

"Hold it, Garth!"

With more than ten feet to go, Garth knew he could not make it. Rather than be shot in the back, he stopped and turned to face the man emerging into the sunlight pouring in through the open doors. "Last chance to give some thought to what you're doing, Burty," Garth said, his own voice sounding distant and metallic in his ears. "You're not going to get rid of any aliens by killing me. You're just going to end up spending the rest of your life clawing at your worms in some cell."

"I gotta do it, Garth," Burty Bennett said, raising his rifle and aiming it at Garth's chest. "I gotta do it because of what you and the aliens did to me."

Suddenly there was a flash of gray as Charlotte, running at full speed, came racing out of the darkness, heading directly toward Burty Bennett. Bennett started to turn, but he was too late, and Charlotte collided with the back of his thighs. Bennett flipped backward in the air, landed headfirst on the concrete, and lay still.

Garth staggered over to the unconscious man as Precious emerged from the darkness and nuzzled up to her companion. When Garth saw that the other man was still breathing, he raised the iron bar over his head. He was going to pass out at any moment, and Bennett would shoot him if he regained consciousness before someone came by and looked in through the open doors.

Garth lowered the steel bar, kicked away the rifle. He would have killed Burty Bennett without hesitation if the other man were still on his feet with the rifle, but he could not bring himself to crush the skull of a helpless, unconscious man. He took the remaining ears of corn from his waistpack and dropped them on the floor next to the fallen man. Then he sank to his knees beside Bennett. "Sit," he said to Charlotte and Precious as he

113

patted Bennett's chest and stomach, and the last thing he saw before losing consciousness was the pigs doing precisely that.

VEIL

THE LAZARUS GATE

Veil dreams.

Vivid dreaming is his gift and affliction, the lash of memory and a guide to justice, a mystery and sometimes the key to mystery, prod to violence and maker of peace, an invitation to madness and the fountainhead of his power as an artist.

The Lazarus Person standing under the streetlight on the sidewalk outside the former warehouse Veil Kendry owned was an attractive woman in her late thirties or early forties. From the vast loft on the fourth floor where he painted and lived, Veil watched her through the one-way glass of his window. Although her face was impassive and her expression distant, he sensed her discomfort. Despite the fact that this was New York City's East Village, the woman was not in danger, for Veil had taken steps when he had first bought the building fifteen years before to make sure that the few blocks surrounding his building were crime-free; drug dealers and others who committed violent crimes in his immediate neighborhood invariably chose not to return a second time, and some disappeared altogether. There was   no bus stop in the middle of the block, no apparent reason for her to be standing there for almost forty-five minutes, and the fact that she was a Lazarus Person made him doubly suspicious. If she somehow knew about him and wanted to talk, she had only to press the buzzer at the entrance on the ground floor.

When an hour had passed and the woman still had not moved, Veil went to the telephone and called Dr. Sharon Solow at home. She was not there, and her answering machine did not come on. When there was no answer at her office in the Sleep Research Laboratories at St. Vincent Hospital, he went down to his arsenal of weapons and equipment on the third floor. He took a pair of night-vision binoculars off a shelf, turned off the lights, and went

117

to a window at the front. First he scanned the rooftops of the buildings across the street, but saw no one there. In the darkened doorway of a storefront directly across the way, however, he spotted a man standing by himself, and he was wearing headphones. Veil peered into the night on the other three sides of the building, but saw nothing out of the ordinary. Satisfied that the watcher and listener in the doorway were alone, Veil left the building through a freight-delivery entrance at the rear, went to the end of the block, around the building, crossed the street, and then came up on the man as silently as a shadow within the shadows and hit him in the solar plexus. As the man doubled over and gasped for air, Veil grabbed the back of his coat collar and marched him across the street. The woman now looked sad, and she remained motionless, watching him as he approached.

"I'm sorry," the woman said quietly as Veil dragged the man up over the curb and shoved him toward the entrance to his building. "The man in green said he would—"

"You don't have to explain," Veil interrupted. "I know you meant me no harm, and I know you didn't agree to act as a lure out of concern for your personal safety. I promise you they won't threaten your family again. You're free to go. There's a subway station a few blocks north of here, and you'll be safe walking there."

The woman nodded, then turned and disappeared into the night. Veil pulled the man through the doorway into his building, and then shoved him hard against the doors of the freight elevator in the small foyer. He closed the entrance door behind him, and then turned to the man, who had slumped to the floor and was still holding his stomach. The expression on his face was a mixture of fear and wonder. He had fiery red hair, green eyes, and thick fields of freckles on his cheeks and forehead. Veil estimated him to be in his mid twenties, although he could have passed as a teenager—a potentially dangerous teenager who, for some reason, was prying into some very dangerous secrets.

118

"My God!" the young man said excitedly, shaking his head and licking his lips. "It's true! You recognized what she was! The two of you must be able to com—!"

"Stop jabbering, or I'll smack you again," Veil said curtly. "Who the hell are you?"

The young man with the red hair and green eyes swallowed hard, then removed his headphones, which hung askew around his neck. A single droplet of sweat had appeared in the center of his forehead. "I . . . won't tell you anything. You can't make me."

Veil grunted. "Really? You look awfully young to be working in the field for the CIA, but when you reach middle age just about everybody starts looking young."

"I said I wouldn't—" The young man stopped speaking and cried out as Veil abruptly grabbed the lapels of his overcoat and yanked him to his feet, once again slamming him against the slatted elevator doors. "Are you going to torture me?"

"Nah," Veil replied evenly. "I hate torture. I don't mind torturing torturers, but you don't look like one of those. But I will show you a trick your chiropractor probably doesn't even know."

Veil jerked the other man around and cupped his chin with his left hand. He twisted the man's neck at the same time as he pressed hard with the heel of his right hand against a precise point on the man's spine. There were sharp popping sounds in the man's neck and back, and he collapsed to the floor.

The man in the overcoat sat on the floor with his legs splayed and his weight balanced on his hands as he stared up into the glacial blue eyes of the rangy man with the shoulder-length, gray-streaked yellow hair who stood over him. What he saw there was death, or worse. He glanced down and began to cry when he saw the puddle of urine forming between his legs. "I'm peeing myself and I can't even feel it," he sobbed. "You've paralyzed me."

"Incontinence is the least of your worries, sonny. Right now you're at least a candidate for a wheelchair. If you don't give simple, straight answers to my questions, you're going to end up being wheeled around on a hospital gurney for the rest of your life.

119

As you may have noticed, I don't bluff, and I rarely even bother to threaten. Now, if you don't want me to shut the rest of you down, stop slobbering and tell me your name."

The young man cut off a sob, breathed, "Denny Whalen."

"All right, Denny Whalen, you work for the CIA, of course. Ops?"

"Yes and no."

"Give me the no part first."

"We don't do ... nasty stuff. No covert operations. We're organized under Operations, but we're strictly research."

"What's your outfit called?"

"Department of Human Possibilities."

"I make it my business to keep up with these things, and I've never heard of you. You need another spinal adjustment?"

"We used to be called the Bureau of Unusual Human Resources."

"Ah yes," Veil said, and sighed. "BUHR. The 'chill shop.' I thought the dwarf put you people out of business last year."

"We've been . . . reorganized."

"Right. Just what the world needs now: a reorganized 'chill shop.' If you're not a field operative, what were you doing with eavesdropping equipment outside my building tonight?"

"It was an experiment. The woman was wired, and I would have heard anything you said to her. I had to see for myself if it was true that Lazarus People recognize each other and are capable of some degree of telepathic communication. I wanted to see if you'd come down—which you did. You two didn't have a real conversation, but you did recognize what she was."

"You're a damn fool, Denny Whalen. How the hell did BUHR find out about Lazarus People? The Lazarus Project was a decade ago, and all the records were destroyed."

"The Lazarus Project was mentioned in KGB files. A lot of their people are working for us now, and they brought a lot of their records with them."

120

"If you've got reports on the Lazarus Project, then you should know it was a complete bust. You can't get to where they wanted to go from here."

"The files are incomplete and spotty. .You killed the two KGB operatives who were at the institute and on the army base."

"So I did. You're holding Dr. Solow?"

Denny Whalen again swallowed hard, nodded.

"Kidnapping sounds like nasty business to me, Denny, and it was a very, very bad idea. Where have you got her?"

"A safe house on the Upper West Side. The address is—"

"I know where it is. Has she been harmed?"

"No."

"How lucky for you. How is it that the director of Ops authorized a kidnapping by a bunch of research scientists?"

"Ops has given top priority to finding out exactly what happened with the Lazarus Project. You must have really rattled some cages in the past, because nobody wanted to mess with you. That's why we approached Dr. Solow first. But she wouldn't cooperate. We needed you. Then it was decided that the best way to get both of you to cooperate would be to take Dr. Solow into our, uh, temporary custody. The director gave us a field operative for that, and I was given permission to run my experiment before we contacted you.

"How many of you are there at the safe house?"

'Three. Two researchers and the field operative."

"Where are you keeping Dr. Solow?"

"In a bedroom on the second floor, at the rear. We have an operations center set up in the basement. Look, why don't you let me try to—?"

"Shut up," Veil said, then bent over the other man and searched through his pockets. He found a cellular phone, smashed it. Then he dragged the helpless man into a corner of the foyer before opening the doors of the freight elevator and stepping in. "Your paralysis will wear off in about forty-five minutes, Denny," he continued. "If I were you, I'd just stay put and wait it out. If it does occur to you to try to crawl out of here and look for help so that you can phone ahead, remember the neighborhood you're in. The vultures around here would like nothing better than to find a nice, well-dressed young fellow like you helpless on the sidewalk. How are you on double negatives?"

"What?"

"I will not not be left alone. And I will not allow anyone to bother Dr. Solow. Tell that to your superiors at Langley. The director of Ops will know just how serious I am."

"Yes, sir."

Veil returned to his arsenal on the third floor. He selected a .45 automatic, which he placed in a small duffel bag along with lock-picking tools and a length of light but strong nylon rope. Then he went out and took a cab to the CIA's safe house on the Upper West Side. He disarmed the security system from a circuit box on the side of the brownstone, then picked the lock on the back door and went in. He found the field operative, a bald, burly man dressed in matching green slacks, shirt, and sport jacket, in a room on the ground floor watching television and drinking beer. The man leaped to his feet and grabbed for the gun in his shoulder holster when Veil entered, and Veil whipped the barrel of his .45 against the side of the man's head, knocking him unconscious. Veil tied up the operative with the nylon cord, then left the room and bounded almost soundlessly up the stairs to the second floor. At the opposite end of a corridor an older man with a withered left arm, dressed in a brown tweed suit and smoking a pipe, was sitting in a chair outside a closed door. When the man looked up, he saw Veil stalking down the corridor toward him, gun raised and aimed at his head. The pipe dropped from the man's clenched teeth and the color drained from his face as he leaped to his feet and thrust his hands in the air.

"Open it," Veil said quietly, nodding toward the door.

"It's not locked," the man with the withered arm replied in a choked whisper.

Veil turned the knob and opened the door. Then he grabbed the front of the man's shirt and shoved him hard into the room. The man in tweed stumbled, spun around, landed on the bed, bounced,

122

and fell on the floor on the other side. Dr. Sharon Solow, her long, wheat-colored hair tied back in a ponytail, was sitting under a bright light in an easy chair across the room. She looked up from the book she was reading, and her eyes, almost as blue as his own, went wide when she saw him. She dropped her book, leaped to her feet, and rushed into his arms.

Veil held the woman he loved tightly in his arms, caressing her hair, brushing his lips against her forehead and cheek.

"Are you all right?"

"Yes." Sharon kissed him hard on the mouth, then stepped back and frowned. "Veil, somehow they found out about the Lazarus Project. They came to me, wanted me to fill them in on the details. I told them I didn't know what they were talking about. There wasn't anything I could tell them that wouldn't involve you. I don't understand how—"

"They already knew about my involvement. They got hold of some old KGB files that presumably mention the two of us and what you were trying to do in that little mountaintop hospice at Pilgrim's Institute."

"Oh God. They must know just enough to get somebody killed."

"It appears that way. I wonder how many people the Russians killed trying to get somebody through the Lazarus Gate and back again."

"How did you find me?"

"They decided to use some Lazarus Person they'd found to run a little experiment on me before calling me to tell me they had you. The experiment didn't quite turn out the way they'd expected."

"Veil, we have to talk to them!"

"Talk to them?" Veil paused, glanced at the man in the tweed suit, who had gotten to his knees and was peering at Veil over the top of the bed. "I've been giving some thought to killing everybody in this house."

"No, my love! You mustn't do that! They're just scientists, and they're terribly curious."

"These terribly curious scientists work for a particularly ugly little department in the CIA that was supposed to have been shut down last year."

"But these people mean no harm—except for the man in green."

"He's sleeping this one out."

"It's what they're trying to do that's so dangerous, my love. We have to talk to them, tell them what will happen if they try to repeat those experiments."

"I'll talk to them. You go home."

"No. I want to be with you."

Veil turned to the man in the tweed suit, who had finally risen to his feet and was holding tightly to his withered arm, as if it were a frail captive that might slip away. "It looks like you're finally going to find out what you want to know. Take us to your leader."

The man cleared his throat, drew himself up straighter. "I, uh, I'm the leader. I'm Dr. Schaefer. What have you done with Dr. Whalen?"

"He's taking some time out to rethink his approach to this whole matter, and maybe consider other career options. Who else is in the house, besides the Jolly Green Giant?"

"Just Dr. Leeds. She's downstairs."

"Is she armed?"

"Of course not. What do you think we—?"

"Let's go."

Veil and Sharon followed the man in the tweed suit down two flights of stairs to the basement, which was spacious and had been cleared to make room for a wooden table, a desk, chairs, two hospital gurneys, and an array of medical equipment that was now pushed back against the wall at the opposite end of the room. Half of the wall to their left was covered with a large mural comprised of dozens of separate, framed panels and illuminated by spotlights recessed in the ceiling. A big-boned, white-haired woman who was standing at the table and making notes on a pad looked up and started with alarm as they entered the room.

124

"Just stay calm, Gail," the man in the tweed suit said quickly, walking across the room and touching the woman's hand. "Dr. Solow and Mr. Kendry have agreed to cooperate with us."

"Veil," Sharon said in a voice just above a whisper as she turned to look at the multi-paneled mural. "That's—"

"It certainly is," Veil replied dryly as he stepped closer to the wall to examine his work.

The predominant color of the painting was a brilliant, electric blue surrounded on all sides by clouds of gold-specked black and gray. Brush techniques and alternating patches of thin and thick layers of pigment projected the illusion of movement, of flight toward a gray figure with outstretched arms silhouetted against a pool of brilliant, pure white light. In the space where the figure's heart would be was an open rectangle where the brick wall behind the mural showed through. "I painted 'The Lazarus Gate' a long time ago," Veil continued quietly, turning back to the two scientists. "The Company must have gone to considerable trouble and expense to find and put all these panels together. My work doesn't come cheap."

It was the white-haired woman who answered. "It took years. The individual panels were in museums, galleries, and private collections all over the world. But we never could find the last panel. Would you tell us what's there?"

Veil's response was to point to the strips of paper that were EKG printouts taped to the wall next to the mural. Each clearly showed the signature Lazarus Spike of someone who had been clinically dead and then brought back to life after having seen the Lazarus Gate. "Have you tried to send anybody there yet?"

"No," the woman replied evenly. 'We needed more information before we tried to conduct the experiment. That's why we were so anxious to speak to you and Dr. Solow. Is it true that humans who approach the Lazarus Gate as they are dying become telepathic?"

"Where did you get these EKG printouts?"

"From the hospital records of Lazarus People, men and women who had a near-death experience naturally."

"I assume you questioned all of them. What did they say when you asked them if they'd become telepathic when they were dying?"

The woman flushed slightly. "They just laughed. All of them."

"Well, there you are.

"But there is something there. You painted a picture of it."

"Of course there's something there. Death. That's why we say that people who've seen it and survived have had a near-death experience. It's not complicated, Doctor. For some people, all they have to do to get there is to die. Things are going to become complicated when you start sending living people off to find this place and they don't come back." Veil paused as Denny Whalen, looking thoroughly shaken, walked through the door. Then he turned to Sharon. "Now that everybody's here, tell them what they want to know."

Sharon nodded, said, "I'm a physician, as you know. What you may not know is that I'm a thanatologist—a specialist in death and the dying. For years it has been known that a small percentage of people who 'die,' as it were—that is, their hearts stop beating and they are clinically dead—revive and tell a story about being in a corridor and seeing at the end of it a blinding white light and a shadowy figure beckoning to them. At this moment they report feeling completely at peace, with no fear of death. Every single one of them reports desperately wanting to fly into the arms of this figure and be washed in the white light. Those who don't, who turn back at the last moment from the cusp of death and revive, uniformly do so because of some compelling personal reason, a sense of unfinished business which can be anything from a belief their family can't survive without them to an unpaid utility bill. The experience has been reported by people from all cultures in societies all over the world, by those who are religious and others who are atheists. The vision is seen by about two percent of the people who've had a near-death experience, and we refer to them as Lazarus People. All report feeling remarkably changed, and all had an identical reading on their EKGs a moment or two before

126

they revived. That's what we call the Lazarus Spike, and we say that they've been to the Lazarus Gate."

The man with the withered arm pointed to Veil's mural. "That's what they see? That's the Lazarus Gate?"

"That's it," Veil replied curtly. "Go on, Sharon."

"Years ago I was in Monterey doing secret research—the Lazarus Project—for an ex-astronaut named Jonathan Pilgrim who'd had a near-death experience and believed he'd found heaven; he was looking for a way to control the experience. I worked in a hospice that was separate from Jonathan's main operation, where researchers studied individuals with highly developed talents or unusual traits. Veil had been invited to come there as a test subject, and he wound up with me at the hospice because—"

"That's irrelevant," Veil interrupted.

Denny Whalen shook his head impatiently, said, "But you said you'd tell us what we wanted to know!"

"There's nothing of any value for you to learn from my experience. I ended up in Dr. Solow's hospice by accident because of some funny business with a KGB operative who was monitoring the whole situation at Pilgrim's Institute. My experience is irrelevant to your purposes because I wasn't dying when I wound up in the hospice, and I'm not a Lazarus Person."

The three researchers exchanged puzzled glances, then looked back at Veil. The white-haired woman said, "But there's your painting..."

"How do you know I didn't work from some Lazarus Person's description of the experience?"

"Did you?"

"No. Listen up, folks, because I'm only going to go over this once and I'm not going to answer any personal questions. Denny here will tell you just how jealously I guard my privacy. The problem is that you've already shoved your noses so far into my private business that I have to give you this information to push you back out. By definition, a Lazarus Person is a child or adult who has suffered a very particular near-death experience. A consciousness of the world and a sense of self had been formed in the individual, and it is this perception of the world and self that is so profoundly changed when a person sees the Lazarus Gate and then returns to life. That isn't what happened to me. I almost died at birth, and a newborn infant has no sense of self or the world. I was born with a cawl, and my parents named me Veil as a kind of prayer. Obviously, I lived, but I suffered— suffer —brain damage. I was left a vivid dreamer, a condition that can best be described as a kind of rupturing of the protective membrane separating dreams from reality. I dream in Technicolor and surround sound, and those dreams are every bit as coherent and vivid as what I experience when I'm awake. The condition can drive you insane, and not a few vivid dreamers die in their sleep of heart attacks; vivid dreamers not only get chased by ogres, sometimes they get eaten. Denny here may harbor suspicions that I'm a violent person. I became one because of my vivid dreaming, and I eventually learned to control both the violence and the dreams through painting. Now I can go virtually anywhere I like and do anything I want in my dreams—but I'm still just tucked in bed, dreaming. There's no astral projection, no telepathy, no precognition, and none of those other wet dreams the Russians were having. Just dreams, with absolutely no practical application—unless you want to count my work as an application. It's just imagination. That's how I discovered the Lazarus Gate, which seems to be a kind of shared racial consciousness some people experience as they die. It probably has to do with endorphins and hard-wiring those people have in their brains. The point is that I got there through the back door, in a manner of speaking. I was able to go to the Lazarus Gate and return, literally without losing any sleep over it, because I wasn't dead, just dreaming. I'd learned to control my vivid dreaming, so I just checked out the neighborhood, then turned around and went home. When I woke up, I started this mural. Anyone you try to send there by artificial means, with your machines and your drugs, isn't going to be so fortunate. You can manipulate their brain waves to match that pattern, all right, but anybody you kill and try to send there is going to stay dead. That's all the Lazarus Gate is—death. The drugs you need to use to artificially create that brain-wave pattern block the way back. Your test subjects aren't going to be sending messages from submarines, or anywhere else, to other test subjects because they'll very quickly become biologically as well as clinically dead. End of story."

Again, the researchers exchanged glances. It was Denny Whalen who finally spoke. "What's on the missing panel in the mural?"

"Jesus, Denny," Veil said, then sighed and shook his head. "What a great question; it shows how impressed you are by what I just told you. My work is totally irrelevant. We've told you everything you need to know. You can interview all the Lazarus People you want about those crackpot KGB theories, and they'll laugh at your questions like the others have done. You think they're all involved in some conspiracy? They've all survived a similar, profoundly moving experience that has left them with mixed emotions about returning to life, and they're looking forward to repeating the experience when the time comes. They're not about to be bothered trying to describe the experience or explain themselves to a bunch of science wonks working for the CIA."

Now there was a prolonged silence, which was finally broken by Sharon. "The Russians, of course, knew about Lazarus People, and they'd been conducting their own experiments, probably for years. Because of the well-known phenomenon of Lazarus People who are strangers instinctively recognizing others like themselves, the Russians theorized that some kind of crude telepathy was taking place, and that this telepathic power was greatest in the few moments before death—as certain people approach the Lazarus Gate. One of their many zany notions was to take two people in different parts of the world, stop their hearts, use drugs to get Lazarus Spikes on the subjects' EKGs, have them exchange secrets at the Lazarus Gate, then revive them and recover the information. *Voilà*. An intelligence-gathering system that is instantaneous, and can't be penetrated. This seems to be your Holy Grail as well. Forget it. As Mr. Kendry has explained, you can't duplicate the experience in a lab and have the test subject or subjects survive. The KGB probably tried to do it many times, and kept losing people. That's why they penetrated Jonathan Pilgrim's operation when they found out I was doing similar research. But I was working with people who were already dying and who fit a profile predicting they might be candidates for experiencing the Lazarus Gate. We never tried the experiment you're contemplating, because we'd already done computer simulations telling us it couldn't be done successfully."

"That doesn't jibe with what's in the KGB reports," the white-haired woman said, her tone openly skeptical. "Those records indicate *you* were sent there, and you've obviously survived."

Sharon shook her head impatiently. "Those files are inaccurate. It's true they wanted to use me as a guinea pig, and they got as far as stopping my heart. But then Veil stopped them before they could try to induce a Lazarus Spike, and he revived me."

"But you died and came back," the woman insisted. "You're a Lazarus Person."

"No. I just died and was revived before the KGB could juice me up. I never shared the experience. I don't remember a damn thing."

"Let's go," Veil said to Sharon, taking her arm and leading her across the basement. He paused at the door, turned back toward the others. "Now you know it all," he continued. "You're wasting your time. Don't waste mine, or Dr. Solow's, again. You tell your Company bosses I will not tolerate anyone from your outfit invading our privacy again. Got it?"

Denny Whalen half raised his hand, said in a small voice, "Uh, Mr. Kendry?"

"What part of that statement didn't you understand, Denny?"

"May I ask you just one more question?"

"Not about the missing panel."

"It's not about the mural, sir. It's about you."

Veil shrugged resignedly. "Let's hear the question.

"We learned about your being a CIA operative during the Vietnam War from the KGB files. There's no mention of you in our own files, not anywhere. The only thing we could find was a note on your army record that you'd been dishonorably discharged on a Section Eight; just about everything else had been deleted. The KGB reports say that your CIA code name was Archangel. Why did the Company expunge your file?"

Veil smiled thinly, exchanged glances with Sharon, then replied, "For your own good, Denny, I'm not going to tell you. Don't pursue it; don't even think about it. You ask that question of the wrong person at Langley, and you're going to end up dead. Good night."

Veil dreams.

He senses something is wrong, and he flies to where he has not been in many years, the Lazarus Gate. He is pure blue flight, surrounded by a brilliant electric blue. He is the blue, and when he looks at his hands he can see through them. There are no fixed reference points, no sounds, only the sensation that he is traveling at great speed through no time and no space to a place that for others is death.

As he continues to stare at his right hand a pinpoint of white light suddenly appears in the blue beyond the palm. He puts his hand to his eyes and the light flashes through him, arcing down his spinal cord. He explodes into pieces and is reassembled, floating weightless in a gray void before a shadowy figure silhouetted against a shimmering white radiance that he knows is the Lazarus Gate. The man in green, naked now like everyone who comes here, is just completing his passage through the gate, disappearing from sight as a great chime sounds, and Veil can feel the booming echo in his head, heart, stomach, and groin.

Denny Whalen, his eyes bulging with wonder and a huge grin on his face, is floating on his back, arms and legs spread out to his sides, down the gray corridor toward the beckoning figure. Veil

131

speeds down the corridor, past the scientist, then stops in front of him, blocking the way.

Denny sees him and giggles hysterically, the sound of his laughter emerging from his mouth as a series of tiny bell sounds that cascade like rain all around them. "HEY, KENDRY! YOU DIDN'T TELL US WHAT IT FELT LIKE! WHAT A TRIP! ARE YOU REALLY HERE, OR IS THIS JUST A DREAM?!"

"Precisely," Veil replies evenly.

"WHICH IS IT?!"

"This is a dream you're not going to wake up from unless you do exactly as I say."

"WHO WANTS TO WAKE UP?"

"You don't have to shout. As you can see, there's a great sound system here."

"I'M SO HAPPY!"

"Denny, you're really a glutton for punishment. You and your buddy who just went brain dead simply couldn't resist the temptation to try for the Lazarus Gate, could you?"

"BUDGET CUTBACKS!" Denny shouts, and again giggles hysterically. "EVERYBODY HAS TO PULL THEIR WEIGHT OR GET FIRED! I FIGURED THIS WAS A WAY TO GET AHEAD! WE COULDNT JUST TAKE YOUR WORD FOR IT THAT THERE WAS NOTHING HERE! THE STAKES WERE TOO HIGH!"

"Stop shouting, Denny. Calm down."

Denny, the fields of freckles on his face glowing purple, tries to somersault up and over Veil, but Veil blocks his way. "If you are really here, then it's true," Denny says, his voice dropping to a whisper. 'We're communicating telepathically. You and Dr. Solow lied."

"So sue us."

"Absolute, stone telepathy, complete with bells and whistles, a great light show, and all in living color."

"*Almost* living, Denny. You seem to keep forgetting that little problem. What you are is not quite biologically dead, but you're working on it."

"This is what's on the missing panel in the mural, isn't it? You."

"No. There is no missing panel, Denny. The mural is complete as it is. There's nothing there at the heart of that figure. It's biological death. There is no emptier space."

"Who is he?"

"There's nobody there, Denny. It's a shadow. Superstition. Humans are apparently hard-wired for it. Superstition may have been a very useful survival skill for cave people in the Stone Age."

"How do you know there's nothing there?"

"Because I've been there, Denny. I've passed through the heart of that shadow many times."

"You brought Dr. Solow back from beyond there, didn't you?"

"Yes. But it took years, and a very special lifeline called love. Sharon is a unique survivor, because I'm apparently unique—no other vivid dreamer that I know of has learned to control dreaming as I do, or traveled here. In addition, to find others you need a personal connection. That's why you don't see anybody else around."

Denny giggles again, but his laughter is becoming less hysterical. "You raise the dead."

"I don't make a habit of it, and I'm certainly not available for work as a kind of astral answering machine for the CIA or anyone else. You didn't listen before when I warned you, Denny, but you'd better listen now. Apparently every person experiences some flow of endorphins just before the end; it's life's last gift to us. It's why you feel so good, and why Lazarus People no longer fear death. It also changes the way they view things. Even if you could send intelligence operatives here to exchange messages without killing them, not much of the information they gave back to you would be very useful. Lazarus People make lousy spies, because spying doesn't interest them any longer. Harming people doesn't interest them, nor does lying and secrecy—unless it's to protect life. But that issue's moot. What's happened, as I warned, is that the drug cocktail they gave you to induce the Lazarus Spike after they stopped your heart has resulted in a multifold increase in endorphins; right now your brain is flooded with feel-good juice. You don't want the feeling to end; you can't end it on your own, any more than you can suddenly stop an orgasm. Unless you do as I say, your brain will die before it can reabsorb the endorphins. Right now your people are no doubt frantically trying to restart your heart and wondering why they can't. It's because you don't want the orgasm to end. You could say I'm here to squeeze your dork until the effect begins to wear off."

"Wooaaaa."

"Sorry. I know it's a tacky analogy, but it's the most accurate I can think of."

"But you're absolutely right. I don't want to go back. There's nothing back there that interests me any longer."

"See the problem? Count sheep, Denny."

"What?"

"You heard me."

Denny giggles again. "That's very funny."

"Count sheep — big, fat, ugly sheep. You have to try to distract yourself from the ecstasy long enough for your brain and other organs to reabsorb the drugs. There can't be much time left, because we're drifting closer to the Lazarus Gate. I know we're close, because I can feel the pressure of the light on my back. I won't go through there with you, because you'll be beyond my help. Now close your eyes and count sheep. I'm going to come closer. If you can feel my presence entering yours, wrap your arms and legs around me and hold tight."

"I'm not sure we know each other that well."

"This is about life, Denny. Shared humanity. If you can become one with me, I may be able to take you back. Do it. Quickly."

Denny Whalen continues to grin inanely, but he closes his eyes, and his lips move as he begins to count. Veil moves even closer, entering the mist that is the other man's body. When he feels Denny's presence, he wills himself into flight back down the corridor, slowly at first and then accelerating. Denny, still

134

counting, comes with him. When they reach the field of electric blue, Veil rolls away from the other man and returns to his own darkness.

Denny Whalen stood outside on the sidewalk beneath the streetlight where the first Lazarus Person had been, looking up at his window. Veil did not have to check the streets surrounding the building to know the man had come alone. He selected a bottle of wine, then took two glasses from a cabinet and went downstairs. "Welcome back," he said, walking over to the red-haired man and handing him a glass. "I'd invite you up, but I've been working, and I don't like people to see my works-in-progress."

Denny held out his glass as Veil poured wine for both of them. "It really happened, then, didn't it?" he asked quietly.

"I suppose that depends on one's definition of reality. Are you still interested in sending secret messages from submarines?"

"I came to thank you."

Veil shrugged. "No need. I'm glad you made it back."

"You brought me back. They were just about ready to give up trying to revive me. Another couple of seconds and I would have been dead."

"You were dead."

"I'd have been permanently dead."

"Indeed."

They sat down together on the curb, shoulder to shoulder, and sipped their wine in silence. Finally Denny said, "I lied to them. I told them I didn't remember everything. I told them it didn't work."

"That part isn't a lie. It doesn't work."

"God, dying is so *private.*"

"Indeed."

"I know so much about you now, Veil."

"No, you don't, Denny. You just feel very close to me. There's a difference. This is what you'll feel with every other Lazarus Person you meet for the rest of your life."

135

"No. I *know* you. I know the goodness in you. And I know that somehow the Company hurt you terribly."

"They didn't hurt me at all. I owe everything I am and have to the Company."

"They hurt you."

"You're getting maudlin on me, Denny. Now drop it. That's as private to me as dying."

Denny sighed, nodded. "With the corpse of one field operative and a researcher who says he experienced nothing to explain, I don't think they'll be trying that experiment again."

"Let's hope not."

"I'm quitting the agency."

"Why?" Veil asked in a mild tone.

"I thought you'd understand."

"Tell me."

"You were right about how returning from the Lazarus Gate changes people. Now so much of what the Company does seems just . . . silly. I want to do something else with my life. I want to do what you do."

"Paint?"

"No. Something that's deeply satisfying to me personally. Maybe helping people."

"While you're trying to figure out what to do with the rest of your life, consider the possibility that you could help people by staying right where you are now. There are lots of bad guys in the world who need spying on, Denny. Leave them to their own devices, unchecked, and they'll eat innocent people alive."

"I assumed you hated the Company."

"I hate the bad guys in the Company—and there's a whole passel of them. They're the ones who tried to hurt me. I don't object to the CIA's mission—just the way they go about it. Now, I happen to think having a Lazarus Person in there is a hoot. I also think it's a great idea. You should work hard for promotion, maybe devote your life to becoming Director. A Lazarus Person would make the perfect mole, a kind of ultimate weapon against the bad guys."

136

"I won't be a weapon for anybody, Veil."

"Exactly my point, Denny." Veil smiled as he raised his glass. "Here's to a long and illustrious career in the CIA, Denny. Cheers."

UNMARKED GRAVES

Veil dreams.

Vivid dreaming is his gift and affliction, the lash of memory and a guide to justice, a mystery and sometimes the key to mystery, prod to violence and maker of peace, an invitation to madness and the fountainhead of his power as an artist.

As the A train pulled into the West Fourth Street station, Veil Kendry heard the wail of a human over the scream of machinery, and he turned to his left to see a knot of people gathering around someone lying in their midst on the subway platform. He pushed through a wall of startled and curious commuters and came upon a frail young Chinese woman giving birth.

"Get back and give her room to breathe!" he said sharply, raising and loosening her dress as he knelt beside her in a pool of her burst water. It turned out to be a needless request, for the harried New Yorkers were already surging around them in a rush to get on the train. He shouted to no one in particular, "Tell the motorman to call the paramedics!" The train pulled out of the station, and the few people who had gotten off glanced nervously at the tableau of a man and woman, blood and water on the concrete, and walked quickly away. In a few moments they were alone on the platform. Veil positioned himself between the woman's legs and gently cradled the tiny, bloody head that was emerging from the birth canal. Between gasps and cries the woman spoke to him rapidly in what Veil recognized as Chinese. He spoke, or at least understood, a number of Asian languages, but not Chinese, and so he spoke to her softly and soothingly in English. When the baby emerged Veil wiped away the placenta, bit through

139

the umbilical cord and knotted it, then gently laid the newborn infant on the mother's heaving chest. "Here you are, Mama," he said quietly, caressing her cheek. "Calm down, now. It's all right. People will be here soon to take care of you."

The woman's reaction startled him. Still speaking rapidly and obviously distressed, she picked up her baby and held it out to him, urgently and repeatedly gesturing for him to take it. "I don't want your baby, Mama," he said, shaking his head as he pressed the infant back down on her chest, noticing as he did so the rope burns on her wrists. "She's yours. Take it easy. Everything's going to be fine."

There was a clattering sound behind him, and Veil looked over his shoulder as two paramedics who had just come down the stairway, a Sikh and a Hispanic, unfolded the collapsible stretcher they carried and hurried up the platform, followed close behind by a black patrolman who was speaking into a crackling walkie-talkie.

"Not too trashy, pal," the Sikh said, nodding his approval as he gazed down at the woman and her baby. "You a doctor?"

Veil started to rise, but the woman would not release her tight grip on his wrist, and so he eased himself back down beside her. "An observer," he replied. "I've seen a few babies delivered."

"You work in a hospital?"

"I used to work in a jungle."

The Hispanic grunted as he handed Veil a towel to wipe the blood from his hands. "This is the seventy-fifth subway delivery this year. That puts us a little bit ahead of schedule. The birth rate down here is nice and steady. We'll take care of her now.

The woman looked around, gasped, and then renewed her urgent efforts to hand Veil her baby. Veil turned in the direction the woman had looked and saw that three scowling Chinese youths, one an albino, had suddenly appeared on the platform and were standing just behind the paramedics. They were identically dressed in jeans, black sneakers, and black satin jackets embroidered with red dragons. The policeman cursed under his breath.

"She is our sister," the Chinese in the middle, a husky youth with a tiny spider tattooed on his forehead, said in

140

unaccented English, his tone low and menacing as he glanced in turn at the paramedics, the policeman, and Veil. "We became separated. We will take her now."

The Hispanic said hesitantly, "Your sister's just had a baby here on the platform, mister. It's October, and it's cold. They both need to be taken to a hospital, cleaned up, and looked after."

"She doesn't need a hospital," the albino said, stepping around the gurney and reaching down to take the trembling woman's baby. "We'll take care of her."

"I think not," Veil said in a flat tone, blocking the youth's movement by reaching out and planting his left palm firmly on the husky man's chest. He gently but firmly twisted his right wrist free of the woman's grip, and then straightened up, keeping his left palm on the Chinese youth's chest. The Chinese was pressing forward with all his weight as he glared at Veil, baring his clenched teeth and making low, guttural sounds in his throat. The albino and the third youth, a man in his late teens or early twenties with a pockmarked face, were moving to flank and press him toward the edge of the subway platform.

The policeman moved closer to Veil, said quietly, "These guys are Shadow Dragons, buddy, and we're right on the border of their turf. As a rule of thumb it generally works out best for everybody if the Chinese are left to take care of their own affairs. They say this woman is their sister, maybe we should let them take her and the baby."

"I think not," Veil repeated in the same even tone, meeting the hate-filled gaze of the Chinese pressing against his hand at the same time as he tracked the movements of the other two with his peripheral vision. "They're not her brothers. Look at her; she's terrified. We'll get her and her baby to a hospital, then find an interpreter to tell us what she wants."

Suddenly the youth in front of Veil reached into the right pocket of his satin jacket and withdrew a box cutter, which he used to slash at Veil's exposed wrist. But Veil's left arm was no longer in the space between them, and the razor sliced nothing but air. The sudden and violent movement caused the youth to lose his

141

balance and lurch sideways. Veil stepped behind him, grabbed the back of the youth's jacket and his belt, whirled him around once, and then released his grip, sending the Chinese hurtling through the air like some unwieldy human discus. The youth landed on his face and chest, skidded a few feet, then lay still.

The policeman reached for his gun as nunchaku sticks and a knife suddenly appeared in the hands of the other two youths.

"You won't need that," Veil said to the policeman as he quickly stepped away from the woman and out into the center of the platform to give himself more room. "This is just a friendly discussion about proper health care."

The youth with the nunchakus attacked first, the two hardwood sticks connected by a chain a blur as he whirled them in intricate patterns in front of his body and over his shoulders. Veil spun away from the first strike, at the same time slipping out of his leather jacket, shifting his weight, and delivering a sidekick to the solar plexus of the knife-wielding albino, who had rushed in on his left flank. The breath exploded out of the albino in a great whoosh before he doubled over, grabbed at his stomach, sank to his knees, and began to retch.

Obviously startled by Veil's quickness and skill, the pockmark-faced youth hesitated just long enough to lose his rhythm. Veil darted forward, swinging his leather jacket over his head and snagging the connecting chain between the nunchaku sticks. He yanked, pulling the sticks from the youth's hands and catching them in the air. He tossed aside his jacket, and then began to twirl the sticks as he slowly advanced on the Chinese, whose face had gone ashen. Veil stopped next to a support pillar, beat out an intricate tattoo on the steel, and then casually tossed the sticks to the Chinese, who made no move to catch them. The deadly weapon fell at the youth's feet, and then clattered away on the concrete. Then the youth bolted, darting in a wide circle around Veil and going to the albino, who was still on his knees and clutching at his stomach. The pockmark-faced youth pulled the albino to his feet, and together they went up the platform to help the Chinese with the spider tattoo, who was just regaining

142

consciousness. The three of them disappeared up a stairway at the opposite end of the platform.

"It looks like we'll be using my health plan," Veil said as he walked casually back to where the policeman, paramedics, and woman were all staring at him, wide-eyed.

"The Shadow Dragons are a particularly nasty gang," the policeman said to Veil. "They're likely to come looking for you."

Veil shrugged as he helped the paramedics lift the woman and her newborn baby onto the gurney. "I'm easy enough to find."

The policeman narrowed his eyes as he studied the rangy but solidly built man with the glacial blue eyes and shoulder-length, gray-streaked yellow hair. "Your name Veil Kendry?"

Veil glanced at the man, replied evenly, "That's right."

"I've heard of you."

"I hope it was good."

"It depends on who you talk to. You're a friend of the crazy dwarf, aren't you?"

Veil laughed, but abruptly reached out and grabbed the end of the gurney when the paramedics started to wheel it away. The woman was still staring at him, a naked plea for help in her limpid almond eyes. "Where are you taking her?"

The two men glanced at each other, and the Sikh answered, "You may have a health plan, mister, but it doesn't look like she does. She doesn't even have a purse. We'll take her to the clinic at Bellevue.

"Take her to St. Vincent's. It's closer."

"We don't have a contract with St. Vincent's. They won't—"

"Don't worry. I'll pay."

The paramedics looked at the policeman, who nodded. "He's a hotshot artist with big bucks. He's good for it."

The Hispanic asked, "How are you going to pay, mister?"

"Plastic. What else?"

"What are we supposed to tell them when—?"

"I'll tell them myself. I'm coming with you."

143

The Hispanic nervously cleared his throat, said, "We're not running a taxi service, mister. It's against company policy to transport civilians who aren't relatives of a patient."

Veil took his wallet from his pocket, removed the money from it. "I've got eight dollars and change. I'll get you more if you stop at an ATM machine."

"Big bucks, huh?" the Hispanic said wryly, glancing at his partner, then down at the woman, who continued to gaze imploringly at Veil. Finally the man shrugged. "Come on, buddy. Keep your money. Mama here obviously wants your company, and I guess you've earned the right."

Throughout the short ride to the hospital the woman gripped Veil's wrist with her free hand while Veil spoke to her soothingly in English. At the hospital, where he was known, he arranged to have the woman and her child admitted for postnatal care and observation. He left a credit card at the desk, walked to another part of the building, and then used an electronically coded key card to gain entrance to a private elevator that took him to the top floor. He exited, walked to his right and through a swinging door marked *Sleep Research Laboratories.* In a small, dimly lighted office on the right a woman with long blond hair and dressed in a white lab coat sat with her back to him as she monitored an array of instruments on a console before her and made notes on a yellow legal pad. Beyond her, behind a glass panel, three men and a woman lay sleeping on cots, wire leads running from their heads, arms, and chests.

"Good day, Dr. Solow," Veil said quietly, moving up behind the woman and placing his hands gently on her shoulders.

"Veil!" Sharon Solow said without looking around. "What are you doing here? I thought you were going to the Whitney to supervise the hanging of your show."

"Something came up—or out, actually—and I had to take a detour. Since I was in the neighborhood, I thought I'd drop in and say hello."

144

"I'm glad. I'll be right with you. I want to notate this data while it's fresh. I think I may have resonance here; all four subjects went into REM at virtually the same time."

"How's the kid with the night terrors doing?"

"Much better, thanks to you. He's using the techniques you taught him to simply roll away from the dream and go back to Stage Two sleep, or dream himself someplace else. Most of the time he goes someplace else, probably because he knows you do that. He idolizes you."

"Where does he go?"

"Disneyland, mostly."

"Sounds like a good choice to me. Free admission, and he doesn't have to wait in line for the rides."

"Veil, what's that smell?"

"Probably blood and placenta."

Now Sharon Solow spun around in her chair, and her mouth dropped open when she saw the stains on his shirtfront and jeans. "Veil, what happened?!"

He grinned. "I delivered a baby on the subway platform a little while ago. Mother and baby doing very well downstairs, thank you. But I need to get cleaned up before I go to the museum. I could have gone home, but I seem to remember I have a change of clothes here."

"You always have a change of clothes here, love," Sharon said, squeezing his hand. "You go wash, and I'll join you when I finish here."

Veil showered in the locker room reserved for the laboratory's test subjects, then toweled off and started to dress in clean clothes. Sharon appeared in the doorway as he was slipping on a denim shirt. She came over and helped him button it, then kissed him. "Thank you, love," she said softly.

"For what?"

"Just for being you. For being our baseline research subject and authority on vivid dreaming, and for helping all the other vivid dreamers who come here looking for help because they can't handle it like you do. And, of course, for coming through the Lazarus Gate to save my life."

Veil smiled thinly. "It took me a long time to find a way to bring you back; you were in a coma for almost three years. To my knowledge, you and I are the only two people who have actually gone through it and come back. And you can never do it again. I couldn't help you. You'd stay dead."

Sharon whispered, "I'm aware of that, Veil. No more machines and drugs. Ever."

"You miss the CIA funding?"

"Do roosters crow in the morning? Of course I miss the CIA funding. But I don't miss the CIA. We make do."

"And they still don't know what happened?"

"Not a clue. And they'll never know—unless either you or I tell somebody, and I'm no more likely to do that than you are."

"Good."

"There," Sharon said, helping Veil put on his sports jacket and plucking off an imaginary piece of lint. "That's a great artist's costume. Are we still on for dinner?"

"For sure."

"See you later, love."

Veil arrived at the hospital at noon the next day with flowers and a basket of baby clothes only to be told by the nurse at the reception desk that the Chinese woman and her child were gone. As Veil stared at her uncomprehendingly, the nurse quickly added, "An elderly Chinese gentleman with a lawyer came for her this morning; they'd called the ambulance service to see where she'd been taken. The old man was very polite, and the lawyer had papers showing that the woman was his granddaughter."

"You're sure of that?"

The woman behind the desk flushed slightly. "Well, the papers were in Chinese, but everything seemed in order."

"Jesus Christ," Veil breathed, his eyes suddenly flashing blue fire.

146

"Sir, I was with them when they talked to her."

"In Chinese?"

"Yes, sir. But the woman offered no resistance. She seemed perfectly willing to go with them."

Veil sighed. "That nice old Chinese gentleman and his lawyer probably told her they'd bury her baby alive and kill her family in China if she didn't go with them willingly."

The blood drained from the nurse's face. "What?"

"Never mind," Veil said curtly, placing the clothing and flowers on the desk. "It's too late to do anything about it. Give these to some other patient."

He returned to his loft and worked feverishly, trying to put the mother and baby out of his mind and center himself.

Thousands of vultures of unspeakable cruelty and injustice circled the city day and night, and the fact that the wings of this particular dark bird had brushed his face did not mean there was anything he could do to track and bring it to ground and rescue its prey. The woman and her baby were lost, almost certainly untraceable, beyond his help.

The attempt to blot out rage and memory with canvas and paint did not work, and he finally gave up the struggle. There were still debts that he owed, and he felt he did not have the right to refuse to at least try to repay them when the opportunity arose.

In late afternoon he washed out his brushes and walked over into Chinatown to buy a bird.

Veil dreams.

He is Archangel, the CIA's most efficient and ruthless operative in their secret war in Laos. He gathers intelligence by acting as liaison to the anti-Communist Hmong tribes in the mountains, but mostly what he does is hunt and kill the enemy. This is war, and so he is rewarded for his murderous bent and skills. But he kills not out of love for country, but for himself. Violence is a need. It will be many years before he learns to control the vivid dreaming that is at the root of his battle with insanity and finds both redemption and healing in painting his

147

nightmares. Now it is only extreme violence that holds in check his personal demons and allows him to find rest in the savage dreamworlds of his nights.

Despite the fact that he is constantly teetering on the edge of madness, he does not lack feelings of intense loyalty to, and even love for, the people of these mountain villages he has armed and fought with. Now he is particularly concerned about the safety of one particular tribe, for he has been spotted and recognized by the Pathet Lao on a trail close to the Hmong village. He kills four of the guerrillas and escapes from the others by leaping from a tall cliff into a raging river where he loses consciousness and floats downstream for some distance before finally being washed ashore. It is after nightfall when he regains consciousness. Dazed and cold, he nonetheless immediately begins the arduous climb up out of the gorge, for he knows that he must warn the villagers that they will be suspected of collaborating with Archangel, and all will be made to pay the price.

He completes only half the climb before he leans back on a pillow of air, falls through space, and rolls away from the dream into deeper sleep. He has no need to complete the journey now, for he knows what he will find at the end. He has returned to the village many times before. He has come this far now only to take. the temperature of his soul and test his resolve, to see how far he will go in real time to atone for the past by trying to save another woman and her baby in the present.

Veil arose at 5:30 A.M., washed and dressed, then cut up an old sheet to use as a shroud to cover the birdcage. He disguised himself, then picked up the cage, left the building, and walked the few blocks from his home in the East Village to the Delancey Street corner of Sara Delano Roosevelt Park on the western boundary of the traditional area of New York's Chinatown.

He hobbled on his cane into the park, then sat down on a bench at the southern end and watched from under the wide, floppy brim on his hat as other men, each carrying a shrouded birdcage, entered the park from all directions. They sat on the benches, some

148

together and others alone, and as the sun began to rise and heat the day they carefully rolled the covers on their cages to one side, reenacting a centuries-old tradition. A lone bird began to sing, and soon it was joined by another, and another. Soon the air in the park was filled, filigreed, with the trilling of birds. There were calls and countercalls, and within the space of a few minutes it seemed as if all the birds were singing the same song, improvising on a single melody.

Veil rolled back the cover on his cage, but nothing happened. He bent over and looked inside the cage at his *hua mei*, a brownish song thrush with splashes of olive and gray that was found near the Yangtze River in China and in parts of Southeast Asia. The bird sat silently on its perch, staring back at Veil. Veil clucked and softly whistled a few times, but the bird steadfastly ignored him. Veil grunted and shook his head, and when he looked up he saw the man he had come to talk to enter the park. Veil waited until the silver-haired banker had chosen a spot to sit, and then he rose, picked up his birdcage, and hobbled over to him.

"My bird will not sing," Veil said quietly. "I thought perhaps you might tell me why."

The man, dressed in jeans, sneakers, and a blue windbreaker over a white sweatshirt, looked up, fixed Veil with his soulful brown eyes, and then frowned as recognition came. "Veil?"

"Not my name, Chou. I don't want anyone to know whom you're talking to. You're just having a conversation with an old man. Can you tell me what's wrong with the bird?"

The middle-aged banker hesitated, then pulled back the cover from Veil's birdcage and looked inside. "First of all, it's from Shanghai," he said, a note, of distaste in his voice.

"How can you tell?"

"Its beak lacks the black traces found in the best birds, which are from Guandang Province. How much did you pay for this bird?"

"Seven hundred dollars."

149

"You were cheated. A bird that has not yet picked up songs from other *hua mei* should cost no more than five hundred. What do you know about hua mei?"

"Nothing, really, except I remembered that you and the others bring your birds to the park each morning to sing. It's considered a virtuous hobby, and a distraction from vice."

"The birds won't sing if they don't eat well, and this one looks as if it has not been properly cared for. Without proper food, the feathers get dull, like this one's, and the bird has low morale."

"Birds have morale?"

"Most definitely. They must also be allowed to bathe frequently. I will write down for you a recipe for preparing a proper diet."

"Thank you, Chou."

"What is your real reason for wanting to see me?"

"I need information. I wish to know which of the three tongs controls the slaving business down here. It will be the one that controls the Shadow Dragons gang."

The banker made a sound in his throat like he was choking, then abruptly picked up his birdcage and began to rapidly walk away. Veil remained motionless, waiting, watching the man's back. The silver-haired banker had almost reached the sidewalk when his pace began to slow, and finally he stopped. He remained motionless for almost a minute before turning and walking slowly back to Veil, furtively glancing around him as he did so.

"You shame me," the man whispered to Veil, and then bowed his head.

"Certainly not my intention, Chou."

"My wife and I wouldn't be alive today if it weren't for you. I owe you more than I can ever repay."

"You owe me nothing. I didn't come here to ask you to repay any debt, only to ask for information."

"This is very dangerous talk."

"The reason I'm in disguise and walking my bird like all the other men in the park. The people I'm looking for will not know I've spoken to you."

150

"Now you are trying to help someone else?"

"'Trying' is the operative word. I'm looking for a woman I'm sure was brought into this country illegally. She and her family probably contracted for a lot of money to have her smuggled in, and now the people who brought her have her working in a brothel to pay off her debt—which will never happen. She escaped long enough to have her baby, but her slavers caught up with both of them. It's just a strong suspicion. If I'm wrong, then I suppose I'll never find her."

"These people will not speak with you, Veil."

"My problem."

"Even you could disappear without a trace in Chinatown, Veil. The people you're looking for are not just above the law here; they are the law. The police cannot help you if you get into trouble."

Veil did not reply. He waited, watching the other man. Finally the banker sighed, continued, "The man you want to talk to is Grandfather—Chan Fu Ong. It is his tong that controls the smuggling of Asians into this country."

"Where do I find him?"

"His headquarters is a social club—really a gambling and heroin den and a brothel—on Elizabeth Street. But you—"

"Thank you, Chou," Veil said, slipping the cover back over his birdcage. "May your *hua mei* sing well today."

He returned to his loft to paint, practice, eat and rest, and in the early evening he again shrouded his *hua mei*, picked up the cage, and walked back into Chinatown, to Elizabeth Street. It was not difficult to find the place he was looking for, for a knot of satin-jacketed Shadow Dragons stood around the entrance to the four-story building. The three youths he had confronted on the subway platform were among them. As he approached, all three— surprise clearly etched on their faces—stepped out to block his path. They glared at him, the surprise in their eyes quickly turning to a film of rage and hatred.

"Nice evening," Veil said evenly to the youth in the center, the Shadow Dragon with the spider tattooed on his forehead. The boy had a large bandage over his nose, deep scratches on his left cheek, and both eyes had been blackened.

"You must be crazy!" the Shadow Dragon said in a choked voice, the color draining from his face.

"You aren't the first person to think or say so," Veil answered in the same flat tone. He glanced up at the surveillance camera mounted over the doorway. "I've come to speak to Grandfather."

There were grunts of surprise, whispers among the gang members. The albino said, "Who is this 'Grandfather' you speak of?"

"Don't waste my time, sonny," Veil said, still looking up at the television camera. The other gang members had moved to surround him. He seemed to be ignoring them, but in fact he was very conscious of the position and body language of each youth, and was prepared to move to defend himself at any moment. "Mr. Ong would consider that impolite."

"What do you want?"

"None of your business, sonny.

He sensed the closing of a Shadow Dragon behind him. Veil shifted his stance slightly. He was about to spin around and plant the side of his hand in the youth's throat when the tension was abruptly broken by the trill of a cellular phone. The youth with the pockmarked face took a phone out of one of his jacket pockets, put it to his ear, listened for a few moments, and then said, "Yes, Grandfather," before disconnecting and putting the phone back in his pocket. He looked at Veil oddly, and then continued, "It's the door at the back."

Veil walked down the stairway to the below-ground entrance. The lock on the door buzzed as he reached out to turn the knob, and he entered a large basement hall crammed with tables and chairs filled with Chinese who were gambling at various games of chance. All activity and conversation stopped as he wended his way around the tables toward the door at the rear of the hall. He knocked once on the door, then opened it and entered a spacious, thick-carpeted office paneled in dark mahogany and

152

decorated with antique murals of Oriental motifs. A slight, old Chinese man with a long, wispy goatee and dressed in an expensive suit that was too big for him sat behind a massive oak desk. He was flanked by two tall, heavily muscled Chinese with shaved heads who were dressed in flowing silk robes. Aside from the one the old man sat in, there were no chairs in the room.

"Thank you for agreeing to see me, Grandfather," Veil said as he walked across the room and stopped in front of the desk. "My name is—"

"Veil Kendry," the old man said in a wheezing voice that had a lilting, sing-song quality .to it. "You are a friend of the crazy dwarf."

Veil smiled thinly. "My claim to fame."

"Hardly. You are a well-known artist whose work is displayed in museums and galleries around the world. You create what are called dream paintings, and it is rumored that your style springs from some sort of physical affliction from which you suffer. You were not always so . . . aesthetically oriented. You are a master of the martial arts, with an eclectic style that is largely self-taught. You were a CIA operative during your country's conflict in Southeast Asia. You were considered an insane and merciless killer by your enemies, and your night visits were much feared. Your code name was Archangel. Should I go on?"

"Not if it's meant to impress me. I'm already impressed."

"I have many sources of information in the Asian communities here—as, obviously, do you. After you so efficiently intimidated and dispatched three of my finest young warriors, I felt it a good idea to find out something about you. I asked about a man fitting your description. It was not difficult to obtain information." The old man paused, added somewhat ominously, "I know where you live."

"I'm practically your neighbor."

"It is quite remarkable how you have retained so many of your fighting skills into middle age. You must practice a great deal."

"A great deal."

Chan Fu Ong gestured to indicate the burly, robed, blank-faced Chinese flanking him. "Wing and Kwok were very impressed. I'm sure you would be impressed by their skills. Unfortunately, they cannot give you a demonstration. They were both champions in China, but the rules of the secret martial arts society to which they belong dictate that any combat they engage in must be fought to the death."

"I am not interested in fighting or sowing discord between us, Grandfather," Veil said, stepping forward and placing the shrouded birdcage on one corner of the massive desk. "I bring you this gift as a token of my respect."

The old man leaned forward to draw back the cover on the cage and examine the bird inside, then leaned back in his chair and once again regarded Veil. "You are here about the woman and her baby?"

"Yes, Grandfather."

"Why?"

"They are very important to me."

"Why?"

"It's personal."

"She is not here against her will."

"I don't believe I implied that she was."

"She and her family contracted with our benevolent society to bring her to this country, where she might search for a better life. She is free to do that—after she has worked to pay off what she and her family owe me, which is a great deal of money. This was all agreed upon beforehand. There is a contract."

"Somehow I don't believe she thought she would be forced to work as a prostitute."

"Now you are being rude, Mr. Kendry. She is an entertainer. Businessmen come here to relax. She helps them unwind."

"What about the baby? The baby can't be of any value to you."

"It's an unfortunate situation. We discourage pregnancy until the debt is paid. The woman hid it from us. She was not really

154

trying to run away, you know. She had no money, no place to run to. It's remarkable she managed to get down on the subway platform where you found her. All she wanted was to have her baby away from here. She probably intended to give the infant away to the first person who would take it, in the hope that the child would be raised as an American. Perhaps she even offered it to you. If you'd wanted to make her happy, you should have taken the child—and hoped that we didn't find you. Since the baby was the fruit of her body, which belongs to us until her debt is paid, the baby belongs to us. We will sell it to some childless couple. The child will probably end up being raised American, which is all the woman wanted anyway. We will apply the purchase price to her debt, and she will be free that much sooner. It works out best for everybody."

"I wish to purchase the woman's contract. Her baby will be part of the deal."

The old man smiled thinly, but there was no humor in his icy hazel eyes. He pulled at his wispy goatee, said, "A million dollars should do it. Do you have that kind of money, Mr. Kendry?"

"Now it is you who are being rude to me, Grandfather. Mockery is an impolite response to a serious offer. The top going rate for smuggling a foreign national into this country is thirty-five thousand dollars. That is what I will pay."

The old man made a dismissive gesture, glanced toward the ceiling. "What do you really know about Chinatown, Mr. Kendry?"

"Jack Nicholson. Faye Dunaway. John Huston."

"Mocking me would be very unwise."

"I understand what you're saying, Grandfather. Here, things are done your way. People here do not cooperate with the police, for your word is the only law they recognize. The intrigues of Chinatown are closed to outsiders. If I were to fail to leave here, it would be as if I never existed."

"Correct."

"I just want to make a business deal, Grandfather. I understand that things can get complicated around here, but I don't see why this has to be one of those things. If I'd wanted to waste my time, I would have gone to the INS and complained that the head of the tong that controls the Shadow Dragons gang is running a prostitution ring stocked by illegal aliens, or I could have told my story to the police and put them to sleep. Instead I came to you, with respect."

The old man turned to the Chinese on his right, said, "Inspect the bird, Kwok."

The man called Kwok reached across the desk, opened the cage, and cupped his hand around the bird inside. He removed the bird, gave it a cursory inspection, then abruptly closed his fist, crushing the *hua mei* into a mass of blood, tiny bones, and feathers that oozed through his thick fingers. He threw the bloody remains back into the cage, wiped his hands on the shroud, and then stepped back. "It is from Shanghai," he said in English, his face impassive as he stared straight ahead, through Veil. "It has not been cared for or trained properly, and it does not sing. It is worthless."

"I do not do business with foreigners, Mr. Kendry," the old man said in his soft, wheezy voice. "Leave here now, and be thankful you are still alive to sing your songs.

Veil stood motionless, his face impassive as he returned the gaze of Chan Fu Ong and considered his options, which appeared to range from few to nonexistent. Attempting to reopen the discussion would be futile, and would only earn him the tong leader's contempt—which might prove more dangerous than his anger. Both bodyguards had altered their stance slightly and placed their hands behind their backs, presumably gripping the short fighting swords they would be carrying in the sashes of their robes.

He knew that many lives could depend on what he did in the next few seconds. On the eve of an important show at the Whitney Museum he could be plunged into a war with one or more gangs, and that war could easily spill over the boundaries of Chinatown. All of his resources would have to be redirected to

156

defense and attack, and, in view of the numbers that would be sent against him, he would have to begin hunting again, as he had done many years before. The streets of lower Manhattan could become a killing ground like the ones he had waded through so long ago. He had not come here to atone for personal guilt; in the final analysis, the Pathet Lao had been responsible for what had happened to the Hmong chieftain and his pregnant wife. Prodded by memory, he had come here simply to try to chase a bit of evil from the world and replace it with a bit of good. Now it appeared that could not be done. Killing, or dying, would accomplish nothing; indeed, the woman and child he had come to help could very well end up among the first victims of any conflict that began in this room. It would be a senseless battle, just like so many of the senseless battles he had been a part of in another lifetime.

Veil turned on his heel and walked out of the room.

Veil dreams.

He completes his journey back to the village, his clothes and flesh torn by the numberless tiny claws of the jungle he has surged through in an attempt to warn the villagers before the Pathet Lao come. But he is too late. Every man, woman, and child in the village has been slaughtered. Both the chieftain and his pregnant wife have been tied to stakes, disemboweled, and beheaded. The woman's head lies at her feet in a pool of gore that had once been the child growing inside her.

He uses his bare hands and his knife to dig shallow graves for the chieftain and his wife and their unborn baby, then slips back into the jungle to begin a hunt of vengeance that will last six weeks.

There had been no tears in him then, no ability to cry, but his life has changed and he now weeps copiously in his dream as he flies away from the village, high over the jungle, rolls away, and drifts back down into deep sleep.

It was dusk when Veil finished the first panel in the mural that had become his work-in-progress. He framed it, then went into the

157

kitchen area of his loft and took a garbage bag from beneath the sink. He put the painting in the bag, then went out and walked back over to Chinatown.

He was prepared to gain entrance to Chan Fu Ong's brothel and social club any way he had to, but breaking in proved unnecessary. When he approached the phalanx of Shadow Dragons at the entrance to the building and looked up at the television camera, the door buzzed almost immediately. He entered, walked through the crowded hall that had once more gone absolutely still, and went through the door at the opposite end.

The tableau in the office was the same as it had been the day before, with the two blank-faced, robed bodyguards flanking the old man with the wispy goatee, who sat behind his desk.

"Thank you for seeing me again, Grandfather," Veil said in a flat tone as he stopped before the desk.

"You have the look of someone who feels he has left something unsaid, Mr. Kendry. This is the last time you will be admitted here, for, in fact, there is nothing left to say.

"That is unacceptable, Grandfather."

The old man's thin lips curled slightly at the corners of his mouth. "Unacceptable? I simply refuse to do business with you.

"You caused me to lose face."

Chan Fu Ong laughed scornfully. "Lose face? What do you know about losing face?"

"You killed my bird."

"It was worthless."

"Not to me. I was growing quite fond of it; you could say I always root for the underbird. You humiliated me in front of your men. To make up for that you must agree to turn the mother and child over to me." He paused, took the painting out of the garbage bag, and held it up for the other man to see. "This is what I will give you in exchange for the woman's contract."

The tong leader studied the painting, frowned. "A green blob? This is what you call 'art'?"

"I work on a very large scale—wall-length murals that are comprised of dozens of separate panels that are sold separately. As

158

it so happens, collectors and dealers around the world vie to find and gather together the panels to complete the larger work, like a jigsaw puzzle."

"An unusual commercial gimmick."

"The way I work and choose to present it. The ideas often come to me in fragments, in dreams, and so the work is sold in fragments. In time, this painting could be worth more than the thirty-five thousand dollars I originally offered you."

The old man looked back and forth between his bodyguards, and then giggled. "What will the larger work of yours depict, Mr. Kendry?"

"A place I visited many years ago. There was once a village there but now it is just jungle, completely overgrown. The completed work will be titled 'Unmarked Graves.'"

Chan Fu Ong held out one of his frail hands. "Give it to me. Wing, here, is my art assessor. I will have him evaluate your work as Kwok did your *hua mei*."

"I think not. I have already told you its value. You'll get it when you bring the woman and child to me.

"I have no interest in Western art."

"Develop it. If you do not accept this offer, then you will have made an enemy of Archangel. If you do that, your operations in this particular sphere of yours may not continue to run so smoothly. You've taken pains to warn me that what happens here may never get the attention of the outside world. Fine. Archangel was always at home in the jungle."

"You are a fool, Mr. Kendry," the tong leader said in a tight voice. His flesh had gone the color of faded parchment.

"And you are a whoremaster, a slaver with no heart, no soul, and no honor."

"Kill him!"

Fighting swords suddenly appeared in the hands of both bodyguards. The Chinese raised the swords over their heads and came at Veil from both sides. Veil killed the man on his left, Kwok, first, hurling the throwing knife he carried in a scabbard on has wrist into the man's throat. In virtually the same motion he

159

spun around to his right, avoiding Wing's sword thrust. He completed his spin by driving his stiffened fingers into the man's exposed side, breaking ribs, then gripping the wrist of his sword hand. He broke Wing's arm at the elbow, then put his forearm under the man's chin and yanked. The man's neck snapped with a loud crack.

Now Veil bowed slightly to the ashen-faced, open-mouthed old man behind the desk, said softly, "I am sorry we could not do business, Grandfather."

When he had finished, he hung his painting on a wall, then picked up the garbage bag and walked out of the office, closing the door behind him. His footsteps echoed in the still hall as he approached the albino Shadow Dragon who was standing guard next to a door Veil was certain must lead to the brothel.

"What's your name?" Veil asked as he stopped in front of the youth.

The youth glanced uncertainly back and forth between Veil's grim face and the garbage bag he held slung over his shoulder. "Lee Yeung," the boy said at last.

"I am Archangel. I am death. I have a message for you from Grandfather. This brothel is to be closed, effective immediately. The woman I helped on the subway platform and her baby are to come with me, and the contracts of all the other women are to be considered fulfilled. You and the others in your gang are to see that they are shielded from the immigration authorities and absorbed into the community. You will find them suitable housing and employment—which will not involve prostitution. Naturally, nothing of what has happened here will be told to the police or other authorities. When I walk out of this building, it will be as if I never existed. Otherwise, Grandfather, the Shadow Dragons —and even the leaders of the other tongs—will lose face. If you do as I say, the matter is finished with and forgotten; if you do not, then you will deal with me. Grandfather says I should hold you personally responsible for seeing that his wishes are carried out. Are his instructions clear, Lee?"

The youth flushed, bared his teeth, then took a step backward and put a hand inside his jacket. "Grandfather would not wish for me to take orders from you!"

Veil shrugged, then handed the youth the garbage bag. "Here, sonny. You can talk to him yourself."

Obviously puzzled, the Shadow Dragon opened the bag and looked in, then let out a strangled cry and dropped it. As the three heads rolled out across the hardwood floor and gasps of astonishment rippled through the hall, Veil stepped around the youth, pushed open the door, and passed into the twilight world of cries, moans, tears, and sadness beyond.

PRIEST

PRIESTS

Symbols that had once given him comfort and a sense of belonging to a community of infinite continuity now evoked in him opposite emotions, reminding him of his loss and his isolation from all the people, places, and things that had permeated his soul and defined his being until five years ago, when he had been banished from this world.

Flanked by the plastic statuary of the Stations of the cross in their shadowy alcoves, feeling like a naked, vulnerable runner in a gauntlet set up to test his spirit, Brendan Furie, his footsteps muffled by thick maroon carpeting, strode quickly down the center aisle of the dimly lighted cathedral. He had not been inside a church in the five years since his excommunication, the amputation of his soul from the body of the church engineered by the figure in black who was kneeling, head bowed in prayer, at the railing before the white-draped altar at the front of the sanctuary.

Brendan had the distinct feeling that he was being watched, and he wondered if this might not be a kind of vestigial sense of the eyes of God, a psychological reaction to this return after a long absence to physical surroundings that had once meant everything to him but now seemed only a distant memory from another life, perhaps one only dreamed.

He reached the front of the sanctuary, but the frail, kneeling figure remained still, and Brendan was not certain the other man was even aware of his presence. For a moment he felt the old, virtually instinctive, urge to genuflect before the altar, but he knew he no longer had either the obligation or the right, and so he simply sat down at the end of the first pew and waited for Henry Cardinal Farrell to finish his prayers.

Almost five minutes went by before the old man, without raising his head or unclasping his hands, said in a low voice, "Thank you for coming, Father."

"I'm here because you asked me to come, Eminence," Brendan replied evenly. He swallowed, added softly, "I would appreciate it if you wouldn't call me 'Father.' Frankly, it sounds rather odd when you say it. You, of all people, know that I'm no longer a priest."

164

There was a prolonged silence, and Brendan began to wonder if the cardinal had heard him. But then the kneeling figure said, "Other people still call you that."

"No."

"You've become famous."

"Have I?"

"I've seen it in the newspapers. They call you 'the priest,' or sometimes just 'priest.'"

"It's not the same thing, Eminence."

"No," the old man replied, and then shuddered slightly, as if he had suddenly experienced a chill. "And I'd prefer you not to address me as 'Eminence.' It's been some time since I felt eminent. I appreciate your courtesy, but it isn't necessary."

"As you wish, sir."

"Brendan, are you . . . carrying a gun?"

It seemed a decidedly odd question in this stone house of worship, and Brendan stared at the old man's back for a few moments. But the kneeling figure remained inscrutable, old bones and flesh draped in black. Finally he replied, "No."

"I thought you might be. The stories . . ."

"Sometimes I carry a gun, but not often. In my business, a gun doesn't do much good. I've yet to meet the superstition, ignorance, obsession, or hatred that I could kill with a bullet."

Now the cardinal raised his head, unclasped his bony hands, and straightened his back. He put both hands on the rail in front of him and struggled to rise. Brendan got to his feet and started forward to assist the other man, but stopped when the cardinal vigorously shook his head in protest, Brendan resumed his seat, waited. Finally the cardinal managed to stand. He turned, walked unsteadily to the pew across from Brendan, and eased himself down. Brendan gazed into the eyes of the man sitting across the maroon-carpeted aisle, and was shocked by the stark gauntness of the features, the parchment-colored flesh that seemed almost translucent, the dark rings around the eyes. Henry Cardinal Farrell looked, Brendan thought, like a piece of fruit that had shriveled, or been cored.

The old man's lips drew back in a kind of bemused smile, and emotions Brendan could not decipher moved like moon shadows in the watery gray eyes. "Danger, the world, and good works seem to have served you well, priest. You look very well."

"You do not."

"I shall die . . . shortly."

"I'm sorry."

The frail Prince of the Church made a dismissive gesture with a trembling hand, and once again he smiled. "God really does work in mysterious ways, doesn't He?"

"I've heard it said, Father."

"I suppose it could be said that in a certain way I created you."

"How so, father?"

"I created this 'priest' that you've become, this man of such fame—or notoriety, as some would have it—who is now a private investigator, of all things, specializing in religious and spiritual matters, a fierce defender of children and their rights. Before, you were just a priest. I have heard it argued again and again that you are a far more effective avatar for Christ in your state of disgrace than you ever were before your . . . career change. The implications of this for the church are a subject of some heated debate among certain theologians. My name is almost never mentioned. I actually believe my role in it all has been forgotten."

Brendan said nothing. He felt oddly distanced, separated from this old enemy and the institution he represented by an unbreachable wall of betrayal, loss, pain, and death.

"You were never a good priest, Brendan," the cardinal continued in a voice that seemed to be growing stronger with a passion born of either anger or regret. "You were always a rebel, never at ease with the church. You were always questioning things you had no right to question."

"I questioned things you didn't want me to question, Eminence, but I always obeyed you, didn't I?" Brendan paused as he felt waves of his old resentment and anger rise in him, waiting for them to recede. When they were gone, he continued, "I went into retreat to do penance when you ordered me to, and I came out to do your errand when you ordered me to. It was not the church that made me ill at ease."

The cardinal stiffened. "Errand?"

"That's what I said."

"It was God's business."

"It was your business."

"The reason you were sent to retreat in the first place was to teach you that it wasn't your place to make such judgments."

Brendan suppressed a sigh. "Why did you ask me to come here, Father?"

The old man looked away from Brendan, toward the altar and beyond at the huge, painted wood figure of Christ nailed to a cross. "I've told you I shall die shortly. I have my secular affairs in order, and now I am trying to do the same for my soul."

"What is it you want from me, Father?" Brendan asked in a neutral tone.

166

"I want you to hear my confession."

Brendan could not believe he had heard the other man correctly; if he had, it could only mean that his being asked to come here was the sad joke of a dying old man, or that the mind of that dying old man was deteriorating. Brendan said nothing.

"You would refuse the request of a man who is so close to death?"

"I don't understand the request."

"I don't ask you to understand it, only to grant it.'

"I'm not exactly qualified to hear your confession, am I? Why should you wish to participate in a heretical act? Some of your more conservative colleagues might say you've committed heresy merely by making the request—that's assuming you're serious."

The old man opened his mouth and made a strange, rasping sound. It took Brendan a few moments to realize that the other man was laughing. "Since when have you concerned yourself with what the church did or did not consider heresy? I don't think you much cared even before they defrocked you."

"What concerns me is my business, father," Brendan replied evenly. "Forgive me for saying that you've played games with me before, and I can't help but wonder if this isn't just part of some other game."

The cardinal abruptly looked away; when he looked back at Brendan, his pale, watery eyes seemed unnaturally bright. "This is not a game, Brendan," he said forcefully.

"Your sins have nothing to do with me."

"You know that isn't so." He paused, leaned forward in the pew, added: "Some sins have a way of coming back to punish you in this life. Listen to me."

"I won't hear your confession."

The cardinal sighed, leaned back in the pew. "Why do you accuse me of having played games with you? You were asked to perform an exorcism. As a result of your miscalculations, the mother of the young girl in question committed a mortal sin by killing herself. Church authorities determined that the suicide of this woman was a direct result of your malfeasance - - your lack of proper preparation and perhaps even your lack of faith and purpose; the sin, it was decided, was yours, not hers, and the punishment was your excommunication. That judgment may have been harsh, but it was influenced by your past attitudes and writings and your reputation and actions as a dissident priest. You were consistently involved with organizations, social and political causes that the Holy See deemed inappropriate. You were warned more than once. Those are the facts. Do you dispute them?"

167

"I do not. Those are the facts. But the truth lies someplace else."

"Oh? Just what is the truth?"

"You sent me out to perform a rite for which you knew I wasn't prepared and in which you strongly suspected I didn't believe."

"You don't believe in demonic possession?"

"I believe in obsession founded on greed, lust, hatred, or a dozen other human evils. But it's hard enough to get people to take responsibility for their actions without providing them with the potential excuse that the devil made them do it."

"It's not like you to be flippant or disrespectful of ideas other people take very seriously, Brendan."

"I'm telling you the truth you claimed to want to hear. If you think I'm being flippant, you still don't understand me and you can never understand what happened. Lisa Vanderklaven wasn't possessed by demons; her erratic behavior was, under the circumstances, rational and healthy. She had a very good reason for defying her father and continually running away from home, namely that she was being persistently and brutally abused by the same man who had made her mother his mistress and who was her father's close business associate. When Lisa told her father about the abuse, he refused to believe her. Henry Vanderklaven preferred to believe that his daughter was possessed by demons, for to accept that she was being molested by Werner Pale would have interfered with his business interests and cast considerable doubt on his ability to judge character. Lisa Vanderklaven needed protection, not exorcism.

"In my initial interview with Lisa, she broke down; she couldn't believe that her father could actually believe she was possessed. That was when she told me that Pale had not only been molesting her, but had been involved in a sexual relationship with her mother for some time; Pale had bragged about it to her. At the time, I didn't feel I had any choice but to talk with Olga Vanderklaven, not only to try to confirm Lisa's story but to offer the mother my help, if she wanted it. *That* was my mistake. Faced with the fact that Lisa and I knew about her lover, and that the lover was molesting her daughter, she committed suicide.

"If anybody in that family could have been described as possessed, it was Lisa's father, and he'd created his own hell out of a deadly combination of greed and self-righteousness. Vanderklaven's greed was what led him to employ a man like Werner Pale in the first place. Vanderklaven was an arms dealer, as you well know. What you might not have known was that Werner Pale was a murderous soldier of fortune whom

Vanderklaven employed to train *provocateurs*. Those *provocateurs* were kept busy whipping up brush wars in various parts of the world in order to keep up the volume of sales of the arms Vanderklaven manufactured. He saw nothing wrong with what he did; he was an impossibly self-righteous man who could not see the evil around him that he'd created. He was a zealous Catholic with powerful friends in Rome, a church benefactor who gave millions to various church causes. He was so assured of his reservation in heaven that he could destroy his family and be blissfully unaware of the cause, the evil he had brought home with him, the man he considered a friend as well as a business associate. When Lisa told him that his friend was raping her, Vanderklaven demanded that she see a psychiatrist; when she ran away, he sent Werner Pale to find her and bring her back. When she ran away again he went to his golf buddy—you, Eminence — and asked you to arrange for an exorcism to free his daughter from her demons. Demonic possession was the only explanation he could think of for her behavior.

"I believe, Eminence, that when you heard the story you knew it would not withstand the scrutiny and investigation Rome requires before declaring officially that someone is demonically possessed, and that it was highly unlikely you would be able to get a trained exorcist to intervene in the affairs of this very troubled family. But you were afraid to offend Henry Vanderklaven by telling him the truth; you were afraid he might tighten his purse strings to the detriment of the church's interest, perhaps even afraid he might complain to his friends in the Vatican about your lack of sensitivity. And so you looked around for another solution to the problem he'd handed you, and I was it. You would send this young priest you were trying to break to go through the motions of performing an exorcism; once again you would force me to submit to your will while at the same time making Vanderklaven happy. I failed, Father, yes, and because of my failure as a human being to fully perceive and deal with Olga Vanderklaven's torment, she committed suicide as a direct result of my inquiries. Well, Rome was not about to declare that the soul of the wife of this important lay pillar of the church would burn in hell; in their view, and perhaps yours, it was preferable to consign *my* soul to burn in hell, and I was subsequently excommunicated. I didn't disagree with their action then, and I don't now. I was responsible for the woman's death because I should have ignored your machinations, scrapped the whole idea of an exorcism, and referred the case to social workers. Olga Vanderklaven died because of my failure as a priest, Eminence, but she also died because you sent someone you knew to be spiritually unequipped for the task of performing a rite that wasn't even called for to meddle in an incredibly raw

169

emotional situation. *That,* Eminence, is the truth."

Brendan waited, anticipating defense or denial. Instead, the Cardinal simply said, "You are right, priest. That is the truth."

"If you understand that, it seems to me that you have confessed all you need to."

The old man slowly turned to face Brendan, and his pale eyes went wide. "Understand this, Brendan," he said in a trembling voice. "Satan himself was there. It was Satan himself you were battling against."

Brendan studied the other man's face, saw real fear there— as well as something else he could not read. "I assume you're speaking metaphorically, Father." He paused, frowned when the cardinal responded by shaking his head. "Werner Pale?"

Now the cardinal nodded. Brendan ran his hands back through his black hair, looked down at the floor as he resisted the impulse to say something flippant or sarcastic that he knew he would regret. Finally he looked up, said, "No, Father. Pale was a murderous psychotic and a totally useless human being, not Satan. Believing that is just your way of avoiding taking personal responsibility for what happened. That's what Henry Vanderklaven did, and it's what killed his wife."

The cardinal's eyes went even wider, and his hands began to shake along with his voice. "But what if I'm right, Brendan? What if it was Satan?"

"What you believe is none of my business, Eminence," Brendan replied evenly. "Believe what makes you at peace, but don't then ask me to help resolve the conflicts that remain.

The old man took a deep breath, slowly exhaled. His trembling eased, and he sank back wearily in the pew. "I would very much like to know what happened afterward," he said in a voice so low Brendan could barely make out the words.

"Didn't Vanderklaven tell you?"

The old man sighed, producing an odd rattling sound in his lungs. "Henry Vanderklaven put a bullet in his brain soon after returning here from Europe, which was about three months after the events we have been discussing transpired. I believe it was because of something you said or did to him."

Brendan searched inside himself for some feeling of pity for Henry Vanderklaven, a man who, according to his belief system, had sentenced himself to eternal damnation. He felt nothing. He believed the man had done nothing to himself except end his life. He found he no longer believed in hells or heavens save for those created by living human consciousness and deeds, and perhaps never had. His faith had always been about living each day as a human trying to live up to the example set by Christ, not eternal rewards or punishments. What he did believe, what he knew, was that Henry Vanderklaven had created a hell for others that still tormented them, and he was glad the man was no longer alive.

"Brendan?" the cardinal continued softly. "What happened?"

"After Lisa ran away for the second time and came to the children's shelter, I promised her she would be protected from any kind of demons, human or otherwise, until I had investigated to try to determine the truth," Brendan said in an even tone that belied the turmoil once again building inside him. "I failed her. Not only did her mother commit suicide as a result of my bungling questions, but Werner Pale, acting on the father's orders, kidnapped her a second time while I was otherwise occupied trying to defend myself against excommunication. Then father, daughter, and Werner Pale left for Europe. As far as law enforcement and social welfare agencies here were concerned, the matter was out of their jurisdiction. But it wasn't a situation I could live with. I'd promised Lisa she wouldn't be harmed. I searched for them, and I found them. The details aren't important. What matters is that I finally found a way to make Henry Vanderklaven face up to the fact that the friend he relied on to stir up his business of death had cuckolded him and raped his daughter repeatedly. He saw, finally, how his own greed had blinded him, destroyed his wife, and caused his daughter to hate him. I didn't know he'd killed himself. For all his outward zealotry, he apparently didn't believe in forgiveness, not even for himself, and he certainly must not have believed in redemption."

"And where. . . is the girl now?"

"In New York. She's happily married, with a child. She works for a private children's social service agency.

Now the old man again slowly turned to look at Brendan, studied his face for some time. Finally he said, "Ah, yes. It's the same agency, I presume, for which you have done such good work, the one operated by the former nun with whom you are rumored to have a . . relationship?"

"I don't think that's really a part of this story, Eminence, is it? The point is that Lisa is safe now, with her own life to lead. She still has nightmares, but those will pass with time."

The cardinal nodded slightly. "And Werner Pale?"

"He's dead. I killed him

Brendan watched the other man react with what could have been surprise, but also with something else Brendan could not quite determine. "You, priest, killed this professional soldier?"

"He was trying to kill me. We fought, and I was lucky. He'd planned to burn me to death, but he was the one who fell into the fire."

171

Once again the old cardinal, apparently lost in his own thoughts, was silent for some time. At last, he said, "I've heard it said that you've killed a number of men since you left us. Can you have changed so much, priest?"

"How much I have changed is not for me to say, Eminence. I've harmed no one who was not trying to harm me, or sometimes a child. I've told you what you wanted to know. Are you satisfied?"

"Would you care to hear what has happened to me over the past five years?"

"If you feel the need to tell me, I will listen."

"God has turned his face from me, Brendan. I wronged you, and I've been punished. While it's true that the decision to excommunicate you came from Rome, the same people ultimately blamed me, for they knew the truth you spoke of. I often feel as if I have been excommunicated along with you. There has been no peace for me during the past five years.'"

"It sounds to me as if you've been busy punishing yourself, Eminence. You made a mistake, and God will forgive you. Where is your faith?"

The cardinal shook his head impatiently, with renewed vigor. "It was more than just a mistake. It's true that I never believed the girl was possessed, and yet I sent you to perform a sacred ritual simply to mollify her father. That is blasphemy, sacrilege. I need not only God's forgiveness, but yours as well, Brendan."

"You have it."

"Hear my confession."

"I believe I already have."

"In the confessional. Please."

"I don't think so, Eminence. This is the second time you have asked me to perform a sacred rite under inappropriate circumstances. The-"

"Precisely!"

"—first time neither of us believed in what we were doing, and death and my excommunication were the results; now that I have been excommunicated, church authorities would not recognize the sanctity of any confession you made to me. I don't understand what it is you really want, but I do know that it can't be the sacrament of confession."

The old cardinal slowly rose to his feet, turned to face Brendan, and then drew himself up very straight. Suddenly his eyes were very bright. "If you do not understand, priest, then you have not been listening to my words carefully, as I asked you to. I need to confess to you so that I can hear you say the Hail Mary."

Suddenly Brendan felt the hairs rise on the back of his

172

neck, and he resisted the impulse to make any sudden movement. "As you wish, Eminence," he replied in an even tone, bowing his head slightly.

"The confessor will come to you," the cardinal said in the same strong voice, and then turned away.

Brendan forced himself to remain still, to breathe evenly, as he watched the old man hobble across the sanctuary and disappear through a door to the right of the altar. He waited a few seconds, then rose and walked toward the ornately carved wood confessional stalls to his left. He hesitated just a moment before entering the priest's section of the confessional and sitting down.

Sins have a way of coming back to punish you in this life. Listen to me.

Almost five minutes passed, and then Brendan heard the door in the section on the other side of the wood screen open. Brendan glanced through the screen and watched as a stooped figure wearing a white robe with a cowl entered.

Even without the Cardinal's cryptic request to hear him speak Hail Mary, which was a reversal of the rite and all wrong, he would have sensed danger now, for this robed and hooded figure wore the white sash, the alb, around his neck, and that was wrong; a priest wore the alb to receive confession, not to enter the box as a penitent.

His earlier sensation of being watched had not been a fantasy, Brendan thought, but the eyes watching him had definitely not been those of God.

Are you carrying a gun?

Brendan stood and hurled himself at the screen, hitting the wood with his right shoulder and placing his left forearm across his face to protect his eyes from splinters. He hurtled through the fragile latticework, landing against the robed figure, and they both fell to the floor of the stall. Brendan used his left hand to grab the wrist of the man's right hand, which had emerged from the robe holding a .22 caliber pistol, while he drove his right fist into the man's midsection.

The cowl slipped back, revealing a face that was a nightmare mass of milk-colored, puckered scar tissue and lines of pink scars that could only have been the results of a series of failed operations. Werner Pale writhed beneath Brendan with the strength born of bottomless hatred and rage, swung at his head with the steel hook that had been used to replace his left hand. Brendan ducked under the blow but felt the sharp tip against his back as the steel began to dig its way through his leather jacket toward his flesh. He reached out with his free hand, found a shard of wood from the shattered screen, and wrapped his fingers around it. As the steel tip sliced through his jacket and touched skin, he raised

173

the stake in the air, and then drove the tip down into Werner Pale's throat.

Blood spurted from the pierced jugular. The scarred 0 of the man's mouth opened in a silent scream, but almost immediately the one Seeing Eye began to glaze over. The body beneath Brendan twitched violently for a few moments, and then was still.

Brendan rose from the corpse, threw open the door to the confessional and, wiping blood from his face, ran through a labyrinth of narrow stone and wood corridors toward the Cardinal's private chambers.

He found the old man, looking even paler and with pain clearly evident in the watery eyes, sitting at the desk in his study, seemingly holding himself upright with his palms on the polished oak surface before him.

"Brendan," Henry Cardinal Farrell breathed as Brendan came through the door, stopped. "Thank God. My prayers have been answered." He paused and squinted, as if he was having trouble seeing. "You're hurt."

"The blood is Werner Pale's, eminence, not mine.

"Thank God."

"Thank you for your warning. It saved my life."

"I couldn't warn you outright, priest. He was listening."

"I understand," Brendan said and again started forward. He stopped a few feet from the desk when the Cardinal raised one trembling hand with the palm outward, as if to push him back.

"He came to me . . . to kill me, of course, since I was responsible for sending you into his life. He wanted to know where to find you and the girl, and he said that he would kill me quickly if I told him. There is nothing he could have done to make me tell him, Brendan. Believe me."

"I do, Eminence. You don't have to explain."

"But I want to," the old man said in a voice that was growing progressively weaker.

"I believe he spent most of the past five years in hospitals, or he would have known how famous you've become. He would have had no trouble finding you, and you would have had no warning. He might also have traced the girl, Lisa. I decided to gamble for your life and the girl's; you had defeated him once before, and perhaps you could do it again. I sensed that he was afraid of you. But I also sensed that he badly wanted to make you suffer, and that shooting you down from some rooftop would not be satisfying for him. I acted well, Brendan. I got down on my knees before him and begged him for my life. I told him I would bring you to him and extract the information he wanted, if only he would spare my life. I also told him I would help trap you in a closed space, where you would be at his mercy. He was very

174

pleased with the idea of killing you in the confessional booth, positively delighted when I suggested that he could pretend to be me. He said he was going to shoot you in the belly or kneecaps first, and then carve you up. He couldn't stop laughing when I showed him the robe and sash he could wear. He loved the idea of dressing up like a priest to kill you." The old man paused, and the broad smile that suddenly appeared on his face seemed to belong to a much younger and less troubled man. "That's when I knew we had a chance, priest, for you, of all people, would find it rather odd that I, of all people, would ask you to join me in an act of heresy."

Then the cardinal coughed blood and pitched forward on the desk. Brendan rushed forward, lifted the old man by the shoulders, saw the blood, and the handle of the stiletto that was protruding from the other man's stomach. He also saw that it was too late.

"Pray for me, priest. God listens to you. Pray for me. Help my soul find its way to heaven."

"I will."

"Do you . . . understand what I . . . mean?"

"Yes. I will."

And then the old man was gone. Brendan walked to the wardrobe in a corner of the office, removed a robe, and put it on. He removed the crucifix from the cardinal's neck, put it around his own. Then he knelt beside the old man's body and began performing the last rites, his last rite. For the first time in five years he prayed in the old way, as if it mattered.

LETHAL BELIEFS

The sign crudely painted on the stained and pitted concrete foundation of the house read, "This Way To Hell", and the excommunicated priest with the widow's peak, raven-black hair and eyes followed the arrow down At the bottom of the trash-littered stairwell he knocked once on the door of the basement apartment; when there was no answer, he knocked again. The door was suddenly yanked open and Brendan Furie found himself staring into a deadly Cyclops eye that was the bore of an AR-15 assault rifle. The face at the other end of the weapon was that of a young man who had perhaps just left his teens. His pale green eyes were filmed with suspicion and not a little fear. Perspiration glistened on the pink scalp visible beneath stubble of blond hair on his shaved head. He was dressed in camouflage fatigues that were too big for him. At that moment Brendan feared as much for the young man's life as he did his own, for he could feel Marla's presence close by; Marla always seemed to be close by when there was danger present. When he had first met the woman he had been struck by her physical presence and beauty, but he had quickly become even more impressed by the fact that she could move more quickly and quietly than any person he had ever known.

"Who the hell are you?!" the boy with the pale eyes snapped. He was obviously trying to sound intimidating, but his voice squeaked.

"My name is Brendan Furie," the defrocked priest relied evenly. "I'm a private investigator. You're Jack Kellerman. I'd like to speak with you and your brother. I'll pay for your time."

"How the hell do you know who I am?!"

"Your father showed me your picture and told me where to find you."

177

Jack Kellerman blinked in surprise, and then nervously licked his lips. "You talked to my father?"

And mother."

"Liar! You're a goddamn federal agent come here to spy on us!"

"Hardly, Jack. It's a bit difficult talking with a rifle pointed at my nose. Would you put down the gun?"

"Admit you're working for the feds!"

"But I'm not working for the feds, Jack. I don't have the slightest interest in your militia membership or your activities. I'm here to talk with you and your brother, if you'll agree, about what the doctors did to you and your parents."

Once again the boy blinked rapidly in surprise, and then shadows that could have been shame, guilt or remorse passed over his sea-colored eyes. He looked away, and then abruptly lowered the gun before turning and walking back into the dingy, windowless room that was his home. Furie followed, glancing around the basement of the home of Floyd Kuhns, leader of the Patriot Militia. There were two cots, only one of which was made, a shower stall, toilet, and washstand. A battered cardboard wardrobe propped up against one pitted wall served as a closet. On the floor next to the unmade cot were a mug, a half-empty jar of instant coffee, and an electric heating element.

Jack Kellerman had set aside the assault rifle and was leaning on the washstand staring at himself in a mirror that was hung above the stand. The glass was spiderwebbed with cracks.

"Is Robby around?" Furie said to the boy's back.

"No," Kellerman answered, his voice muffled by the wall. "He ain't here. How come you want to talk to me about that doctor business?"

"Seven years ago your mother went to a psychiatrist seeking help for mild but persistent depression. She was promptly diagnosed by the man as having a multiple personality disorder. Not long after that the good doctor and two of his colleagues managed to persuade your mother that she was not only a victim of ritual Satanic abuse, but that she was actually the high priestess of an ancient Satanic cult that was responsible for the murders of dozens of infants in a seven-state region. They made your mother believe it, and then she voluntarily admitted herself to the first psychiatrist's clinic to be 'cleansed' of her demons. For a time they had your father believing that he was also a member of this cult, but he dropped out of the program after a couple of months. Then the psychiatrists convinced your mother that she should divorce him. And then they came after you and your brother. Somehow, probably with your mother's help, they managed to convince a court that the two of you had repressed memories, were victims of Satanic abuse, and required long-term care in another facility they owned. It was all nonsense; none of the cult activity or abuse ever happened. Yet the two of you were put away, and then simply released when you turned eighteen. Neither the doctors who diagnosed you nor the judge who put you away even offered so much as an apology.

The boy with the shaved head, who continued to stare into the mirror, asked in a small voice, "You don't believe in Satanic possession?"

Furie felt a whisper of cold at the base of his spine. He could tell Jack Kellerman a thing or two about the consequences of belief in Satanic possession, he thought, but he simply said, "No." He paused, smiled grimly, continued, "The doctors who did this to you and your family and dozens of other victims will have to take responsibility for their own actions. It wasn't the Devil who made them do it. It was an elaborate insurance scam; all of the victims targeted by those crackpot therapists had very rich health insurance benefit plans. Your mother's insurance company paid out more than three million dollars for the so-called 'treatment' of your mother and the two of you."

"So you're trying to nail those bastards?"

"No. Your parents are suing them, so maybe some good will come of that. In the meantime, the therapists are still trying to drum up business by appearing on talk shows. There doesn't seem to be any shortage of willing victims."

"If you're not after them, then why do you want to talk to me and Robby?"

"I work for a private foundation funded by a few wealthy men and women who have some interesting notions of their own. We're approaching the Millennium. Historically, susceptible people around the world get even more antsy than usual around this time. There's a general rise in the level of anxiety, and numerology, astrology, and all sorts of other superstitions become growth industries. Large numbers of people become infected, if you will, by some very strange belief systems, and they're willing to act on their beliefs. Some of these belief systems are lethal. You get lots of people killing each other because God has told them to. In this country you have groups like your own that are absolutely convinced that United Nations troops in black helicopters are coming to take away your guns. There's an increase in the level of violence; you have more incidents like the bombing of the federal building in Oklahoma City, Waco, Ruby Ridge; you have a guy wandering around carrying a cigar box full of enough Ricin, the deadliest poison on earth, to kill upwards of a million people.

"Belief in Satanic possession is potentially lethal because it allows people to shed responsibility for their own actions, and it strangles the intellect and spirit. The difference between this Millennium and the last is that now we have nuclear warheads, nerve gas and biological weapons to sling around instead of rocks and arrows. The people I work for are concerned about this. They believe that this kind of anxiety and random violence could reach a kind of critical mass where civilization explodes into chaos, wars, mass murders and disease on an unprecedented scale. They want to try to stop it. To do this they're attempting to develop statistical proof that such a global flashpoint could be reached, and then they will try to develop a kind of education program that could be used by governments and world health organizations. At this time they're trying to understand the process of what might be called socially acceptable insanity, and that's where I come in. I've been hired to research the bizarre. The FBI profiles serial killers; I try to profile serial victims. Your family is the victim of nonsense, Jack.

I've already interviewed your mother and father, and now I'd like to talk to you and Robby. I'd like to tape record your recollections of how those doctors trashed your family, and then I'd like you to fill out a questionnaire. Some of the questions are highly personal, but I'd like you to answer all of them. I guarantee your anonymity. You'll be assigned a code number when the data is compiled, and your name will not appear in any final report or literature. I need about two hours of your time, and I can pay you two hundred dollars for your cooperation."

Now Jack Kellerman finally turned back from the mirror, and Furie could see that he had been crying; tears still welled in his pale green eyes, slid down his cheeks, dripped off his chin. "Hell, why not?" he said in a voice that cracked. "It'll be the first and probably only time in my life I'll ever be paid a hundred bucks an hour."

The boy spoke into Furie's tape recorder for almost ninety minutes, ending with the account of his release from the therapists' institute and his aimless wandering with his brother until they both found a home with Floyd Kuhns and the Patriot Militia.

When Jack Kellerman had finished speaking, Furie handed him a five-page questionnaire, a ballpoint pen, and four fifty-dollar bills. The boy, sitting next to Furie on one of the cots, had just completed the first page of the questionnaire when the door slammed open and a huge man stepped into the room. The man, whom Furie immediately recognized from news reports as the obese and bellicose leader of the Patriot Militia, stood well over six feet, with a belly that hung like a flooded awning over the buckle of the belt he wore with his camouflage fatigues. His khaki shirt was open, and the T-shirt he wore beneath it was stained with sweat and spaghetti sauce. His huge hand, which he raised to point a finger at Furie, was shaking, and the muddy eyes in his bearded, doughy face glittered with rage and suspicion.

"Jack, who the hell is this guy?!" Kuhns bellowed.

Furie rose, said, "My name is Brendan Furie, and-"

"Shut up! I didn't ask you! Jack, what's this guy doing in my house?!"

The young man, thoroughly intimidated, put the clipboard with the questionnaire aside, stood up, then stepped away from Furie. His voice quavered slightly when he spoke. "He ain't nobody who wants to hurt us, Floyd. He's just a guy come to talk to me about what the doctors did to me and my family."

Kuhns, face flushed, slammed the door shut behind him, and then abruptly began to pace back and forth across the opposite side of the cramped space, slapping the palm of his hand against the side of the stained porcelain washbasin each time he passed it. Finally he stopped and shouted at the boy, "How could you have been so *stupid*?! You think anybody is really interested in how your mother swallowed all that Satan crap, Jack? You really think this guy wants to know about you and that bunch of weirdo doctors? I thought you'd put that behind you and could think straight now. The only devil around here is this guy you let into the house! He's a fed, you idiot! I can smell 'em a mile away! He's here to spy on us!"

"Begging your pardon, sir," Furie said evenly, "I-"

"It's *General* to you, fed!"

"What Jack has told you is true, General. I'm involved in a private research project. I don't work for the government."

The big man suddenly stopped pacing and walked over to Furie, coming so close that the ex-priest could smell his sweat and the beer on his breath. "The reason you and your people are going down is because you underestimate people like me," Kuhns said in a low, rasping voice that issued from him against a background of wheezing that sounded like static. "You think we're stupid. You think we don't know what you and your pud-pounding, kike paymasters are up to. You think we don't know how you're letting the UN bring in niggers from Africa to help American niggers take away our guns and kill us? You think I'm blind? You think I haven't seen your black helicopters?"

"I'm sure you've seen fleets of black helicopters," Furie replied quietly, meeting the other man's gaze. "But I wasn't flying in any one of them, and neither were the people I work for. Your political beliefs, and what you do with your friends and followers, doesn't interest me at the moment; I've already interviewed a dozen people like you, and you all sound the same. It's not the fault of government, blacks or Jews that life has disappointed you."

"You're a wise guy," Kuhns rasped, his murky eyes narrowing. Suddenly he reached around Furie and snatched the clipboard and questionnaire off the bed. "Let's see what you've got this other idiot writing about. Jack Kellerman flushed in embarrassment and shifted his feet slightly. "Floyd, please . . ."

"Hey, kiddo! You let a fed spy into the house, and then you start whining to me because I want to know what he's been asking you?!"

"He didn't ask me any questions about the group, Floyd, and I didn't talk about it."

Kuhns grunted as he scanned the questionnaire. After a few moments he tore the papers in half, dropped them and the clipboard on the floor. "Gee, I'm really glad you're not a bed wetter, Jack," the big man said sarcastically, and then abruptly shoved Furie aside and reached for the tape recorder laying on the cot. "I want to hear for myself what you've been talking about."

Furie stepped back between Kuhns and the cot, placed his right hand on the man's barrel chest, blocking his way. "I think not," he said softly.

Floyd Kuhns seemed genuinely bewildered to find Furie's hand on him. He stared down at it for a few moments in disbelief, his mouth opening and closing to reveal rotting teeth, and then suddenly slapped the hand away. "You *think not*?!" He shouted in Furie's face. *"Why* not?!"

"Because it's confidential. If you want to hear what's on this tape, you have to get Jack's permission, in writing. Or you can simply ask him what we talked about."

A scarlet cloud spread across the pasty flesh of Kuhns' cheekbones. "Ask his *permission*?! I'm going to bust your ass, you son-of-a-bitch!"

"I have resources, General."

Kuhns swung a wide, roundhouse right toward Furie's head. Furie ducked, shifting his weight to the balls of his feet as the fist sailed harmlessly over his head, then came up fast, driving his weight with his legs and using the stiffened fingers of his right hand to jab Kuhns just above his enormous gut and below the sternum directly into the man's solar plexus. Kuhns' breath burst from his wheezing lungs in an explosive gasp. His eyes widened and his face turned purple as first he doubled over, and then dropped onto the cot and bounced off it to the floor. Furie waited a few moments while the other man made desperate, sucking sounds, and then knelt on the floor beside him, intending to loosen the man's belt in an effort to help him breath. Then he straightened up and jumped back as Kuhns slashed at him with a huge combat knife that had suddenly appeared in his hand.

"You sucker-punched me," the big man wheezed. He was still gasping for breath, but he managed to get to his feet. "We'll see how good . . . you fight . . . when I cut off your fingers."

Furie crouched slightly and backed away, keeping his gaze focused on the other man's chest as Kuhns waved the knife in the air and lurched toward him. Then the militia leader stopped and spun around as the basement door crashed open. The sharp, clean sound of a hammer being cocked was amplified in the small, enclosed space. What Kuhn saw was a stunningly beautiful woman, six feet tall, with short-cut blond hair, finely chiseled features, and velvety brown eyes that displayed no emotion whatsoever. The woman was dressed in white tennis sneakers and a loose-fitting, blue nylon running suit. Her right arm was fully extended, and in her hand was a Smith and Wesson .38 caliber revolver that was aimed directly at the startled man's head.

"*What the-?!*"

"The resources I mentioned, General," Furie said in a flat tone. "My employers insist that she tag along with me because they think I might run into dangerous people from time to time. I can't imagine where they got that idea. I assure you that Marla is as deadly as she is attractive. If I were you, I'd drop the knife and back off."

Floyd Kuhns' response was to raise the knife even higher and move toward the woman. The report of the gun was thunderous in the small room. Kuhns grunted as he stopped and put a hand to his left ear. There was a look of almost childlike amazement on his face as he took his hand away from his ear and stared at the blood on it. "She shot me," he said in a high-pitched nasal tone. "My God, that woman shot me."

"It looks to me like she just nicked your ear. Be thankful your ear's still there, not to mention your head to keep it hanging on. Your brain may be not much larger than a peanut, but she could still have put a bullet in it. Now drop your knife and back off. My business here is finished."

This time Kuhns did as he was told, but as soon as Marla put her gun in the pocket of her nylon jacket he spread out his arms and rushed at her, spittle flying from his mouth as he bellowed with rage. Marla barely moved - - a small step to her left as she turned slightly and arched her back like a matador preparing to meet the charge of a bull. There was a blur of movement as Kuhns reached the spot where she had been standing only a moment before. Then, like the judo master Furie knew her to be, Marla assisted Kuhns in using the combined forces of his weight and charge to drive the big man into the concrete wall directly behind her. Furie winced at the sound, which he imagined was not unlike the crunch a sack of potatoes would make if it were dropped to the sidewalk from the roof of a tall building.

Furie shook his head as he walked over to the heap of smelly flesh sprawled unconscious on the floor. He felt for a pulse, and when he was satisfied that the militia leader was still alive he straightened up to find that Marla had already retrieved the pieces of the questionnaire and tape recorder, and she was holding the door open for him. Jack Kellerman was still standing where he had been, his hands clasped tightly in front of him. He looked astonished and very lost.

"We'll be going now, Jack," Furie continued. "Thank you for your cooperation. The information you gave me may help save others from the kind of abuse suffered by you and your family. I'm sorry if I've caused you any trouble. Good luck."

"Mr. Furie . . .?"

185

Furie was already halfway out the door, but now he turned back. "What is it, Jack?"

"I'd like to go with you," the boy said in a small voice.

Furie frowned slightly. "Have these people been holding you prisoner?"

Kellerman shook his head.

"Then I think it's best we travel our separate ways. We don't have time to wait for you to pack."

"I don't have anything to pack. I've got the two hundred dollars you gave me, and I'd be grateful if you'd just give me a lift to the next town where I can catch a bus or maybe hitch a ride." He paused, and then added, "The fact of the matter is, I'd like to talk to you some more."

Furie felt Marla's hand on his shoulder. He turned to look into her deep brown eyes and she slowly shook her head.

Normally Furie would defer to Marla's judgment, for he had learned to trust her instincts, but as he looked back at the forlorn figure standing in the room he felt the powerful pull of his past. He'd found the social work he'd done as a priest extremely satisfying, and he'd been happy with his life before he had been forced by his Cardinal, for political reasons, to perform an exorcism he hadn't been trained for and in which he didn't believe on a young girl who had been clearly possessed by nothing more than a well-founded terror of one of her wealthy father's business associates who had been sleeping with her mother as well as occasionally raping her. Death had followed in the wake of that lapse in his judgment and moral courage, the truth had come out, and he had been made the scapegoat for an extremely embarrassed and embattled church hierarchy. In fact, he no longer missed the priesthood; he was no longer sure he even believed in God, and he had found new satisfaction and purpose in a second career as a private investigator specializing in searching for young people who were lost, physically or emotionally. Then he had reluctantly signed on to work exclusively for this band of dreamers who believed it possible to somehow educate away evil, poke a finger in the massive, cracked dike of human irrationality and stupidity, save a world perhaps beyond saving by saving from themselves people who had no interest in being saved. It was at times like these, after encounters with men like Floyd Kuhns or after hearing reports on the almost unbelievably cruel and greedy actions of the predator psychiatrists, that Furie felt dangerously close to being overwhelmed by bitterness and a sense that he was wasting his time trying to help paint a big picture when what he should be doing was tending to the needs of the dark little splotches of people spattered across the canvas.

"Come on," Furie said, motioning for the boy to follow them. "We'll drop you off at a train or bus station.

As they left the basement room, Marla walked backward, gun in hand, guarding their rear. When they reached the car she got behind the wheel, as she always did. Furie slid into the back seat next to Jack Kellerman.

They rode in silence down dusty roads and through orchards for almost five minutes before the young man spoke again. "Talking to you made me feel better," he said to Furie.

Furie nodded. "I'm glad to hear that."

"The people you work for are really serious about their thinking that the world is in really big trouble?"

"Not the world, Jack. Just humans. And yes, they are very serious."

"Is it some kind of religious thing?"

"No. What they believe in is a mathematical model."

"I don't understand."

"It's complicated."

Kellerman stiffened. "You're saying I'm too stupid to understand?"

Furie sighed, shook his head. "I don't understand the math; but I believe their projections may be accurate, which is why I agreed to work for them. They've come up with a mathematical model, which they call the Triage Parabola. You might compare it to the computer programs meteorologists use to predict the weather, except that this program predicts human behavior and its consequences. There are a series of very complex equations.

Historical data is transformed into numbers, and the numbers are plugged into the equations to get predictions of future events. The news isn't good."

"The world is going to end?"

"Not the world, Jack. Just our species."

"Nuclear war?"

"The model can't predict things that precisely. What it does predict is a sharp increase in mass paranoia, anxiety and hysteria in the decade ahead. A kind of psychological critical mass is reached, and then things start to fall apart. You have the rise of Messianic movements all over the planet. A lot of these competing groups start throwing things at each other - - nerve gas, biological weapons, and nuclear weapons when they can get hold of them. There are no rules of engagement because each group believes it is acting on God's will. Whole governments begin to break down, and with them go hospitals and medical research facilities. In the American Civil War, two thirds of the casualties died from disease, not combat wounds. That could happen again - - will happen again, if the model is accurate. The computer program takes into account not only manmade viruses and bacteria, but also new, natural diseases that are released as the rain forests are destroyed. The model predicts that a new Black Plague - - actually, a whole series of them - - is coming, and this time up to ninety percent of the human population on earth could die. The survivors would be too few and too scattered to form a viable gene pool. The Triage Parabola predicts that we could be extinct as early as the year 2035."

"Jesus," Jack Kellerman whispered.

"Don't blame Jesus."

"You don't seem all that concerned."

Furie turned in his seat to face Kellerman. "Look, Jack," he said in an even tone, "it's only a theory, so don't waste your time worrying about it. In the end you can only be responsible for your own behavior, so do what you can to clean up and polish your life every day. Live *smart* and forget everything else I've told you. Those divided-memory quacks ruined your family and your childhood, and those militia maniacs were getting ready to ruin the rest of your life. I have contacts with a number of organizations that will give you a place to rest and counsel you, help you get your own life back on track. If you'd like, I'll make some calls when we reach the next town."

"Yes," Kellerman said. "I'd like that." There was a prolonged silence, and then he continued, "If I'm going to start fresh, then I have to clean up the past. There's something I have to tell you."

"What's that, Jack?"

"I was at Oklahoma City."

Furie saw Marla's shoulders tense slightly, and she glanced quickly in the side and rear view mirrors. His mouth had suddenly gone dry.

"The Murrah Building?"

Kellerman looked away from Furie, slowly nodded. "I was in on the planning. We all were. We had to show we were committed to the cause. The bombs weren't supposed to go off when they did. My brother was inside the building checking a charge when they blew, and he was killed along with the others. Next week I was supposed to plant another bomb in the county courthouse."

Furie took a deep breath and slowly exhaled, then turned around and glanced out the rear window. The road behind them was empty. For now. "This changes things, Jack."

"I know."

"I'm going to have to make some other calls besides the ones I mentioned."

"It wouldn't be a good idea to talk to any of the local cops, Mr. Furie."

"I'll be calling the FBI. The fact that you're coming forward will carry a lot of weight in the courts, and those organizations I mentioned may still be able to help you."

"Will you wait with me until they come to pick me up?"

"Yes."

Marla suddenly braked hard, throwing both Furie and the young man beside him up against the front seat. Furie recovered, then glanced up and felt his stomach muscles knot. Parked across the road, blocking their way, was a police cruiser with its rack of red and white lights flashing. Emblazoned across the side of the cruiser were the words, *SHERIFF'S DEPARTMENT*. Standing in the middle of the road was a trim, broad-shouldered man in a deputy sheriff's uniform. He wore a stiff-brimmed trooper's hat low on his forehead, and his mouth was set in a grim line. In his hands was a double-barreled shotgun that was aimed at their windshield.

"Oh, Jesus," Jack Kellerman whispered.

"Is he a member of the militia?"

"Yeah."

"Stay here," Furie said as he opened his door and got out. Marla was already out of the car.

"Won't do no good," Kellerman said, getting out and following after Furie. "He wants me."

Furie stepped into the middle of the road, stopped in front of their car as Marla slowly began to move off to her right. The deputy's shotgun followed her.

"Stay right where you are, cupcake," the man said to Marla in a deep, gravelly voice. "I heard all about you. Try any funny stuff with me, and I'll blow you in half."

"My name's Brendan Furie," the excommunicated priest said to the deputy as Jack Kellerman came up beside him. "There must be some kind of mistake, so there's no need for you to be pointing that gun at us. What's the problem?"

"There's a mistake, all right, mister, and you made it. You damn feds are always making mistakes, just like that rat traitor standing next to you."

Kellerman took a tentative step forward. "Harry, I never said anything about-"

"Shut up and stand still, rat traitor! You're a damn liar! It's written all over your face! You've been spilling your guts!" The

190

deputy abruptly swung his gun back on Marla. "What's your name, cupcake?"

"Her name's Marla," Furie said. "She's mute." He paused for a few moments, then asked, "What now?"

"We wait."

Furie looked over his shoulder, saw in the distance a plume of dust that was moving rapidly toward them. He turned back to the man with the shotgun. "You look like a smart man, Deputy. There are two very big reasons why you should let us go on our way before General Fruitcake gets here. He wasn't in a good mood when we left him, and things could get out of hand when he gets here."

The deputy grunted. "That right? Give me one good reason, you lousy Communist loving fed bastard."

"There's no good end for you in keeping us. I'm not a federal agent; I'm a private investigator, and Marla and I work for some very powerful people. If you kill us, I assure you we'll be missed. There'll be media coverage."

"You're full of crap, fed. And the Commie-loving media can go to hell."

"It's not the newspapers and television you're going to have to worry about, Deputy. Our employers know exactly where Marla and I are, and why we came. They know all about your organization. If I don't report in six hours, you and General Fruitcake are going to be swimming in real federal agents right up to your eyeballs. Harm us, and you'll get exactly what you're most afraid of."

"We're not afraid of the feds," the deputy said, but now there was a tinge of uncertainty in his tone. "What's the second reason?"

Furie again glanced behind him. The plume of dust was much closer, perhaps only two or three miles away. He turned back, pointed to the plastic figure of Jesus mounted on the cruiser's dashboard. "Are you a Christian?"

191

The deputy spat. "Of course I'm a Christian. What, do I look to you like a Jew? I never met anybody in my whole life who wasn't a Christian."

"Roman Catholic?"

The man narrowed his eyes. "Yeah. So what?"

"I'm a priest - - or I used to be. I'm a man of God. Kill me, or anybody under my protection, and you'll be committing the worst kind of mortal sin. You'll be condemned to hell."

"Used –to-be doesn't count," the deputy said uncertainly.

"Are you so certain that in God's eyes I'm not a priest that you're willing to risk your immortal soul? Think about it: What you do in the next minute or two could determine whether you spend eternity in heaven with God or suffering the fire of hell with Satan. Eternal agony or ecstasy. Which is it going to be, Deputy? Remember that it's you God will hold responsible if General Fruitcake harms us."

"We're soldiers for Christ," the man said, licking his lips. "We're fighting for God's country, so God's on our side."

Furie took a deep breath, fighting against the frustration and desperation that were making him feel nauseous. "What about the Rapture, Deputy?"

The other man frowned slightly. "What's that?"

"There are a lot of good Christians like yourself in this country who believe we're in the End Times. The final battle of Armageddon could begin at any moment. Instead of federal agents to worry about, you're going to be fighting demons from hell - - and demons take no prisoners. Christ will return to establish the Kingdom of God on earth, but only after the wicked have been destroyed. What you're doing here is wicked, Deputy. I can see by the statue of Christ on your dashboard that you're a devout man, and before you stopped us the chances were probably good that you'd be Raptured off the face of the earth to sit at Christ's side until the battle is over and Jesus returns. But that isn't going to happen if you kill a man of God and the people with him. In a single moment, with this one bad decision, you could be throwing

192

away paradise and buying yourself a ticket to hell. Think about it very carefully, Deputy."

Shadows of doubt, and perhaps even fear, filmed the other man's eyes, but it was too late to let them go. A battered red pickup truck had skidded to a halt with a squeal of brakes and a shower of pebbles on the shoulder of the road. Floyd Kuhns leaped out of the cab and limped toward them. Blood was still streaming from his bullet-nicked ear, and his face was a patchwork of bruises and cuts. His nose had been pushed to one side of his face, and both eyes had already started to blacken.

"Jesus, Floyd," the deputy said in a low voice, "what the hell happened to you?"

"Shut up!" Kuhns barked as he raised the .357 Magnum he carried and pointed it at Marla. "Did you get her gun?!"

"I don't remember you tellin' me she had a gun."

"You're a real cheesebrain, Harry," the militia leader growled as he slowly advanced on Marla, keeping the gun trained on her chest. "Step over here and put the shotgun to her head. If she so much as hiccups, blow her brains out."

"Floyd . . .?"

"*Do it!*"

The deputy stepped closer to Marla and placed the barrels of his shotgun against her right temple as Kuhns, moving very cautiously, reached into the pocket of her nylon jacket and retrieved the revolver she carried there. Then he hit her in the mouth with his fist. Marla collapsed and lay still, blood dripping from her split lower lip, but Furie did not think she was unconscious, although her eyes were closed. He started toward her, then stopped when both the shotgun and .357 Magnum swung in his direction.

"Listen to me, both of you," Furie said with quiet intensity. "Stop this now, before you dig yourselves a hole you can't climb out of. Marla and I aren't federal agents, and we didn't come here to spy on you. I came to talk to Jack about his experiences, not about you. Listen to the tape in the car, and you'll see that what he talks about is personal, about himself and his family. Marla and I

193

don't give a damn about your militia. Kill us, and your whole organization goes down the toilet right after you. You'll be caught and executed. If you've got something to hide, this isn't the way to do it."

"Maybe we should listen to the tape, Floyd," the deputy said to the other man, watching him out of the corner of his eye. "He could be telling the truth."

"Like I said, Harry, you're a cheesebrain. Even if there's nothing about us on the tape, how do you know what they talked about in the car? How do you know what the rat traitor is going to say if we let them go? There's too much at stake. Shoot 'em."

"Remember that this is about your soul, Deputy," Furie said softly. "Think about where you want to be in the next minute if the End Time comes then."

"I don't know about this, Floyd," the deputy said in an uncertain tone as he shook his head. "Maybe we should talk about it some more."

"*Talk about what?!*" Kuhns roared, spraying blood from his broken mouth.

"Maybe we should just let them go like this guy says. He used to be a priest, so he knows things we don't know. He says Jesus could be coming back soon, and we'll all be judged. Maybe this isn't such a good time to be killing people."

"You are an *idiot*, Harry! He's been trying to brainwash you with a bunch of religious crap to try to get your mind off the mission! What God wants is for us to get rid of the federal government so they won't be messing with our lives and trying to take away our guns! Now, *shoot 'em!*"

"I . . . I don't think I care to do that, Floyd."

"Then I'll do it myself!" Kuhns snapped, and aimed his gun at Furie's chest.

"Floyd, don't do it!" Jack Kellerman shouted, leaping in front of Furie just as the gun exploded. The Teflon-coated slug passed through the boy's body, and Furie felt a tug on the right sleeve of his jacket as the bullet sliced through the fabric. A moment later the gun had dropped from Floyd Kuhns' grip and he

194

was making gurgling sounds as he clutched with both hands at the knife that protruded from his throat. Blood spurted from his jugular vein, ran from his mouth and nose. He turned around once, very slowly, and then his knees buckled and he went down.

Furie glanced down at the young man with the hole in his chest, and knew that Jack Kellerman was dead. He glanced over at Marla, who had risen to her feet. The expression on her face was as impassive as ever. The left sleeve of her jacket was pulled up to her elbow, revealing an empty wrist scabbard. Furie walked over to where Floyd Kuhns lay, his eyes as wide and unseeing in death as they had been unseeing in life.

"Oh, man," the deputy said in a low, strangled voice. "Oh, man, how am I going to explain this?"

"We'll explain it to the authorities together," Furies said carefully. watching the other man. "The important thing is that you haven't murdered anybody today."

The deputy grimaced, his mouth twisting in anguish, and shook his head. "Everything's going to come out. I'll go to prison. That's no good for me. I've got a wife and kids."

"Deputy, put down your gun and listen to me. Two people are dead already. That's enough. Your soul is clean of the sin of what happened here."

Again the man shook his head. Now his eyes looked vacant. "My life's going to be hell, priest. I can't let them make me into a rat traitor and send me to prison. I'll be killed there. I gotta' do what I gotta' do."

With the deputy distracted by Furie, Marla had been slowly circling around toward his rear, but now the man sensed her presence. He abruptly wheeled and leveled his shotgun on her. Furie snatched the Magnum from the ground beside Floyd Kuhns' body, aimed and fired. The gun had a tremendous recoil, kicking up in the air, but Furie's aim had been true. The shotgun discharged into the ground as the bullet hit the deputy in the right cheek, just below his eye, and tore off the top of his skull.

Furie threw the gun to one side, then leaned over and vomited. Gasping for breath and retching, he was only half aware

195

of Marla's presence as she knelt down beside him and used her jacket to wipe her fingerprints from the handle of the knife sticking out of Kuhn's throat. Then she did the same to the grip of the Magnum. Furie wiped his mouth, then walked unsteadily toward the police cruiser. He opened the door and reached inside for the radio, but stopped when Marla's hand firmly gripped his wrist. When he looked at her, she slowly and firmly shook her head, just as she had done back in the basement room when Jack Kellerman had asked to go with them. She wiped his prints from the car's door handle, and then motioned toward their own car.

This time Furie took her advice.

TOMB

Somehow he had to find a way to do things differently from the others, quickly and as often as alternatives, no matter how seemingly illogical, occurred to him, or he would surely die like them, and at the moment the only thing he could think of to do that the amateur and professional cavers and team of Army Rangers had certainly not done during their descent down the glacier wall was to turn off the powerful light mounted on his helmet, and the instant he did so he was enveloped in a darkness so complete and almost palpable, and he felt so alone, that it paradoxically reminded him of the shimmering light on the surface of the glacier he now embraced and the scene of spiritual and physical chaos that had greeted him when he had arrived at the site the day before, parked his rented snowmobile at the edge of a sort of improvised "lot" filled with other snowmobiles, dogsleds, cross-country skis, and snowshoes, and then climbed up the polar white and emerald green face of the glacier on crude steps that had been cut into the ice.

At the top he put on his sunglasses and scanned the area, which was littered with garbage, portable toilets, multicolored pup tents, rough wooden crosses mounted on tripods, scattered urine and feces stains, improvised lean-tos, three igloos, and even a large, prefabricated aluminum Quonset hut he presumed had been erected by the missing five-man team of Army Rangers that had disappeared a week before into the cave that so far had claimed seventeen lives.

After forty-five minutes of walking around the campsite, occasionally peering into sleeping bags, he had not found the boy, which disappointed and surprised him, but he did find Dylan Parker. The tall man with the full head of bushy white hair and piercing blue eyes swimming with madness was standing at the head of a knot of his followers staring, transfixed, at the entrance

197

to the cave, a secret tens—perhaps hundreds—of thousands of years old finally revealed, millimeter by millimeter, by the eons-long whisper of a receding glacier. The opening in the stone—merely the top of an ice-blocked cave entrance estimated to be upwards of two hundred feet high—was perhaps two feet at its highest point, twenty-five yards long, as black as a stain of India ink splashed against the gray-brown rock of the mountain that erupted like a great god's tooth from the bluish-white gum of the ice sheet that encased it.

As if sensing Brendan's presence, Dylan Parker suddenly wheeled around, and his eyes with their gaze that was slightly manic even when he was calm suddenly glittered with excitement. He threw back his head and shouted like a man in the throes of ecstasy, "Priest!"

"Hello, Dylan," Brendan said, and winced when the tall man threw his long arms around him and squeezed.

"Even *you* know it's true this time, don't you?" Parker shouted hoarsely in Brendan's ear. "It's why you've come to join us!"

"Take it easy, will you, Dylan?" Brendan said not unkindly, extricating himself from the cult leader's grip and stepping back. "I'm sorry to disappoint you, but I'm here on business."

Dylan Parker shook his head determinedly. "God's business. The fact that you're here is one more sign."

"I gave up the presumption of trying to know God's business ten years ago, Dylan. It's the same situation as when I met you the first time. I'm looking for another kid."

The big man in the silver and orange parka spread his arms in a gesture that seemed at once benediction and supplication. "Why bother? In a very short time you'll be reunited with everyone you've ever loved or looked for, have everything you ever wanted or thought you wanted. We all will. We're going to heaven."

"His father doesn't want him going to heaven just yet, at least not without his medication. I was certain he'd be with you, and if he's not, I've wasted a lot of my time and his father's

198

money. He's a nineteen-year-old boy by the name of Hector Martinez. Is he here, Dylan?"

"Yes," the other man said simply.

Brendan let out a deep breath he had not even been aware he was holding. The simple affirmation meant he had not traveled more than six thousand miles by jumbo jet, bush plane, dogsled, and snowmobile for nothing. "Thanks, Dylan. I appreciate it."

"What are you thanking me for, Priest?" Parker asked, a slight edge to his voice. "My telling you that Hector is here? You know I don't ask anyone to follow me against his will. People who are with me are free to come and go as they wish. I don't hide things, and I don't try to brainwash anybody."

"I'm aware of that, Dylan. Where is he?"

"In town getting supplies. He should be back in an hour or so."

"I hope he took a barrel of cash. The Indians in that native village are having a field day, thanks to you. It's costing me two hundred dollars a night to stay in a tool shed with a kerosene heater, and that snowmobile I rented must have been the last one in town because it's costing me three hundred and fifty dollars a day. The Indians should give you a cut, or at least make you an honorary tribal chieftain."

"I have my own money," Dylan Parker said stiffly. "It's given to me by my followers of their own free will, and it all flows back to them. You know that, Priest. If you thought I was a thief, I suspect your attitude toward me would not be quite so benign. I helped you find that girl; she wanted to go back with you to her family, and I didn't object in the least."

Brendan sighed, and then nodded in the direction of the black gash in the mountainside at the edge of the glacier. "Just what is it you think is down there?"

"The end of the world. Jesus is coming."

"Out of the cave?"

"I'm not sure what's coming out of the cave. Perhaps Jesus - - perhaps demons, or angels. It doesn't matter. It's the end of the

199

world as we know it, because Jesus is coming back to rule His kingdom."

Brendan grunted. "You thought it was the end of the world five years ago, Dylan. You and twenty-seven of your followers, including the girl I was hired to find, went to New Mexico and sat in the desert for a month, waiting, until your food and money ran out, and you all decided that your timetable had been a bit off. What makes you so certain you've read the schedule right this time?"

Dylan Parker pushed a long strand of white hair out of his eyes and back under the hood of his parka, then half turned and waved his right hand to indicate their surroundings. "Look around you, Priest. There are hundreds here, camped out in the cold. They're not here because I told them to come. They're here because of the discovery of the cave; they've been called to this desolate place by God to witness the beginning of our entrance into Paradise."

"They're here because they read or heard news reports about the cave and your prophecy, Dylan. The entrance to a cave that's been hidden since at least the last ice age suddenly appears and starts swallowing up people, and then somebody with your charisma starts telling everybody it's a sign of the Second Coming. It's powerful imagery, and it appeals to a lot of people who are miserable with the present version of their lives. They want an easy way to start over, and they think a Second Coming will give it to them. Also, it's Millennium Fever. You're going to see a big increase in this kind of nonsense in the next few years."

Parker squinted. "You may call it nonsense, but the fact that you've come here, for whatever reason, is still a sign. It's what God wants."

"If you say so."

"Why did the Church excommunicate you, Priest?"

The abrupt change of subject, and the question itself, startled Brendan, and he was momentarily taken aback. "It's none of your business, Dylan," he replied at last, softly, and twenty-four hours later, suspended in darkness and listening to the faint but distinct scratching sounds of moving things on the stone of the cave floor far below him, he realized that what he was feeling was the same almost overpowering sense of mystery and awe he had once experienced when entering a church and thinking it was God's home. He was as surprised at the intensity of the emotion as he was by his lack of fear. Although he had not yet even made it to the floor of the cave, and was surrounded by clicking and scratching sounds that could signal the presence of whatever it was that had killed the others, he was not sorry he had begun this journey into a place possibly millions of years old where humans had only recently come, and disappeared. He knew what he had told Philip Imukpak, and he knew what he had told himself, but now he wondered if the real reason he had started on this journey was to experience an emotion, a kind of ecstasy, he had thought lost to him forever, as well as a kind of faith as powerful as any he had ever felt.

He could traffic in crackpot ideas with the best of them, Brendan thought as he smiled grimly to himself in the darkness; he actually believed that he was not going to die in this cave.

He estimated it had been more than five minutes since he had turned off the lamp on his helmet, and the scratching sounds in the darkness below him had become even more pronounced. When he heard something climbing up the ice wall toward him, he locked off the bosun's chair on the line, then took his automatic and a powerful flashlight out of the smaller pack strapped to his chest. He aimed the flashlight down into the darkness, flipped the switch.

"Christ!" Brendan cried out when he saw the black, leathery thing with long fangs and claws and no eyes clinging to the ice wall barely two feet below him.

He was about to fire the gun when the thing began to thrash wildly in the bright light, then lost its grip on the ridged ice. It emitted an extremely high pitched squealing sound as it plummeted to the stone floor below, where it exploded in a burst of blood, bone, and tissue that appeared black in the beam of light. When Brendan swept the beam across the floor, two other black leather creatures shuffled away into the darkness, their extended claws clicking and scratching on the stone.

The creatures looked like bats, Brendan thought—except that they were almost the size of a man and waddled like penguins rather than flew.

And they were obviously carnivorous; as he continued to sweep the beam of the powerful flashlight across the floor he could make out bloodstains, scattered bones with pieces of flesh still clinging to them, and scraps of clothing. However, he did not see any army uniforms or equipment, and he did not see a green-checked flannel shirt or red cap.

This sealed-off, domed entrance to the cave system was the size of a massive cathedral, and tributary caves of various sizes radiated off from the stone wall in all directions, at varying heights, and Brendan knew that, even without the threat of the creatures in the darkness who viewed him as their latest entree, it was hopeless to even think of trying to explore all of them. *He needed a sign*—and he received it.

When he swept the beam of light across the curved wall to his Left, his heart began to pound, not with fear but with hope. At the mouth of one of the larger tributary caves, placed on top of a pile of stones as if it had been left there intentionally, was a red baseball cap.

He knew he could descend to the bottom of the hall and climb up a slope of riprap to the cave, but the stone floor, with its pools of gore, did not look like a particularly safe place to be. Consequently he pushed off the ice wall at an angle, swung out, then extended his legs and pushed off even harder, in the opposite direction, when he came back to the wall. After fifteen minutes of considerable exertion the arc of his swing carried him over the ledge that held the pile of stones and red cap. He released the safety mechanism on his rigging, dropping to the ledge. He immediately grabbed for the rope, but missed; the line swung away into the darkness, out of reach. It meant he would have to descend to the killing floor to climb back up, but Brendan decided that was the least of his worries at the moment. He picked up the cap, stepped into the mouth of the cave.

"Hector!" he shouted. *"Hector, can you hear me?"* He waited, listening, but heard nothing but the hollow echoes of his own voice, and then silence once more.

"Hello, Priest," Hector Martinez said evenly as he pulled his red supply-laden snowmobile into the area near the edge of the glacier where Brendan was waiting, cut the engine, and got off.

"You don't look surprised to see me, Hector."

The slight boy with the handsome face and hair and eyes as black as Brendan's merely shrugged. "My dad sent you, didn't he?"

"Yes."

"Are you going to try to persuade me to go back?"

"If I did try, would I have any chance of success?"

"No."

"Then I won't try."

The boy looked up, fixed Brendan with his sad eyes. "It's almost time, you know. Jesus is coming out of the cave. I want to be here to meet Him."

"Fine. You're of legal age now, Hector. Nobody can make you do anything you don't want to do. If you want to sit around on a glacier and wait for Jesus to step out of a cave that's already killed seventeen people, that's your privilege. It's not like when you used to run away and spend time at the shelter."

Hector Martinez raised a brown hand to shield his eyes from the bright sunlight reflected off the ice and snow around them. "Then why are you here?"

"To deliver a message."

"What message?"

"Is there someplace we can go to sit down and talk, Hector? Maybe the Quonset hut? It looks like the state troopers have set up some kind of first aid station there."

203

"I want to get back to my friends, and I have these supplies to take to them. Why don't you just say whatever it is my father paid you to come all this way to say?"

Brendan studied the boy, felt anger and frustration rising in him. "All right, Hector," he said abruptly. "Your mother's dead. She died in an automobile accident three weeks ago. Your father thought you should know."

Brendan waited for the boy's reaction. He was prepared to take Hector Martinez in his arms to comfort him, but the boy did not seem particularly shocked, or saddened. His eyes misted, and a single tear roiled down one cheek, but that was all. "It's all right," he said softly. "We'll be together again very soon."

"Come back with me, Hector. Your father would very much like you home with him. He loves you. Nothing is going to happen here, except that you're going to get older, wetter, dirtier, and more miserable."

The boy slowly, firmly, shook his head. "The world is going to end. Jesus is coming. I have to be here to meet Him."

"I've brought you something."

"What?"

Brendan took the dark orange plastic prescription bottle out of one of his pockets in his parka, offered it to the boy. "Your lithium."

Hector Martinez looked at the bottle in Brendan's outstretched hand, took a step backward. "You know I won't take that stuff, Priest. God doesn't want me to poison my body with drugs. The doctors couldn't get me to take it before, and I won't take it now."

"This isn't for your body, Hector, and you know it. It's for your mind. You're a severe manic-depressive, and God put a lot of you on this earth. Fortunately, God also made lithium. It's not poison; it won't alter your thoughts, and it won't do your thinking for you. What it will do is give you a level emotional playing field to stand on. It will help you to think straight, and you'll feel better. You'll know you don't really want to be here. You'll understand that you're squandering your place in the world, your life, by sitting around and waiting for it all to end. People who think the world is going to end and that Jesus is coming back really want to end their own lives because they're unhappy; they want God to end it all for them, painlessly, and then give them a brand new off-the-shelf Life that Jesus won't allow them to foul up. I'd have more sympathy for them if they weren't so eager for God to take everyone else's life, too. Take the medicine, Hector. Go back home to mourn with your father, and stop all this stupid screwing around. You've wasted enough of your Life because you wouldn't do what your doctors recommended, and your life isn't going to end now just because you want it to."

The boy stiffened. "Just because you don't have faith, Priest, is no reason why I shouldn't. Jesus is coming soon, and I'm going to be here to meet Him."

"Goodbye, Hector," Brendan said quietly to Hector Martinez as the boy snatched a box off the snowmobile, then turned and started up the steps carved in the ice, and Brendan was still haunted by the conversation as he walked through the intricate labyrinth of caverns, leaving chalked blaze marks on the walls, calling the boy's name, and at the same time experiencing an ever-increasing sense of awe as he passed running streams and coursing rivers, night meadows of strange, dark plants, some as tall as trees, none of which had ever been exposed to a single ray of sunlight. He found the corpse of one of the black, leathery creatures that had apparently died of natural causes, examined it and knew what it was, which he could not say about the myriad other creatures that appeared in increasing abundance as he traveled ever deeper into the mountain, ever closer to the unsuspected heat source three miles to the north that gave life to this world and had sustained the Givers, whose artifacts were strewn all over the caverns. But he had not found the boy, and even in his rapt awe and astonishment he remained haunted by their last conversation, as he had been haunted the night before as he'd lain awake in the tool shed, staring at the glow of his kerosene heater and knowing that in the morning he would cancel his reservation with the bush pilot and return to the glacier and the ages-old secret it had only recently begun to reveal.

"You don't look like the type."

Brendan turned from the cave opening, found himself looking into the handsome, brown face of an Eskimo, one of the state troopers who occasionally stopped by and stayed for a day or two in the Quonset hut, which they had made their headquarters. "What type is that?"

"An end-of-the-worlder."

"What does an end-of-the-worlder look like?"

The trooper casually swept his arm around to indicate the others scattered over the ice, Dylan Parker and his followers. "Like those people."

Brendan grunted. "I'm surprised you haven't sealed off the cave entrance, or at least posted a guard to make sure nobody else goes down there."

The Eskimo shrugged. "This is Alaska. Here, we let people do pretty much as they please.

"Even if it pleases them to kill themselves?"

"Alaska has a high suicide rate; I suspect a lot of people come here to kill themselves, although they may not realize it. We come around to keep an eye on things, but if anybody is stupid enough to go down there after seventeen people, including expert cavers and a team of Army Rangers, have disappeared, it's their problem."

"Sometimes people have to be protected from themselves."

"Not in Alaska; Alaskans don't like to be protected from themselves, which is one reason they come to, or stay in, Alaska. Besides, these people won't be here much longer. If they think it's cold up here now, wait another month. Our summers don't last long."

"When winter comes, do you think the glacier will seal off the cave again?"

"No. It's been slowly receding for the past seventy-five years. In another thousand years or so, the entire entrance will probably be exposed."

"What happens with the cave now?"

"This is federal land, so it's the Feds' call, but the last I heard NASA is sending a team of scientists here. They're going to try to modify one of their robot explorers, then lower it down there to have a look-around with a TV camera. I wish them lots of luck. We've got seismic readings showing there are hundreds of miles of caves honeycombing not only that mountain, but the two on either side of it as well, and they're all interconnected. The system may be bigger than Carlsbad Caverns and Mammoth Caves combined. We may never know what killed those people. The Rangers went down there loaded for bear, with everything from gas masks and oxygen tanks to machine guns; the problem is that whatever it is down there killing people isn't a bear." The trooper paused, looked hard at Brendan. "You're Brendan Furie, aren't you? The man they call Priest."

"I'm not a priest," Brendan replied, making no effort to mask his surprise.

"But you used to be. You were excommunicated for some reason. I'll bet the Church fathers are sorry about that now."

"Somehow, I doubt it. How do you know who I am?"

"You're very modest, Furie. There's been a lot written about you. You work now as a private investigator."

"I investigate sometimes, privately, but I'm not a private investigator in the usual sense. I do a lot of work for social agencies, private, state, and federal, and for a private foundation that studies human belief systems."

"You search for troubled children."

"Sometimes for troubled children, but there are a lot of troubled adults, too. The things that people believe sometimes get them into a lot of trouble, and I'm occasionally hired to get them out of it."

"I'm Philip Imukpak," the Eskimo said, removing a glove and extending his hand. "I'm pleased to meet you, Furie. You do good work."

"Not always," Brendan said quietly as he shook the trooper's hand, and then glanced back at the black gash between ice and rock.

"I take it you're here looking for somebody. You need help?"

"No. I found who I was looking for yesterday—a nineteen-year-old boy by the name of Hector Martinez." He paused, swallowed hard. "He stole some equipment, tied a rope onto one of the pitons left in the rock, and went into the cave last night."

"Oh, Jesus," the trooper said softly. "I'm sorry to hear that."

"Yeah. It's my fault."

"That sounds like a pretty heavy load to put on yourself, Furie."

"But it's a true load. We had a conversation yesterday, and it went badly. I botched it."

"It still sounds like a pretty heavy load to put on yourself."

Brendan took his gaze from the cave entrance and looked into the other man's face. What he saw there was decency, honesty, and courage. He liked and trusted the face with its soulful brown eyes; it was a face to which he could confess, and so he said, "Hector's a diagnosed manic-depressive, severely emotionally disturbed. I've known him for years, from a shelter for runaway children where I serve as a counselor. He always resisted taking the medication that would help him, and so he would suffer psychotic episodes and have fantasies that only reinforced his decision not to take his medication. Three weeks ago his mother died, and his father hired me to try to find him, give him the bad news, and then once again try to get him to come home and get the proper treatment. One of his strongest fantasies has always been that the world was going to end any day, and that he would get to meet Jesus. When I read about this cave, and heard that Dylan Parker was here on another one of his end-of-the-world vigils, I

208

had a pretty good idea I'd find Hector here. I was right. I gave him the bad news, but I didn't get him to go home. I was tired, and I got impatient. I should have handled it differently."

"It sounds to me like he might have gone down into the cave anyway."

"No. He was willing to wait for Jesus to come out. He's gone down there to meet his dead mother. It's why I have to go down after him."

The trooper was silent for some time, studying Brendan's face. Finally he said carefully, "You want to die because you think you made a mistake?"

"I don't want to die; I don't plan to die."

"That sounds like a belief that could get you into a lot of trouble."

"It's something I have to do," Brendan said quietly.

Again, the Eskimo was silent for some time as he stared into Brendan's midnight eyes. Finally he nodded, said, "Yes. I can see that. When do you plan to go?"

"Now."

"Have you ever done any rock climbing or caving?"

"No."

"Do you have any equipment?"

"The rope Hector used is still attached to the piton. I was hoping to borrow or buy whatever else I might need from the other people around here."

"Come with me, Furie."

Brendan followed Philip Imukpak across the width of the glacier, past pup tents and sleeping bags and lean-tos and the blank-faced people who occupied them, to the Quonset hut. The layout inside the metal dome was simple, with wooden slats for floorboards, three kerosene heaters strategically placed at intervals around the perimeter, three cots draped with thick down sleeping bags, an electric generator, and a butane cooking stove on which a pot of coffee simmered. In one corner was a mound of dun-colored equipment—canvas bags, ropes, chain, battery powered lanterns and flashlights, automatic weapons.

209

"This is extra equipment the Rangers left behind," the trooper continued. "I'll show you how to use it. I don't think you'll want to lug everything. The Rangers went down loaded to the ears and armed to the teeth, and it doesn't seem to have done them much good. I suggest you travel light in order to conserve energy."

"Agreed," Brendan said, and watched as Philip Imukpak began to remove various pieces of climbing equipment from the bags and spread them out over the makeshift floor. He was struck again by how much he instinctively liked and trusted this man, who was willing to offer so much help and ask so few questions. He continued, "I told you I didn't handle this business with Hector well. I made a similar mistake once before. I bungled an exorcism.

The trooper stopped what he was doing, glanced up at Brendan. He was too polite to laugh, but curiosity mixed with amusement was clearly reflected in his dark brown eyes. "You bungled an *exorcism?"*

Brendan smiled thinly. "In a manner of speaking, yes. I agree it sounds funny; it would be funny if a woman hadn't died as a result of things I did - - and didn't - - do. It's why I was excommunicated."

The laughter left the other man's eyes. "I'm sorry."

Brendan nodded curtly. "The lesson is that you shouldn't do things you don't believe in."

"Did you believe then?"

"No; not in demonic possession—and so I didn't believe in exorcism.

"Then why did you do it?"

"I was ordered to. I should have refused, but I didn't. It was Church politics. The girl I was supposed to exorcise was the daughter of a very wealthy and powerful man. She was another runaway, staying at the shelter where I counsel. The father gave a great deal of money to the Church, and played golf every week with the cardinal of our archdiocese. The girl's story was that her father's closest business associate, who also happened to be her mother's lover, was repeatedly raping her. The father just couldn't accept this; it was impossible for him to accept that all of this

210

could be happening right under his nose, and so he decided that his daughter must be possessed in order to make up such a story. He asked his friend the Cardinal to arrange for an exorcism. The Cardinal was no fool; he knew he could never get Rome to approve the procedure and send one of their trained exorcists based on the evidence that was presented, and so he pressured me into doing it, simply to mollify the father. I investigated, determined that the girl was telling the truth, and I went to the mother to offer her my help in straightening out the mess. Big mistake. I didn't handle that conversation any better than I handled the one with Hector. The mother ended up killing herself rather than face what she thought would be the shame and humiliation of having the truth come out."

Philip Imukpak made a sound that was somewhere between a sigh and a hum. "Rome needed someone to blame, and you were it."

"Something like that. They weren't wrong. The point is that if that woman had disappeared into a cave instead of jumping off the roof of their mansion, I'd have gone after her, too."

"You got the short end of the stick."

"On the contrary. Now I consider my excommunication a great gift. It changed my life for the better, and I'm grateful I've had the opportunity to do some of the things I've done—except for times like yesterday. If Hector is dead, at least maybe I'll be able to recover his body and take it back to his father."

The trooper simply nodded, then went about instructing Brendan in the use of the bosun's chair and other equipment laid out on the floor. When he had finished, he helped Brendan put on back and chest packs, and the rigging he would use to lower himself to the cave floor. Brendan gripped the other man's shoulders and nodded, then headed for the door.

"You want company?"

Surprised as much by the trooper's casual tone as by the question itself, Brendan paused in the doorway of the Quonset hut, turned back. The Eskimo had picked up a pack and coil of rope, and was looking at Brendan inquiringly.

"What?"

211

"Do you want me to go with you?"

"I don't understand. You're convinced I'm going to die. Why should you be willing to die with me?"

"I'm not convinced you're going to die. And you are a man I would go into those caves with, Priest."

Brendan was silent for some time, staring at the other man. Finally he said, "That's the finest compliment I've ever received, Philip. Thank you."

Imukpak grinned, revealing bright, even white teeth. "Of course, I'm also curious."

Brendan grinned back. "Well, that's understandable."

"My curiosity is a bit more involved than you may think. We Inuit have a very curious Creation myth. It concerns a species of godlike creatures we call the Givers. Actually, the Givers were somewhat flawed gods—not very pleasant to be around. They rounded us up, used us as beasts of burden, and even ate us. The Givers had already lived for millions of years before the Inuit came into being, building a great city inside mountains that were near a volcano—a kind of underground Garden of Eden, if you will. They survived through many ice ages inside those mountains. But then the volcano died, and the Givers died with it when the ice and snow came again. But we didn't die. The Inuit could live in the cold, using the things we had learned from the Givers to survive right up to the present day."

Brendan turned around, gazed across the ice sheet toward the rock face and the entrance to the cave. "That mountain's an extinct volcano?"

"Not that one. But the one behind it is. Interesting, no?"

Brendan turned back. "Your reason doesn't sound as good as mine."

Imukpak thought about it, then shrugged and dropped the pack and coil of rope to the floor. "You're probably right. Good luck, Priest."

"I'll let you know what I find," Brendan said, and thought now as he walked in the direction of the boy's answering shouts that Philip Imukpak, and not a few other people, would be more than a little interested in what was in the caves.

He found Hector Martinez in what could only be described as a chapel, sitting on a stone bench. Strewn about him were dead batteries. The faint glow from his flashlight was just barely enough to illuminate the mummified remains of what could only be a Giver priest slumped over the raised stone rectangle of what could only be an altar. Brendan went to the boy, and they embraced. Then Brendan set out four flares, which were sufficient to light the entire chamber. He turned off his lantern, sat down next to the boy, and put his arm around him. "I'm so sorry about your mother, Hector."

Tears sprang to the boy's eyes, rolled down his cheeks. "Yeah. Me too. I'm really happy to see you, Priest."

"And I'm really happy to see you." Brendan paused, smiled at the boy, and added carefully, "From the looks of all the extra batteries you brought with you, I'd say you weren't all that certain you wanted to die just yet. Also, you left your cap to show which cave you'd gone into. Am I right in assuming that you might want to live a little bit longer—or at least not die down here?"

Hector Martinez slowly nodded his head. He seemed transfixed by the figure on the altar, and by the myriad of paintings and stone sculptures illuminated by the flares. "What were those... things... that came after me?"

"If you're referring to those big, black, ugly critters back by the entrance, my guess is that they're mutated bats—carnivores. They're a hell of a lot bigger than any of the other animals I've seen down here, so they must be at the top of the food chain. That means there aren't too many of them, and they're probably normally scattered all over the place. When people started coming down here, it was like the call went out, 'Look what's coming for dinner,' and they started congregating around the entrance to wait for their next meal to drop in. It's possible you and I got through because they're pretty full right now, and not as aggressive—or hungry, or as numerous as they were when the others went down. In any case, they can be handled if we keep our eyes and ears open.

213

They're blind, but they must have residual photoreceptors in their skulls because they don't like it when you shine a bright light on their heads. If all else fails, I have a gun and lots of ammunition with me."

The boy slowly looked around him, then again fastened his gaze on the mummified priest, shuddered. "It's horrible."

"Horrible? I think this is a pretty cool place."

The boy looked at Brendan, laughed nervously. "That's only because you're pretty cool."

"Hector," Brendan said seriously, "these caves are a place of wondrous mystery, and what's to be found here will change the world forever."

"How could it be, Priest? How could this *place* be?"

"At the bottom of the ocean there are animals, giant tube-worms and blind crabs, that thrive in very small areas around volcanic vents erupting from the ocean floor. They live solely on the warmth and nutrients that spew out of the vents, without benefit of sunlight or any other food. There's also an ancient rock structure, called the Burgess Shale, where there are the fossil remains of millions and millions of tiny, wondrous creatures that all lived, evolved, and finally became extinct, all in an area of a few square miles at most. These species existed over millions of years in that one area, and no trace of them has ever been found anywhere else. Now think of what you have down here; it's the Burgess Shale phenomenon magnified thousands of times, and it's still alive. You have a living ecosystem, an entire world that has evolved over millions of years and is still evolving, in the total absence of photosynthesis. *That,* my friend, is truly remarkable— miraculous, if you will. My guess is that the energy source for the system comes from a volcano near here that isn't as dead as the people on the top floors think. It supplies warmth and nutrients for the creatures and plants at the bottom of the food chain, which in turn are eaten by the bigger guys. There are chemical processes down here we've never seen before in nature. There will be new medicines, maybe a cure for cancer—or even the common cold— derived from the vegetation that grows here."

214

The boy raised a hand that trembled slightly, pointed at the dead priest on the altar. "What about that? What about *them?*"

"What about them?"

"They used us like animals."

"First of all, Hector, don't jump to conclusions about what you've seen down here. These caves are millions of years old, and the creatures that are going about their business now are only the latest inhabitants. There have probably been all sorts of species, including Neanderthals, Cro-Magnon, and early humans, who have called these caves home at one time or another, but they didn't all live here at the same time. Then the last ice age, or even the one before it, came. The glacier sealed off the cave entrance, and the things that are here now began to evolve."

"But those things and humans lived at the same time. You saw the paintings and the carvings in the rock. They kept us. They *ate* us."

"So what? So do lions, tigers, and sharks."

"It's different."

"No, it's not. We eat other animals, like whales and porpoise, that, in their own way, may be as intelligent as we are—or close to it."

"But how could *they* have existed, and accomplished what they did, without our finding out about them before now?"

"Remember the lesson of the Burgess Shale, Hector."

"These things had language, art, and writing. They kept us as *slaves*. How could they only have existed here? They walked on two legs, and they were smart."

"Ah, but they were also cold blooded—at least the guy laid out on the stone over there looks pretty cold blooded to me. They couldn't survive—or at least couldn't function effectively for any extended period of time—away from the warmth that was radiated throughout those caves by the volcano. That, or they may have lacked one ingredient of consciousness that led our species to scatter ourselves all over the world: human curiosity. These caves were the entire world, and they simply may not have *cared* what went on beyond it. There's no other trace of them to be found

215

anywhere else over the tens of thousands, or even millions, of years of their existence, because they never *went* anywhere else. They were the ultimate home-bodies, Hector."

The boy was silent for some time, and then asked, "What do you suppose happened to the Army Rangers?"

"I haven't the slightest idea. We may never know—or they may pop out of these caves next week, or even be waiting for us right now up above. They went a different way, and we don't know what they found, or what found them. This is truly a different world, and there are probably hundreds of ways to die down here that we can't even imagine; it's no different from what could happen to some Amazon pygmy suddenly dropped into Times Square. What would he or she know about cars and trucks, or muggers, or Saturday Night Specials, or traffic lights?"

Hector Martinez looked into the face of the tall, powerfully built man sitting beside him. "None of this bothers you, does it?"

"What's to bother me? I'm alive; even more important, I found you alive. Now, *there's* a sign."

"How could God have created Man in His image, and then created *those* . . . things to do all of the things we did, and eat us besides?"

"Let me tell you a little personal secret, Hector. I've always considered it a rather curious conceit for a species as brutal and cruel, insensitive, and occasionally downright stupid as humans to presume that God would create *them,* of all things, in His image. If that were true, then we'd *really* be in trouble."

"Then why did you become a priest in the first place?"

"It seemed like a good idea at the time. Then I needed to express what I'm not content merely to continue to feel—a sense of awe, of breathlessness at the world, and the gift to me of my presence in it. The basic lesson of all of humankind's sacred texts is that humans invariably create all of our gods at least with our mindsets and prejudices, if not always in our image. They don't glorify God, they diminish Him. God can only be an infinitely wondrous, and ultimately unknowable, mystery—like these caves."

"Jesus looked like us; He was one of us. You don't believe Jesus could have been God's Son?"

"Look, Hector, I'm not going to tell you any more about what I do or don't believe when it comes to faith in the supernatural. It's irrelevant, and it wouldn't do you any good. What I believe has changed before, and it will probably change again—evolving under the pressure of sunlight, rain, wind, love, hate, fear, observation, and reason. So I'm not going to tell you what to believe. But I am going to caution you to be *careful* what you choose to believe, because you become what you believe. What's important is that you realize what's being offered to you now, perhaps by God, at this moment. These caves are a tomb for a species that came before us, enslaved us when we came on the scene, and probably taught us a great deal. Let this place also be a tomb for your past life, for the beliefs and behavior that initially brought you down here to die. There's an awesome amount of work to be done down here, and generations of scientists are going to spend lifetimes doing it, poking around and discovering the secrets of this place. Whole new sciences are going to be born. Be a part of it."

"I don't have any training."

"Get some. In four years, or however long it takes you to get an appropriate degree and training, they'll barely have scratched the surface of this world. People will *want* you to be a part of it. You have a franchise: a kind of spiritual survivor to religious people all over the world, of whatever faith—because I assure you there are going to be lots of folks who are going to be extremely upset by what's been discovered down here. You can assure them that it's not-if you'll pardon the expression—the end of the world. You'll be able to afford to do anything you want. There'll be book and movie offers, and it wouldn't surprise me to hear that some William Morris agent tries to book a dogsled team minutes after word of our return gets out. You're going to be a very wealthy young man."

"What about you, Priest?"

217

"I make all the money I need doing what I like to do. I don't need the distraction. It's your opportunities we're talking about. You were waiting for a Second Coming, Hector; let it be yours. Be something different when you leave here."

The boy looked at Brendan, his dark eyes now filled with hope—but also fear. "But how do we get out? How can we get past those bats, or whatever they are?"

"No problem."

"No problem?"

"They may be a lot bigger, blinder, and meaner than your average bat, but they still must function with sonar capabilities. We're going to scramble their screens, jam their radar. First, we're going to load our packs with your dead batteries and lots of stones. Then we're going to be *very* cautious walking back. When we get to the big dome at the cave entrance, I'm going to stay up on the ledge and throw batteries and stones all around to distract them while you climb down, scamper across the floor to the rope, and climb out. When you get to the top, you'll return the favor. Then, when we're out of here, you and I and a certain Alaska state trooper who's waiting for me are going to that native village and probably spend half of your movie money for a good hot meal. Simple. You ready?"

Hector Martinez threw back his head and laughed loudly - but there was no hysteria in the echoing sound, only excitement and joy. Finally he stopped, slowly shook his head, and put out his hand. "I hope you brought my lithium with you, Priest. I'm going to be needing a little emotional pick-me-up if I see one of those black things lumbering after me, so I may as well start taking it right now."

MODEL TOWN

"Should I call you Father?"

"No. My name is Brendan Furie."

Father Gary Walsh smiled shyly, shifted in the chair behind the small desk in his small, bare office, then ran his hand back through his thick brown hair, which he wore in a blow-dried pompadour that made him look even younger than his twenty-four years. "Word's gotten around since you've been in town. I heard you used to be a priest, but you were excommunicated. Now you're a private investigator working on some special assignment."

"I think your story is far more interesting, Father Walsh. That's what we're here to talk about."

The young curate flushed. "Of course. I didn't mean to pry. He abruptly rose and stuck out a pink, pudgy hand, continued, "Call me Father Gary. Everybody does."

"Pleased to meet you, Father Gary. I appreciate your cooperation. You seem nervous. There's no need."

"I'm not nervous," the other man said quickly, dropping rather than sitting back down in his chair.

"Okay. That's good."

"I'm just kind of puzzled that Father Reilly would allow you to interview me—I mean, he made it plain that I should answer all your questions."

"Father Reilly was the first person I interviewed a week ago. I've also interviewed twenty-four of your parishioners who have seen the weeping Madonna, or had other miraculous experiences."

"There are a lot more than twenty-four."

"It's a sufficient number for the statistical sample I need. Since all of the unusual occurrences that have happened in

219

Craiggville in the past three months began with you, I figured I'd end with you. Why are you puzzled?"

Again the curate shifted in his chair, fidgeted with his Roman collar. "It was Father Reilly, on the orders of the bishop, who told me to stop talking to the press. The bishop himself turned down an offer by one of those psychic researchers to come in and try to prove that the incidents were either really miracles or a hoax."

"It's not my task to prove or debunk anything, Father Gary. I do field research for a group that's studying human behavior in response to extraordinary events like the things that have happened here. I make no judgments on the events themselves, which is probably why your bishop and senior pastor agreed to cooperate. You shouldn't take their previous actions personally. You have to understand that, from the Church's point of view, the question of miracles puts them in a no-win situation. If the Church officially declares some incident to be a miracle and it turns out to be fake, the Church looks ridiculous; if they declare something a hoax, it discourages the faithful who may have come back to the Church because of what they perceive to be miracles. Usually the Church takes no position, which is the case here. I'm allowed to interview the people who believe, but I can make no pronouncement on the belief itself."

"They've already discouraged and driven away the faithful," Gary Walsh said, a trace of bitterness creeping into his high-pitched voice. "In the first few weeks after the miracles first began there were thousands of people flocking to Craiggville every weekend. There wasn't enough room for everybody at each Mass, and we had to install loudspeakers on the front lawn and in the parking lot. One weekend we had more than ten thousand people come here, and there were traffic jams on every road and highway in all directions. That was when the bishop ordered the publicity blackout. Now we're just about back to where we were before—a dying town with only maybe a quarter of the pews filled for Sunday Mass. When God shows us a sign, you'd think the Church would want the whole world to know."

220

Brendan studied the other man—who seemed to be having trouble meeting his gaze—for a few moments, and then said in a flat tone, "You do seem to be taking it personally. In the last two centuries the Church has officially recognized only a dozen weeping Madonnas and visions of Mary. New Jersey has more than that in a year."

Now the priest looked at Brendan out of the corner of his eye. "What did he say?"

"Who?"

"Father Reilly."

"Among other things, he said that the Madonna here in your church now weeps so much that he has to have a maintenance worker mop up the floor every morning."

"Did he say anything about me?"

"What people tell me is held in strictest confidence, Father. I probably shouldn't have shared with you what I just did."

"But everybody knows that that Madonna weeps all the time."

"Indeed."

"You can see for yourself."

"I have."

Father Gary Walsh swallowed hard, licked his lips, and then said, "Okay, what do you want to ask me?"

Brendan opened the briefcase he carried, took out a small tape recorder and a five-page questionnaire, placed the items on the desk in front of the curate. "Actually, I'd prefer not to ask you much of anything. I'd like you to fill out this questionnaire, and then I'd like you to relate your story into the tape recorder. You can take as much time as you like."

Walsh nodded, reached out and pulled the questionnaire toward him. Brendan sat down in the only other chair in the room, leaned back, crossed his legs and waited as the other man leafed through the questionnaire.

"Some of this stuff is really personal," the young priest said, his face reddening. "In fact, I'd have sinned if I'd done some of these things.

221

"All of us have sinned, Father, and there's no admission you can make on that form that will threaten your mortal soul. I guarantee your privacy. You'll be assigned a code number, and your name will not appear on any report. It's important that you answer all the questions. If you can't do that, I'd prefer to end the interview now"

"I have to do it," the other man mumbled. "Father Reilly made it clear that I should cooperate."

"What is said or written in this room is between you and me."

Walsh shook his head, then hunched his shoulders and began to rapidly check off the boxes on the questionnaire. When he had finished he shoved the form to the edge of the desk. Brendan rose, slipped the questionnaire into his briefcase, then turned on the recorder and sat back down. He waited as the priest stared at the recorder. Walsh cleared his throat several times, but said nothing.

"Father Gary. . . ?

"It's... uh. . . it's kind of hard to get started."

Brendan uncrossed his legs and leaned forward in the chair, resting his elbows on his knees. "Father Gary;" he said in a neutral tone, "about three months ago you walked into this church and saw the Madonna in the apse outside the sanctuary weeping. The statue is still weeping—literally in buckets. Since that time you've suffered stigmata twice.

"The Madonna in your parents' home weeps; in fact, there are weeping Madonnas everywhere you go. Since that first incident you've performed dozens of healings, and dozens of others have been performed in your name. People all over town have seen visions of Mary, and two families have seen the sun begin to spin and radiate all the colors of the rainbow. There have also been six murders, three times the number Craiggville has had in the past decade, and a rash of teenage suicides. Considering—"

"The murders and suicides can't have anything to do with the signs from God!"

"—all that's happened since you saw the first weeping Madonna, I would think you could spend hours recollecting your experiences and feelings."

"It's . . . just kind of hard. Maybe you could ask me questions?"

"All right. Tell me how it began."

"I came into church one morning and saw the Madonna weeping," the priest replied, averting his gaze.

"And?"

"I went to Father Reilly and brought him back to see it. He didn't know what to make of it. Then it happened again the next day."

"And you began to suffer stigmata."

"Yes."

"It happened twice. The last time, your palms started bleeding when you were giving a homily before your congregation."

"Yes."

"And?"

The curate shrugged. "Word got out. Reporters started showing up to interview me, and then thousands of people started coming to town to see the weeping Madonna."

"And then the Madonna in your parents' home began to weep. And then there were others. It seems that everywhere you went, you would cause Madonnas to start weeping."

"Yes."

"And?"

"Then Father Reilly told me that the bishop disapproved of all the attention we were getting, that it was unhealthy. I can't imagine why he thought that. I was to stop giving interviews, and I was temporarily suspended from assisting in the Mass. Without the publicity, we didn't get the same number of people coming to town and Mass."

"But the Madonnas continue to weep."

"Yes."

Brendan Waited, but the young priest with the pompadour continued to stare at the top of his desk in silence. "That's it? That's all you have to say?"

Gary Walsh nodded.

"All right, Father Gary;" Brendan continued as he rose, shut off the tape recorder and put it back into his briefcase. "Thank you for your time."

Suddenly Walsh looked up, and Brendan was surprised to see what looked like fear in the other man's eyes. "Brendan?"

"What is it, Father?"

"Can I talk to you?"

Brendan suppressed a smile. "Of course. That's precisely what I've been trying to get you to do, Father."

The priest pointed to Brendan's half-open briefcase. "Without . . . that."

"Is it personal, or does it have something to do with what's happened in Craiggville?"

"It's . . . uh, both."

"Then I'd like to tape what you have to say;"

"Do you have to?"

"If it has to do with what are perceived as these miracles, yes? That's why I'm here, Father. It's my job."

"But you did say it would be confidential."

"Absolutely."

"Like confession."

"No, Father, not like confession. The tapes won't have the legal shield enjoyed by confession, but I don't see how that would be relevant. I guarantee your privacy. The tape will be transcribed into a written report that's correlated to the answers on your questionnaire. Then your name disappears. Certain people who occasionally check the accuracy of my work may hear your voice, but they wont know who you are."

The young priest's face had gone pale. He licked his lips as he thought about it, and then finally nodded. Brendan took out the tape recorder again, turned it on and put it back on the desk. Gary Walsh rose, walked to the far end of the room and bowed his head

224

slightly. He took a deep breath, and then said to the wall, "Craiggville is very economically depressed."

"I know," Brendan replied evenly;

"Coal mining is virtually our only industry. We were doing just fine up to a couple of years ago, until new EPA laws went into effect. The coal that comes from here has too high a sulfur content to meet the new environmental standards, so the mines were shut down. Hundreds of people lost jobs. When their unemployment benefits ran out, they had to go on welfare. There was no money to support the other businesses in town, so they began to fail. People were losing their faith."

"So you decided to do something about it."

"God decided to do something about it!" Walsh said in a voice that had suddenly become clear and loud. He abruptly turned to face Brendan. His eyes had grown bright. "I had a dream, Brendan. I've never had a dream like it before—it was so clear, so real. God spoke to me in that dream. He told me He wanted to send a sign to the people of Craiggville to give them hope and bolster their faith, and I was to be His messenger.

"So you faked the tears on the Madonna."

"No!" the curate exclaimed, shaking his head so hard that his hair fell around the sides of his face. Color rose in his cheeks. "You can't call something which is God's will 'fake'!"

"You put water in the Madonna's eyes and on her face because God told you to."

"Yes."

"How many times?"

"Only twice. After that, God provided the signs Himself"

"What about your stigmata? Did God tell you to use phony blood?"

"It was real blood. I cut myself with broken glass. But then other people around here began to exhibit genuine stigmata."

"The healings?"

"They really happened. I know these people, and they were sick. They came to me for help. I put my hands on them, and they got better. I swear I'm telling you the truth, Brendan."

225

"I believe you, Father," Brendan said quietly; turning off the recorder and replacing it in his briefcase, which he snapped shut.

"Brendan . . ."

"Is there something else, Father Gary?"

The curate walked closer to Brendan, said in a small voice, "It isn't working out like it was supposed to."

"How was it supposed to work out?"

"At the beginning, things went just the way God said they would. The church was full every Sunday; People came to town and spent money; God had smiled on us. Then the bishop and Father Reilly discouraged people from thinking these were really miracles. They rejected God's signs, and now God has turned His face from us again."

"I'm not the one to talk to about that, Father."

"You're well known. People trust you. If you were to say that you believed most of the miracles were real, then people would—"

"I can't do that, Father Gary;"

"Why not? I swear it's the truth. The Madonna here is still weeping. You've seen it."

"God spoke to you, Father Gary; not me. I can't tell people what to believe or not to believe. All I can do is my job, and part of that job is not expressing opinions on the events I observe, or intervening in any other way; You have to find your own way to deal with the forces you've unleashed, good or bad."

The priest sighed, then turned and went back to his desk, where he sat and put his face in his hands. Brendan stepped forward and put his hand on the man's shoulder, then turned and walked from the office, closing the door behind him.

Marla was waiting for him in the sanctuary. The six-foot, statuesque blond woman with the velvety brown eyes was standing in a side aisle, head tilted back and hands clasped behind her back as she studied a stained-glass depiction of one of the Stations of the Cross. In her short, plaid skirt and yellow blouse, she looked like a

226

college student, giving no indication of the deadly skills she possessed.

Someone else was also waiting for him. Father John Reilly, a balding, portly; kind-faced man who was perhaps in his mid-fifties, rose from the front pew where he had been sitting as Brendan entered the sanctuary through a door next to the altar.

"Brendan, may I speak with you?"

"Of course, Father," Brendan replied, smiling as he motioned for the priest to sit back down. Then he sat beside him. "What can I do for you?"

"I'd like your advice."

Brendan turned to look at the other man, who was staring straight ahead of him at a crucifix affixed to the wall behind the altar. "I can't imagine what useful advice I could give you," he said quietly;

"I've known you only a week, Brendan, but you still seem like a priest to me."

"I take that as a compliment. Thank you, Father."

"A very good priest. I can't imagine why you were excommunicated."

Brendan did not reply;

"Brendan, Craiggville is a very troubled town. Some of the things that have happened here aren't good."

"No. Murder and suicide are certainly never good."

"Do you think miracles have really occurred here in Craiggville?"

"I can't answer that, Father."

"But you have an opinion?"

"I'm not allowed to have an opinion on that."

"I don't know what to do, Brendan. Things have gotten out of hand. I feel like I'm caught in the middle between very powerful opposing forces."

"The middle isn't where you should be, Father. You have to lead. I think people are waiting to see what you say and do. Silence isn't a viable option."

"I don't know how to lead, Brendan. On the one hand I have a young priest who makes statues weep wherever he goes, and on the other I have a Church hierarchy which just wants the whole thing to go away; They're scared to death that all this talk of miracles will blow up in the Church's face. But what if these things are miracles, signs from God of His presence? How can we ignore them? Is it right to encourage people not to believe in miracles?"

"I don't see the point."

Now the priest turned to look at Brendan, frowned slightly; "I don't understand."

"There are millions of weeping children all over the world, Father. I've seen more than my share of them. They're not made of plaster. They weep from hunger, pain, disease, and terror."

"Then you don't believe the things that have happened here are miracles?"

"I didn't say that, Father."

"You don't seem impressed."

"On the contrary; I'm very impressed by the events in Craiggville. But if God were to send us a sign of His or Her presence, I would have preferred manna from heaven, food and medicine for those children, not tears on statues. I would have preferred She sent us a cure for AIDS."

The older man stared at Brendan for some time, and then his oval face broke into a smile. "I think you've given me the subject for next Sundays homily;"

"I'm sorry I can't be in town to hear it."

"I—"

"Brendan Furie?"

"Excuse me for interrupting, Father. I need to speak with this man."

Brendan looked up at the group of men who had suddenly appeared in front of them. The man who had spoken and who seemed to be their leader was in his late thirties or early forties, lean, just under six feet, with hard gray eyes. He wore boots and matching khaki shirt and trousers. He wore his hair combed and

228

slicked over the bald patch on top of his head. He had thin lips, and the rosy nose of a heavy drinker.

"Pardon me, Brendan," John Reilly said in a low voice, then abruptly rose and walked quickly away without making any introductions.

"You are Brendan Furie," the man with the hard eyes said.

"Yes," Brendan replied evenly.

"I'm Frank York. I'm a lay deacon of this church. These are friends of mine."

Brendan rose to shake Frank York's hand; he glanced over the man's shoulder to see that Marla had turned and was watching them. A little girl who was perhaps four or five sat very stiffly; hands clasped tightly in her lap, in the first pew across the aisle. The child was dressed neatly in a white dress and saddle shoes, but there were Band-Aids on both legs and a smudge on her left cheek that might be a bruise. "What can I do for you, Mr. York?"

"I hear you've been asking people about the miracles that have been happening around here." The man had a rasping quality to his voice that Brendan found unpleasant.

"You heard right, Mr. York."

"Some people say you're famous."

"Do they? I can't imagine why;"

"What are you doing here?"

"I was talking to Father Reilly;"

"I mean, what are you doing in Craiggville? Why are you asking questions?"

"I'm conducting a research survey of people's reactions to the weeping Madonna."

Movement across the aisle caught Brendan's eye, and he glanced in that direction and was surprised to see the little girl, unbidden, get up and walk over to where Marla was standing. She said something to Marla, and the blond woman picked the child up in her arms and began to gently caress the girl's bruised cheek. York turned, flushed angrily; "Hey, you!" he shouted. "That's not your kid! Put her down!"

229

Marla hesitated, then hugged the girl and put her back on the floor. Clearly frightened, the child ran back to her place, where she sat and once again clasped her hands in her lap.

"I want you to talk to me and my friends, Furie," Frank York continued, turning back to Brendan. "We've got lots of stories to tell you about the miracles. As a deacon, I spend a lot of time here in the church. One time I actually heard the Virgin sob and call out my name."

"That's very interesting, Mr. York. I'm sure all of you have fascinating stories to tell. There seem to be hundreds of people who live here or visited Craiggville who've seen the Madonna weep, or visions of the Virgin. I've already talked to a good number of them, and I have all the interviews I need. But I do appreciate your volunteering."

"You're going to get the word out, right? You'll be writing articles and telling reporters about the miracles that have happened here?"

"No, Mr. York. That isn't what I'll be doing."

The puzzled expression on York's face wrinkled into an angry frown. "Then what's the point of talking to people?"

"I'm involved in an academic survey," Brendan replied, glancing at his watch. "Excuse me. I have to be going."

He caught Marla's eye, and they walked quickly down the parallel aisles, meeting at the rear and exiting from the church together. Suddenly Brendan felt a hand grip his shoulder, and he was pulled around. He found himself staring into the angry face of Frank York, who was standing so close that Brendan could smell the morning beer on his breath. His friends were standing a few yards behind him, at the entrance to the church, looking thoroughly embarrassed.

"You can't just walk away from me like that, Furie! I wanted to tell you about the miracles I've witnessed! People around the world have a right to know what's happening here, and you're a big shot; people will listen to you!"

"I did walk away from you before, Mr. York," Brendan replied evenly; "and now I'm about to do it again."

Brendan started to turn away, and York grabbed the front of his shirt. "Listen, big shot—!"

It was all he managed to get out before Marla abruptly stepped forward and gripped his elbow with her fingertips, pressing into the nerve cluster there. Frank York's gray; angry eyes went wide with pain and surprise as his fingers, clutching Brendan's shirt, opened of their own accord. York cursed and tried to shove Marla away with his free hand. Marla's response was to grab that wrist and twist. Her face with its exquisite, chiseled features showed no emotion as York's mouth dropped open. As he started to go down to his knees, Marla shoved him back.

"Jesus," York said, cradling his twisted wrist as his gaze shifted back and forth between Marla and Brendan. "What is she, your bodyguard?"

"She's my arbiter of etiquette, and she doesn't like it when people put their hands on me. Try to have a nice day, Mr. York."

They drove out of town for lunch at a restaurant overlooking a lake they had come to enjoy, and then returned to their motel. Marla went to her room, and Brendan to his. He took out his laptop computer and began the task of assigning codes to the names on the questionnaires, then transferring the answers from the forms into the computer. When he had finished doing that, he would start doing the same with the tapes. He hoped to have most of his work done by midnight, so that he could go on to his next assignment with the paperwork for this one almost completed.

At four thirty there was a knock on the door. Brendan did not rise, for he assumed it was Marla, who would come in after she had knocked. When there was a second knock, Brendan got up and opened the door to find a man in a sheriff's uniform standing outside. He was a burly man, heavily muscled, and his two-tone blue uniform fit him tightly; He wore a trooper's hat low on his forehead, just above green eyes that were watchful but not hostile.

"You Brendan Furie?

"I am."

231

"I'm Sheriff Warwick. I'd like to talk to you. Would you mind coming back with me to the station house?"

"Actually, I would mind," Brendan said, moving out of the doorway and pointing to his computer and the forms and tapes piled beside it. "I'll be leaving tomorrow, and I have a great deal of work to finish up. What's the problem?"

"There's been a death."

Brendan frowned. "Who?"

"Father Reilly; It looks like a suicide. I understand you were among the last people to talk to him, which is why I'm here to talk to you.

Brendan felt his stomach muscles tighten as a wave of sadness washed through him. Something cold touched his heart. "Come in, Sheriff," he said, opening the door wider. The sheriff entered the room, and then turned when Marla suddenly appeared behind him in the doorway; "This is my associate, Marla," Brendan continued. "She's mute, but she'll answer any questions you may have in writing. As for me, I don't believe Father Reilly committed suicide. First of all, he's Catholic, and suicide is a mortal sin. When I last saw him, he was in a good mood and looking forward to preparing his homily for Sunday."

The sheriff took off his hat and nodded to Marla, then turned back to Brendan. "I don't believe he committed suicide either."

"When did it happen?"

"The coroner's guess is somewhere between eleven thirty and one thirty, just after you finished talking with him. You mind telling me where you were then?"

"Marla and I were having lunch at the Lakeside Inn. We got there about eleven forty-five. We were just leaving about one thirty.

"Witnesses?"

"Sure. There were about a dozen other diners, and the owner knows us. We've been eating lunch and dinner there all week."

232

The sheriff sighed, then reached up and ran a hand back through his short-cut brown hair. "Yeah, well, I didn't think there was much chance you did it, but I have to touch all the bases. You two are the only strangers in town."

Brendan pulled the chair out from under the tiny desk and motioned for the sheriff to sit down. The other man hesitated, and then did so. He looked tired. Brendan asked, "How was he killed, Sheriff?"

"He cut the end off an extension cord and stripped the wires. Then he plugged in the cord and put the wires in his mouth. Or it was made to look like that's what he did."

Brendan winced. "Why would you think there was any possibility that I killed him?"

"There was a note.

"Handwritten and signed?"

"Nah. Written on a typewriter. Whoever wrote it can't spell, and Father Reilly was a literary man. He didn't write it."

"What did the note say?"

"It kind of rambled, but the gist of it was that he'd been wrong to choke off publicity about the miracles. It said he'd been cooperating with the Antichrist and woman demon who'd come to town—which I assumed referred to the two of you. It said he understood now what God's purpose had been in providing the miracles, that God wanted Craiggville to become the Lourdes of America so that people from all over the world would come to Craiggville to be healed. Lourdes was spelled wrong, by the way;"

"It sounds like whoever killed Father Reilly may have a strong economic interest in getting a new wave of publicity for Craiggville."

The sheriff grunted. "That would include just about everyone in town. What were the two of you talking about this morning?"

"Father Reilly was very concerned about the atmosphere that has developed and events that have transpired since these so-called miracles started taking place."

The other man narrowed his eyes. "So-called?"

233

"Poor choice of words. I should have said apparent."

"How can they be 'so-called' or 'apparent'? Man, you've got statues all over town crying tears by the bucketful, people whose palms start bleeding spontaneously; and the healing of sick people through prayer. If these aren't miracles, what are?"

Brendan looked at Marla, who was leaning against the doorjamb, arms crossed over her chest, listening. She raised her eyebrows slightly and shrugged.

"You aren't one of the people I interviewed, Sheriff, so I can be a little more forthcoming with you. There are any number of ways to make a statue weep".

Now it was the sheriff's turn to raise his eyebrows. "You don't say?"

"I do say; You can smear cold grease, oil or lard, on the eyes, and the grease will begin to drip as it warms to room temperature. Calcium chloride will cause water vapor to condense. If you're mechanically minded and want to get fancy, you could run a tube up the inside of the statue, attach it to a small water pump behind a wall or under floorboards, and have your Madonna weep on cue. If you'd like, I'll introduce you to a physicist who'll explain to you in detail how he can make anything in sight start to shed water the moment he enters a room. A simple squirt gun will do the trick, especially if you're good at using the magician's trick of misdirection. Stigmata are easily faked—all you need is something sharp and a tolerance for pain, or even fake blood from a theatrical supply shop. There have been verified cases of actual stigmata and spiritual healings, but psychiatrists and other doctors will tell you these are examples of a phenomenon called psychogenesis, not miracles."

"Jesus," the other man said quietly;

"Jesus has nothing to do with it, Sheriff."

"How the hell do you know so much, Furie? Who are you working for?"

Once again Brendan glanced over at Marla, who this time gave him a nod of encouragement. Brendan turned back to the sheriff, said, "We work for a private foundation made up of

234

scientists, philanthropists, sociologists, and maybe one or two retired intelligence agents. These people think they have good reason to believe the human race will become extinct within the next few decades, probably before the middle of the next century".

"What? That's crazy;"

"Let's hope so. They base their opinions on a mathematical model that can track and project human behavior on a global scale—something like long-range weather prediction. According to their data, large masses of people all over the world will become increasingly anxious, tense, and irrational as the millennium nears. This spreading neurosis could, if their supercomputer knows what it's talking about, lead to mass hysteria and a sort of global nervous breakdown that will lead to mass destruction and death, most likely from new plagues that will ravage the planet when medical facilities break down. My job is to collect data from places where some form of mass hysteria has already taken place, or where lethal belief systems have taken shape. Their hope is to gather enough data to feed the equations, which in turn may spit out some solution to the problem, say a finely tuned psychological and educational program that can be used by national and world health organizations. That's the nickel tour of what I do and who I work for."

The burly sheriff sighed heavily, shook his head. "Well, you've certainly got a lot of craziness here—statues crying, the sun spinning, sightings of flying saucers, people killing each other, and kids killing themselves. And it seems to be getting worse, not better. People thinking and acting nutty because they believe God's rented a condo here, Or something. The other day I overheard two of my deputies talking about how maybe we didn't need law enforcement any longer because Jesus is coming back any day. How can I trust them to do their jobs? I'm afraid Father Reilly's death could lead to a lot more bad stuff, and I'm not sure how I can deal with it. I can't stay on duty twenty-four hours a day."

"If this town has a fever, maybe you have to lance the boil that's causing it," Brendan said carefully;

235

The other man blinked slowly; "What do you mean?"

"The fever started with the weeping Madonnas. Maybe you should look into that as a public health issue."

"You mean prove they're phony?"

"If they are phony;"

"But you believe they're phony;"

"I'll stand by what I said."

"You really think Father Gary has been faking all these weeping Madonnas? In case you didn't notice, he's not the brightest bulb in the hardware store. He grew up in this town, and he never much impressed anybody—not even when he came back here as a priest. Before this weeping Madonna and stigmata business, most people thought of him as a kind of joke in a clerical collar."

"I'm not offering up any suspects, Sheriff It's possible there's more than one person involved, and they're all operating independently of one another. They might even have different motives, but the majority, most likely, would have a vested interest in seeing Craiggville become the Lourdes of America mentioned in that suicide note we both agree is fake." Brendan paused, then continued. "Look, Sheriff, you'll never convince some people— sincere people—that every one of the incidents isn't a miracle, and these people will continue to be enraptured and unpredictable. But you might convince enough that what's happened here is earthbound, and the results demonstrably dangerous to the mental health of the community. They could convince others, and then the heated atmosphere around here might cool down."

"Why can't you issue a statement telling people what you just told me?"

"Because this isn't my town, these aren't my people, and it isn't my job. I've already been labeled the Antichrist, remember? This is your job, Sheriff Analyze some of the 'tears' from these weeping Madonnas, and I'll bet you any sum you like that you'll find they're common tap water. Check the faces for any residual traces of grease; take a couple of them apart and see what's inside. Investigate these so-called miracles, and you may even turn up

236

your killer along the way; You'll be working in an official capacity, investigating a suspicious death, so you won't need anyone's permission or cooperation."

"Jesus, Furie. People will hate me. They'll try to run me out of town. They want to believe."

Brendan sat down on the edge of the bed, spoke in a low, deliberate tone as he stared hard at the other man. "Listen to me carefully, Sheriff I can't be certain of it, but my guess is that the people I work for are going to be watching very carefully what happens here in Craiggville over the next few weeks and months. This town is a kind of model for what they believe is going to happen in other communities all over this country and the world as the millennium approaches. You no longer trust some of your own deputies to keep the peace because, in a virtually literal sense, their heads are in the clouds as they anticipate the Second Coming.

"We've already had a Secretary of the Interior who was giving away public lands because he thought Jesus' landing on earth was imminent. He may have been a harbinger of the future. How long before the people elect a president who may harbor the same beliefs and who thinks it may not be such a bad idea to lob a few nuclear warheads into trouble spots around the world so as to make Jesus' job easier when He does arrive?

"This is only one of dozens of scenarios produced by this mathematical model I mentioned. Impossible? My employers not only think it possible that something like this is going to happen, but probable, and they're putting their money where their minds are. They estimate it will take hundreds of millions of dollars to develop an educational program and train mental health officials to administer it in order to bring our species back from the abyss.

"But maybe they're wrong. Maybe all it takes in each community is a single person—someone like yourself—who is respected, clear-headed, and courageous enough to say that these miracles are only a miasma, and the real demons in our midst are the Bible- and Koran-thumping demagogues. I plan to include this conversation in my report—I have to. With your permission, and only with your permission, I'd like to identify you by name as the person I said these things to."

The sheriff was silent for some time. Finally he rose, put his hat back on his head. "I don't care what you put in your report, Furie. What I do care about is doing my job."

"An excellent response.

"There's one more base I have to touch, Furie. I know you interviewed Father Reilly at the beginning of the week. I'd like to hear what he had to say to you".

"There's nothing on that tape that will help you find his killer."

"I can't take your word for that."

Now Brendan rose to his feet, stiffened slightly. "I can't allow you to listen to the tape, Sheriff"

"Why not?"

"I guaranteed that whatever he said to me would be held in confidence.

"He's dead."

"His family, friends, and colleagues in the Church aren't, and he may not have wanted to share his thoughts on this matter with them. I assure you that nothing he said gave the slightest indication that he wanted to kill himself."

"I'll get a court order."

Brendan shrugged resignedly; "There's nothing I can do about that. Serve me with papers, and I'll have to play the tape for you. When you verify that I've told you the truth, I trust you'll respect his privacy."

"I'll be back in the morning," the sheriff said, moving toward the door as Marla stepped to one side. He paused in the doorway, turned back, continued quietly; "I'll give some thought to what you said, Furie."

Brendan nodded, and the other man walked quickly to his car. Marla smiled at Brendan, then left, closing the door behind her.

Brendan was deeply saddened by the death of Father John Reilly; but he forced himself to go back to work at the small desk in the motel room. He had made his way through about a third of the material when he glanced at his watch and found it was after seven, an hour past their regular dinnertime.

Normally, Marla would have come and gotten him. He turned off the computer, splashed his face and put on a clean shirt, jacket, and tie, then went out of the room. The first thing he noticed was that their car, which had been parked in front of Marla's room, was gone. When he knocked at her door, there was no answer. It was decidedly odd, he thought—odd that she would go anywhere without telling him, and even odder that she had not returned by dinnertime.

He was not overly concerned about her safety. The beautiful, silent, blond woman that the mysterious Mr. Lippitt, to whom Brendan reported, had assigned to travel with him was, he had discovered early on and to his considerable amazement, not only a judo master, but an expert with both knives and guns. He often wondered what her previous occupation had been, and how she had met Mr. Lipitt, but he had never inquired, one reason being that he suspected she would not tell him. He returned to his room and phoned for a pizza to be delivered, and then went back to work.

At ten fifteen there was a soft knock on the door. A moment later the door opened and Marla, dressed in black leather jacket and pants, entered the room.

"Marla. . . ."

The woman came over to him and squeezed his shoulder. She picked up his briefcase from the floor, took out the tape recorder and a questionnaire. She put the items into his hands, then motioned him toward the door.

"Marla, it's past ten o'clock at night. Where the hell do you want us to go?"

The woman's response was to gesture toward the door even more urgently; When Brendan did not move, she pulled him to his feet, smiled sweetly; and gave him a hard push. Shaking his head, Brendan walked from the room to their car, which was now parked outside his room.

In the six months they had worked together, the woman had already saved his life three times, and she was an expert at quickly shepherding him out of situations that threatened to grow ugly; but it was not for these reasons that Brendan was willing to go out with her at night on an unspecified task. Above all, he had come to trust Marla's instincts and judgment, and if she wanted him to come with her now, it was for a very good reason.

As always, Marla slipped behind the wheel. She drove them back into and through Craiggville, to a gas station and convenience store on the highway at the edge of town. She drove into the darkened parking area, stopped beside a gas pump and motioned for him to get out.

Now thoroughly puzzled, Brendan looked through the window, surveying the scene. Hung above the row of three outdated gas pumps was a freshly painted, hand-lettered sign that read,

MIRACLE GAS STATION AND CONVENIENCE STORE.

The prices posted on the pumps were about the same as at gas stations throughout the region, even a cent or two lower. But stacked haphazardly next to the pumps were other, crudely lettered signs with different prices indicating that, at some time in the past, this particular station had charged upward of fifty cents more per gallon. The owner had started to paint the exterior of the otherwise shabby convenience store, where signs advertising exorbitant prices had not been taken from the windows, but had apparently abandoned the job halfway through. Piled on the sidewalk outside were rain-soaked cartons of merchandise that had not been sold.

Marla reached over his shoulder and pointed off to his right, and then gave him a not-so-gentle nudge in the back. Brendan opened the door and got out, angling through the gas pump parking area toward the corner of the convenience store.

When he rounded the corner he could see light spilling from living quarters, little more than a shack, behind the store. He glanced down at the tape recorder he carried, and was surprised to

240

see that Marla had flipped a switch changing its recording mode from manual to voice-activated, which he never used.

He reached out to switch the mode back to manual, then dropped his hand back to his side. Hefting the recorder, which now felt like a weapon, in his palm, he walked up to the door.

He stiffened in alarm when he heard the screaming of a woman and the crying of a little girl coming from inside, then the harsh sound of a palm striking flesh. More screams. Brendan knocked hard on the door, and when the screaming and crying did not stop he began to pound.

Suddenly there was silence. The silence lasted almost half a minute, and then the door opened a crack to reveal the flushed, suspicious face of Frank York, who reeked of bourbon.

York blinked his bloodshot gray eyes a few times, and then recognition came. "What the hell do you want?" he growled, slurring his words.

"You said you wanted to be interviewed," Brendan replied evenly. "I'm here to interview you."

"It's eleven o'clock at night!"

Brendan glanced over the man's shoulder, and between the doorjamb and the man's head he could see the startled and terrified face of a woman whom he judged to be no more than middle-aged, although her hair was snow white. Her bruised face was puffy and streaked with tears, and one of her eyes was turning purple. Clinging to the woman's torn dress was the little girl Brendan had seen in the church.

"God doesn't keep a timetable," Brendan said, looking back into Frank York's face with its alcohol-ruptured veins.

"You comparing yourself to God?"

"I'm saying you're a man who claims he not only saw the Madonna weep, but heard her cry out and call your name. As I was sitting in my motel room, it occurred to me that this was just too important to leave out of my report. I have to leave town in the morning, so I came right over. Considering the sign God sent to you, I didn't think it would matter to you what time it was."

"How'd you find me?"

241

"I'm a crack private investigator," Brendan answered dryly.

York's bloodshot eyes opened and closed a few times while he thought about it. "Just a minute," he said, and closed the door.

Brendan heard him shouting at the woman and child, ordering them to leave the room, and a few seconds later the door opened again.

"C'mon in," York said, stumbling slightly as he moved to one side.

Brendan entered the cramped living room that smelled of cooking grease and body odor, stopped in the middle of the room.

"You're gonna' make sure people in the country hear about all the miracles happening here, aren't ya?" York continued.

"A report will be made, Mr. York."

"Why don't you sit down?"

"No, thank you. This won't take long. I don't want to take up any more of your time than is necessary;

York slumped in a torn, overstuffed chair, belched, and then reached out for a can of beer on a dust-streaked side table. "So, you want me to tell you how the Virgin talked to me?"

"First I want you to fill out this form," Brendan said, taking the questionnaire from his pocket and handing it to the other man. "When you finish, you can talk about your experiences into the tape recorder."

York took the five-page questionnaire and held it close to his face. His lips moved as he scanned the questions on the first page. He had read halfway through the second page when he suddenly looked up sharply; "What's all this business about bed-wetting, masturbation, and sexual fantasies? What the hell does that have to do with the Virgin talking to me?"

"I don't make up the questions, Mr. York."

"Yeah? Who does?"

"A team of psychologists and social scientists. They're quite insistent that anyone I interview completely fill out that questionnaire."

Frank York slowly and deliberately tore the form in half, dropped the pieces to the floor. "Well, you and your psychologists and social scientists know what you can do with this. I ain't answering none of these questions. I don't need you. By this time tomorrow night Craiggville's going to be in the news again. Everybody's gonna' want to know about the miracles happening here. There'll be television reporters all over the place, and then word will get out again."

Brendan felt a chill, and he stared hard at the other man. "Why is that, Mr. York? Why will reporters be coming to Craiggville tomorrow?"

York leered, revealing bad teeth. "You'll know soon enough, big shot. Wait'll you see the papers tomorrow."

"It doesn't make any difference whether you answer the questions or not, Mr. York," Brendan said quietly; putting the tape recorder in his pocket. "I realize now why I was sent here."

York frowned. "What do you mean, 'sent here'? Who sent you here?"

"I'm here to stop you from abusing your wife and child."
York's face darkened even more. He tipped over the can of beer, then lurched to his feet, where he swayed unsteadily; "You got a hell of a nerve, mister! My family ain't none of your business!"

"An abused child is everybody's business."

"I got a good mind to -."

"Shut up," Brendan said evenly; "Here's the drill. After I talk to your wife and daughter, I think they'll agree to come with me. There must be a woman's shelter somewhere in the county; if there isn't, I'll find someplace else to put them for the night. In the morning I'll make some calls and see if I can't arrange some help for all three of you."

"It'll be a cold day in hell before I let my wife and kid walk out of here with you. They won't want to."

"In that case, you're going to help me convince them that it's the right thing to do. Because, if you don't, I'm going to make sure that Frank York gets more publicity than he can handle. I'll tell all those reporters who'll be gathering here tomorrow about how a lay deacon of the local church where the Madonna first wept, a man who actually heard the Madonna speak to him, still couldn't find it in his heart to stop brutalizing his wife and child. We'll see what miracle they make of that."

"I'm going to kick your ass," York mumbled, staggering toward Brendan.

"Frank, stop it!"

Brendan glanced to his right to see Frank York's wife standing in the room, having just entered from the kitchen. Her white hair was still disheveled, and dried blood stained her lips, but her head was held high and her mouth was set in a firm line as her pale eyes blazed. The terror Brendan had glimpsed in her before was gone, replaced by an air of steely determination. Her daughter was with her. Standing between them, an arm around each of them, was the source of the woman's strength: Marla.

It took York a few moments to comprehend the situation, and then he bellowed, "I told you two to stay in the kitchen! What's that bitch doing in my house?"

The woman ignored him, spoke directly to Brendan. "I heard that you were a man of God, mister, and who else but God could have sent you and this woman to this house tonight? It's a miracle, and I'm going to listen to God and thank Him for sending you to save us. I realize now that we don't have to live like this."

"God wants us to be safe and happy. Dotty and I will be grateful if you'll take us with you. Frank did something real bad today; I know it. He started to get drunk even earlier than usual, and he started ranting about teaching some priest a lesson. Finally he started beating on me and Dotty, like always. This time I thought he was going to kill me, but then you and this woman came."

"Now I will kill you, bitch!" York roared, and stumbled toward his wife.

Marla stepped in front of the woman and child and brought the heel of her right hand up sharply under the man's chin. Frank York's head snapped back and he slumped to the floor, unconscious.

The woman started to go to him, but Marla held her back, gently folding her in one arm at the same time as she caressed the

244

cheek of the child standing next to her. Brendan went to the phone and dialed the sheriff's office. As the phone began to ring he turned and smiled at Marla, who smiled back at him.

Craiggville was the last place on earth he would have expected to feel the breath of God.